Amelia Gittens, a black female, has the distinct honor of being the first female to be admitted to the US Army's elite group of snipers, fighting in Afghanistan. It doesn't come without its price, though, as she comes back as so many veterans do with post-traumatic stress syndrome complete with major flashbacks. Working as a New York City police officer, she is involved with a suspect shooting. Unfortunately for her, it is the cousin of a major international drug dealer who seeks revenge on her and her partner, as well as the departmental psychiatrist. Amelia responds the only way she knows how, falling back upon her military training to keep her ward safe while the situation is being resolved. The whole while, she is battling her own inner demons, fighting with herself to keep them at bay, nearly tearing herself apart.

A HOLLYANNE WEAVER NOVEL

Coming soon by HollyAnne Weaver:

THE PLAID SKIRT

HOLLYANNE WEAVER

LEAVING AFGHANISTAN BEHIND

Published by:
Shadoe Publishing
Copyright © September 2015 by HollyAnne Weaver

ISBN-13: 978-0692524893
ISBN-10: 0692524894

Copyright © September 2015 by HollyAnne Weaver

All rights reserved. No part of this book may be reproduced, stored in a retrieval system or transmitted in any form or by any means without the prior written permission of HollyAnne Weaver or Shadoe Publishing, except by a reviewer who may quote brief passages in a review to be printed in a newspaper, magazine, or journal.

HollyAnne Weaver is available for comments at hollyanneweaver618@gmail.com and https://hollyanneweaver.wordpress.com as well as on Facebook, or on Twitter, if you would like to follow to find out about stories and books releases or check with www.ShadoePublishing.com or http://ShadoePublishing.wordpress.com/.

www.shadoepublishing.com

ShadoePublishing@gmail.com

Shadoe Publishing is a United States of America company
Cover by: K'Anne Meinel @ Shadoe Publishing
Edited by: Deb Amia

LEAVING AFGHANISTAN BEHIND

PUBLISHER'S NOTE

This is a work of fiction. Names, characters, places, and incidents are the product of the author's imagination or are used fictitiously, and any resemblance to actual persons, living or dead, business establishments, events, or locales is entirely coincidental.

The publisher does not have any control over and does not assume any responsibility for author or third-party Web sites or their content.

LEAVING AFGHANISTAN BEHIND

CHAPTER ONE

"Dispatch, 168. Show me 10-7 at East 46th and Avenue N."

"Roger, 168."

The thought of actually getting thirty minutes to sit and eat was particularly tantalizing to me at this point. It was pretty chilly, even having my Second Chance and my heavy coat. I should have worn long johns underneath everything. What I wouldn't give to be a weatherman. I could be wrong more than forty percent of the time and still get paid like I was a damned genius. Especially with all the forecasts coming from the National Weather Service and purchased software that processed that data.

Then again, even when it was sweltering in the summer and freezing in the winter, I got to be outside and take it all in. You couldn't get me to trade places with one of the desk monkeys at One Police Plaza for all the tea in China. Not a chance! So naturally, when given the choice to eat inside where it was warm, I was stupid enough to take my food out on the sidewalk to a table and eat there. Partially to be outside, and partially to be alone. I'm not a loner, per se. I mean, I have Theresa. She's the love of my life, but I do embrace solitude, for the most part.

"Amelia, sit your ass right back down. You'll catch your death of a cold if you eat outside tonight," said Mama. Make no mistake about it, it was her little restaurant, not the family's. "Are you listening to me?"

"Yes, Mama. I promise I'll come back in for a refill of coffee in just a minute. Let me sit down and take a load off first."

"Take a load off in here, you crazy child!" I laughed under my breath. I felt privileged. She didn't treat just anyone that way. "I don't know why I try with you. You never listen to my advice anyway."

"Not true! Didn't I listen to you when you set me up with Theresa? You were the one that pushed me to ask her out. You practically pushed me in front of a train… or should I say train wreck?" Mama laughed and dismissed me with a wave of her hand. "Come back for that refill or I'll haunt your dreams tonight."

"I don't doubt you will, Mama." I sat my food and coffee on the table and relaxed. As much as I like walking a beat (unlike most cops these days who prefer a cruiser), I do like to sit down and take a load off periodically. I'd no sooner unwrapped my sandwich, when the stupid radio went off.

"All units, vicinity of Flatbush and Quentin, shots fired. 10-32. Approach 10-39. Units in the area respond."

"Dispatch, 168. Show me 10-8 en route, two blocks out. Request 10-78 from 10-60."

I ran like the wind. Shots fired, no other information. Naturally I was the closest respondent. All I wanted was a measly half hour for a meal. Was that too much to ask? I'm not only a marathon runner, I can sprint a 5K. I'm now thirty-one years old, but have never been in better shape. The United States Army took a wiry Flatbush girl, with no experience other than the ability to play basketball, and shaped her into what I am now. I am daily grateful. My mom is so proud! She and papa came from Bermuda with little to their names after paying for college, dragging a few suitcases and me and my sister, Cheryll Anne. We'd all flourished here in the United States, but papa had died the year before I went into the army. I always wished he'd lived just one more year to see me graduate from basic training.

I don't think I ever considered being a lifer. That was brought home to me when I pulled my gauntlet in Southwest Asia. That's where you pull your fifth tour. Supposedly it means that you never have to go back, but that doesn't apply to certain specialties. My best friend growing up, Vam Dho, came back from her sixth deployment in a coffin aboard a C-17. She was Psychological Operations. I did five tours and they wanted me to go again. I would have had to extend my

LEAVING AFGHANISTAN BEHIND

enlistment before I left though, since it ran out about the third week of what would have been a six to nine month deployment.

I was, officially, a military policeman - whatever - I was a sniper!

These things were running through my head while I was beating boots down the sidewalk as fast I could, toward the vicinity of the call. Just as I got there, two men ran out into the street ahead of me. I could clearly see the gun that one of them held, even in the dimly lit street. It was a large automatic pistol, either nickel or stainless steel, with light glinting off it.

"Stop! Police!" I shouted at them, which, of course, both ignored. I pulled my weapon and held it up as I ran, pushing the safety off simultaneously. "Stop! Police!" I repeated, to no avail.

Suddenly the one with the shiny gun turned toward me. I didn't know if the other had a gun, but I definitely knew this one did. I immediately got down into a crouching stance and lowered my weapon at him. "Drop your weapon! Now!" I screamed. Nobody said criminals were smart. I heard a bullet whiz by my head, then heard it strike the brick in the building behind me. I firmly pulled the trigger three times. He dropped. The other man continued to run.

I quickly moved up to the suspect I had shot. He still had a fairly strong pulse, but I knew I'd hit him three times in the gut. I grabbed my radio. "Dispatch, 168, two suspects. One down, three shots. Other suspect is heading south on Hendrickson. Send an ambulance and a squad, 10-18."

"168, 10-4. Stand by." While I waited, I tried to find the wounds through the suspect's coat, after first recovering his pistol and sticking it in the back of my Sam Browne. "168, ambulance and squad dispatched. Ambulance ETA, five to six minutes. Squad ETA, less than two minutes."

"168, 10-4." For a two minute ETA, they sure were quick. The squad fishtailed around the corner and came to a screeching halt about twenty feet from me, their headlights and both spotlights focused on the scene. They killed the siren, but left the flashing lights on.

"I've got this one. The other one ran down Hendrickson on foot. Five ten to six feet, dark hair, light complexion, jeans, dark, heavy coat. Sorry I don't have more!" I yelled out.

The other two officers jumped back in the squad. With a wave from each, they hit the siren again and screeched the tires. I had the suspect on his back. I was trying to apply pressure to his midsection, but he was bleeding too badly. I had a terrible feeling. Even when the bad guy shoots first, even when it's a completely justified shoot, you still feel it. If you don't, you should quit and find a new job.

Finally, the ambulance came lumbering up the street. They pulled up beside me. The driver and passenger hopped out with their bags. The paramedic in the back opened the door from the inside and pulled the stretcher out, joining the other two. There was so much blood! It was all over me, all over the victim, and all over the street. The paramedics took over for me. I stood back, really feeling the lack of food now.

Within four or five minutes, there were four more squads on scene. The first one had gone down the street and found nothing. Another squad close to the site, the patrol sergeant on duty, and the patrol training officer pulled up. The sergeant was there to fill out the reports on weapons discharge and the suspect's condition after a physical confrontation resulting in medical treatment. While the sarge was filling out his paperwork, the second squad was filling out the incident report and had already called in Crime Scene Investigation. The good news was that it was a relatively slow night, and CSI were expected within about fifteen minutes. Even though I was the officer involved, they had to fill out the report for the investigation. My report would be just for the record.

The paramedics had put in a mainline and gone through many pints of blood and plasma, but they couldn't slow the flow of blood enough to transport him. About thirty minutes into it, they pulled the parachute cord and bailed. They'd have to wait for CSI before they could leave, but in the meantime it took them a good twenty minutes to get everything squared away.

The paramedics had begun cleaning me up and making sure that I had no injuries. My right knee was a little out of sorts from all the pounding on the pavement getting over here, plus the chase... I'm not twenty-one any more. They gave me some naproxen for that, along with a twenty-four ounce bottle of water with added electrolytes to keep me hydrated. I thanked them for their help. They'd also given me a couple of Mylar blankets to wrap up in and let me sit in the back of the ambulance until I could get some replacement clothes. My shirt and coat were soaked with blood, but at least it was off my hands and arms now.

LEAVING AFGHANISTAN BEHIND

The back of the ambulance opened and the sarge and the reporting officer got in, shutting the door behind them. "Amelia, from what I've gathered already, it was a good, clean shoot. No worries there. Glen here is going to drive you over to the precinct so that you can finish your report while it's still fresh in your head. Then we're going to kick you loose, with pay of course, and you'll have to drive a desk for a few days until we get the official okay from 1PP." He handed me the business card of the head doctor, as required by departmental regulations. "Dr. Feynman is the duty shrink for this week. Call her! Let her do her job! Even if you feel fine. I'm not kidding!"

"No need to shout, Timmy. I heard you the first time."

"I could bust you for insubordination. Not for not using my rank, but for calling me Timmy instead of Tim. For God's sake, Amelia, you're not my parents. I could get away with kicking your ass," he said playfully, punching me in the arm. "I'm going to head home now. I've been on duty since six thirty this morning. Call Dr. Feynman. Promise me."

"I promise, Sarge. Go on home to Rita. Glen will take care of me."

"Good night, you two."

"Good night, Sarge," Glen and I said in unison.

Glen looked me right in the eyes. "Does this bring anything back? I have never discharged my weapon, but I've drawn it, and it takes me back."

Glen was in my unit at the same time, but we always deployed opposite each other, so we never met until we joined the force at the NYPD. On paper, we were the XVIII Airborne Corps, 16th MP Brigade, 91st MP Battalion, 32nd MP Company out of Fort Bragg. When we were deployed, we became the 10th Mountain Division, 1st Brigade, 10th Military Police Battalion, 1st Platoon. Officially you had to be an infantryman, a Special Forces member, a Stryker, or a cavalry scout, but since women weren't allowed in those jobs, they allowed me to be selected from an MP unit that was embedded in an infantry division. But then, in those blurred lines that sometimes present themselves, life wasn't what it seemed.

I said nothing. He helped me into the squad he was driving and took me back to the precinct. I had a couple of spare shirts in my locker and he managed to find me a couple of hoodies to put on. They were both oversized for me, so I had no problem getting them on. I put my beat cap in my locker and picked up a snapback and threw it on. I also got my chain out and put my ID on it so that I could be identified throughout the building. After I finished filling out my report, Glen, who was about ready for his coffee break, came in where I was set up and took my reports to turn in. Then he picked up the phone, slammed it against the desk in front of me, picked up the handset, and shoved it in my face.

"I'll do it."

"When."

"Later. I promise."

"You'll do it now!"

I sighed, pulling out the card for Dr. Feynman. I punched the numbers into the phone as Glen was leaving the office, gently pulling the door shut behind him.

"This is Elizabeth Feynman. May I help you?"

"Dr. Feynman. This is Officer Amelia Gittens. I was just... involved in a suspect shooting." Dr. Feynman immediately lost the sound of sleepiness in her voice.

"Amelia, are you there?"

"Yeah. Look, I can call you tomorrow if you'd like. It's almost midnight now."

"Which precinct are you at right now?"

"67th Flatbush."

"Give me twenty-five minutes. I'll be right there."

"Really, I can do this tomorrow."

"Nonsense. The sooner we do this, the better it will be. See you in a few. Just don't make fun of me without makeup," she laughed. I tried to laugh, but it didn't come.

Next, I pulled out my cell phone. "Hi, baby. How are you tonight?"

"Knowing you're going to be walking in that door in less than an hour, how could I not be perfect?"

"About that... I'm... uh... going to be a little late. I've got to hang out here at the precinct for a while. I'm waiting on the departmental psychiatrist to have an hour visit with me before I can leave, and she won't be here for about half an hour. Then I have to get a ride home. They won't let me drive tonight."

"Baby! What's wrong? Are you all right? Did you get hurt?"

"No, I'm fine actually. It was just... well, you're going to hear about it anyway. I was involved in a shooting tonight."

LEAVING AFGHANISTAN BEHIND

"But you're fine, right? Tell me you're fine."

"Yeah, I'm just fine. I had a suspect shoot at me. He missed. I didn't."

"...So, you shot him? Or her? Or whatever?"

"Yeah. I shot him three times. The ambulance couldn't even get him stable enough to transport."

"Baby girl, are you sure you're okay?"

"I'll be fine. I don't technically have to see the shrink tonight, but I won't be allowed to do anything without talking to one of them, so I might as well get it over with. I'll see you in a couple of hours. I just wanted to let you know I'd be late. Scratch Ferdinand for me. See you in a while. Love you."

"I love you too, baby. So much."

Theresa Biancardi was almost an empath, she cared so much. Not just about me, about everybody really, but especially towards me. Her family had some trouble getting used to me. Not because I'm black, but because of my sounds-sort-of-British-but-not-quite accent.

Finally, the doctor showed up. "Hello, Officer Gittens. I'm Elizabeth Feynman. Please, let's find some place a little more conducive to a chat than this office." We found a lounge area, where she took out a large sticky note and put it on the door. She wrote on it with a big marker, 'IN USE'. "Please, come in. Sit down and make yourself comfortable."

We both got seated, but neither of us spoke, initially. I understood quickly, she was waiting for me to go first in order to judge my condition. I played it coy for a few minutes before finally deciding to speak, "So when you go out on one these little ventures, do you jump on the departmental database and do a quick dossier scan before coming out, or something like that?"

"Or something like that," she responded.

"So you already know what I did before joining the NYPD. Right?"

"You were an MP in the army."

"Does my quick record show what my TDYs were?"

"All I know is that you were in the army as an MP for thirteen and a half years, and that you retired honorably as a Sergeant First Class. It takes an absolute minimum of twelve and a half years to make SFC and yet you achieved that grade and functioned there for some time. It also says that you have a Bronze Star with two oak leaf clusters and two Vs, Global War on Terrorism medal with three clusters, a Commendation

Medal with oak leaf cluster, Afghanistan Campaign medal with three clusters, Distinguished Service Medal, Good Conduct Medal, two Purple Hearts, Army Achievement Medal twice, and a Combat Infantry Badge. Christ! That's only the first quarter or so of the alphabet. And that's only medals, not to mention ribbons and awards. It doesn't say why, it just says that you have them. If you don't mind my asking, what were the extent of your wounds?"

I stood up from my chair, pulled my tee shirt up and my sweat bottoms down about four inches. That let her see the scars from four bullet holes. "Dr. Feynman, I rarely performed MP duties in the army."

"Being from an enemy weapon, those would be thirty caliber wounds, correct?"

I nodded my head at her. I was impressed that she knew the difference and the implications that went along with them.

"So what did you do?"

"I was a sniper. I was already in the 10th Mountain Division, firmly embedded in Afghanistan, but worked primarily in the forward combat brigades. I still wore my MP insignias, in addition to the ones for the unit I worked with. That's what I did for about eighty percent of my time, both at home and deployed. My rotations home were always short, and my deployments always long."

"Well, that explains the CIB. I wondered about that. Most MPs don't get those."

"You do if you're working in a forward area, actually. Glen Parsons, the officer that wrote up my incident tonight, was in my unit at the same time. Never met him until we both started working here. Sort of funny. He has a Silver Star, a Commendation Medal, and a CIB, but he wasn't a sniper."

"Let's talk about being sniper a little bit before we move on. Do you have any confirmed kills?"

"Yes."

"Do you know how many?"

"Yes."

"Would you mind sharing that with me?"

"Yes."

"Amelia, I'm not the enemy here, I'm your friend. I'm not going to be asked to testify at your review board. In fact, I'm prohibited by both licensure and law (not to mention the union), from doing so. I'm just

LEAVING AFGHANISTAN BEHIND

trying to get a baseline for you. The more I know, the more I can help you."

"Who says I need help?"

"That was poorly worded. How about the more I know, the more I can make myself available to you for whatever support I can give? Is that better?"

"Much." I paused for a couple of minutes. What the hell. "Seventeen confirmed, thirty-one suspected."

"And how do you feel about that, after the fact? Not at that moment, but now."

"Whatever."

"Does it bother you? Do you ever have nightmares? Have you ever been diagnosed with PTSD, even mild?"

"Yes, yes, and yes."

"Okay. Let's move on to tonight. What happened?"

"I'm a beat cop. I responded to a call. I gave chase to two suspects. One had a gun that was easy to see, even at night. Shiny. Forty-five caliber. I identified myself twice and gave them warning to stop. Both suspects failed to respond. Shortly after that, the suspect with the gun fired one round that missed me. I did hear the bullet whiz by, so it must have been fairly close. I fired three rounds into the suspect. Guaranteed to immobilize, but not overkill. The other suspect ran away. I radioed in the situation to dispatch and immediately cleared the suspect's weapon and begin giving him first aid as best I could. The paramedics weren't able to save him."

"How did it make you feel, hearing the bullet go by you?"

"I didn't particularly have an opinion one way or another about it, ma'am."

"Please, no need for ma'am. You can call me Elizabeth if you like."

"Actually, I'd prefer Dr. Feynman."

"That's okay as well. So you didn't get upset? Angry? Scared? Nothing particular regarding being shot at?"

"No, but it was because of that I returned fire. I would never have shot first. I would have let them escape and evade before shooting first."

"Departmental policy does give you circumstances where you not only should, but are required to, shoot first if there is a safety issue for the public or yourself."

"Are you going to report me for what I just said, ma'am?"

- 9 -

"No, of course not. I wish I could get you to understand that I represent your interests here, nobody else's. I tell you what, I want some time to review my notes, develop a little plan of action if you will, for you to follow. We'll talk again."

"How often will I have to report to you before returning to duty?"

"Officer Gittens, I really want to see you again. At least a few times. Maybe three or four if you would consent, but as far as I'm concerned, I'll sign off for you tomorrow. I'll have your notice of record included in your jacket to go to the review board, to allow them to rest assured. Okay?"

"Thank you, ma'am."

"On one condition…"

"What's that?"

"Just once, say it. Say Elizabeth. Then I promise you, I'll clear you," she smiled.

I managed to smile back at her, even if I didn't mean it wholeheartedly. I stood up from my chair and stared her down for a minute. I extended my hand to her and said, "Elizabeth. Thank you."

As she shook my hand, she said, "You're welcome. Now was that so hard?"

"No, ma'am." We both broke out laughing then. A long, hard, belly laugh. It broke the tension tremendously. That alone made me feel better than everything else did. There was something about talking to a shrink. I kept having to do it on active duty, and with the VA for the two or three years after I got out because I had PTSD. The day you go in and talk to them, and even the day after, you feel like crud. Then you get better, better than if you hadn't gone. Maybe it was just stirring everything up that created that feeling.

Since Elizabeth was going my way, she offered to give me a ride home. I took her up on it. I thanked her again as I closed the car door and waved goodbye. I went to the door and was fumbling with the lock and my key, when Theresa yanked it open. She grabbed my hoody and jerked me inside. "Hi, baby girl. How are you doing?"

"I'm fine," was about all I could muster.

"Are you sure?"

"Yeah. I'm fine."

"Do you maybe want a little *happy time* tonight?" she asked.

"Not really. I just want a hot shower and to go to bed."

LEAVING AFGHANISTAN BEHIND

"Are you sure?" she asked, grabbing the hands on my hips, her thumbs tickling me playfully.

"I'm sure," I said, pulling her hand away. "Let me take a shower, and then we'll cuddle up together in bed. Would that be okay for tonight?"

"No problem."

"Are you disappointed?"

"Baby, I just want to do everything I can to make you as happy as I can tonight. You've had the shittiest of all possible nights, I suspect. I'll do anything, not do anything, you just tell me what you need and I'll make it so. I'll even get you a hooker if it helps," she joked.

"Now that sounds pretty darn good. The thing is, my girlfriend, she's sort of the jealous type. She doesn't snoop my email or anything like that, but I hardly think she'd take kindly to my fooling around with another chick," I cracked back at her, jokingly.

"You got that shit right! She's a whack, totally wicked bitch when it comes to that. I don't see what you'd want in another woman anyway. After all, she's so cute, and adorable, and funny, and loving…"

"Or so she thinks," I said with a grin.

"But she loves you. More than anything in the world."

"Next time you see her? Tell her that I was the one who fell in love first. I was the one who told her first, and I was the one who asked her to marry me first…"

"What?"

"You heard me. Tell her that I was the one who asked her to marry me first."

"So you're…" she started, shaking her head. "You're asking me to marry you?"

"I was thinking of the right way to tell you. I've been carrying this damn thing around with me for three days at work, thinking about it while I was out pounding the pavement. Usually, I'm pretty good at presenting myself, but this one was different." I got down on the floor on one knee, in front of the couch where she was sitting, and pulled out the ring box. "Theresa Rosanna Biancardi, will you marry me, and live with me, and have babies with me, for the rest of my life?"

She launched herself up and on me, with her arms around my neck, and began crying uncontrollably. Finally she stepped back, tears still flowing, and put her hand out so I could put the ring on her finger. It was a little difficult because she kept shaking her hand up and down. Finally, I took my left hand and grabbed her thumb to hold her hand in place, and used my right hand to slide the ring up. She kept her hand flat to see what it looked like on her. Still, she cried and cried. I wrapped her arms around my neck again, and I encircled her waist and picked her off the floor. I carried her like that into the bathroom, then put her down. She took off her night shirt and her underwear, then reached in to turn on the water in the shower. I took my clothes off and made a little pile on the floor. She stepped in first, then held out her hand, beckoning me. I took her hand, then stepped in beside her. Her tears were gone and now she was simply beaming at me with those crystal clear, blue grey eyes, so common in the north of her country of origin. We washed each other, rinsed each other, dried each other, and dressed each other. Then we crawled beneath the covers and snuggled in tightly. We were both asleep in minutes. Unfortunately, I didn't stay there.

LEAVING AFGHANISTAN BEHIND

CHAPTER TWO

My observer picked up a few grains of sand and let them fall. "Looks like five to seven kilometers per hour. From here, bearing two-two-five. Range is four hundred thirty-seven meters. Combatant is in the second floor window, third from the right. The tan building. I say again, the tan building."

"Roger, Sniper Three. Sniper Two, we have the tan building, third floor, second from the right. The signal is on countdown of three."

"Sniper One, understand countdown of three. We have the tan building. Say again, tan building. Third floor, second window from the right. Time on target. Countdown by Snake Six."

"Snake Six, roger. Holding for countdown from three. I have two squads moving into place at this time. Expect thirty second deployment. Time is on my count. Countdown is from three."

"Sniper One, roger."

"Sniper Two, roger."

"Sniper Three, roger."

"Snake Six, moving, moving, moving. Snap count from three... two... one... Mark!"

Three shots rang out simultaneously, with three bodies in two different windows completely disintegrating under the violent impact of Barrett fifty caliber sniper rifles, with each shot coming from over fourteen hundred feet.

"Snake Six, all squads, go, go, go! First platoon circle building from western aspect and feed to rear of building. All squads move up. Sniper teams, good job. Thanks for the help, guys. I think we got it from here."

"And girls," I muttered under my breath, my mic on mute.

My observer tapped the back of my leg a couple of times in recognition of my accomplishment.

"And that is how it's done. Your first kill. Well?"

"Well what?"

"How do you feel?"

"All I could picture was the explosion of the enemy sniper's head. Total obliteration. From living to dead in under half a second."

I violently lurched up in bed. It took me a minute to get used to the fact that it was almost completely black in our room, yet I'd just been awash in tremendously bright sunlight. It was slowly starting to come back, that it was just another nightmare. One of many, many such occurrences. I reached over to the night stand, took a pill out of the bottle, and chased it down with a drink from my glass. I lay back down on the bed, my heart still up in my throat. Theresa wrapped her arm around me and scratched at my chest for a few seconds.

"Sorry I woke you up. Go back to sleep."

She patted my chest, made a slight sighing noise, and pulled me in tight to her. I picked her arm up off me and laid it down as gently as I could on the bed. I gingerly crept out of the bed and into the living room, picked up my wallet and pulled out Elizabeth's card. I dialed the number, hesitating only a minute.

"This is Elizabeth Feynman. May I help you?"

"Dr. Feynman? This is Officer Gittens. I hate waking you up twice in the same night, and I realize it's really, really late…"

"What can I do for you, Amelia?"

"I need to see you. Today. Is that possible?"

"I don't know when I'll find time, but if I have to, I'll eat my sandwich while we talk, if you don't mind? I'll make time. Are you okay right now?"

"Not really. That's why I'm calling."

"I have to ask you two questions. It's a formality. Right now, are you a danger to yourself? Do you have any thoughts of harming yourself?"

"No, of course not."

LEAVING AFGHANISTAN BEHIND

"At this time, do you have any thoughts of harming anyone else?"

"No. No one."

"I hope you understand, I have to ask."

"What time do you start in the morning?"

"About seven thirty."

"I'll call your office about eight and see when you can have me come in. Would that be all right?"

"That would be great."

I hung up the phone and turned around. By the streetlight, I could see Theresa standing behind me, one arm around her back locked into the other, weight on one foot, obviously having stood there for some time.

"They're back, aren't they?"

I just nodded my head.

"Come to bed, baby. Come to bed with me. Let me make you all better." I followed her to bed, and I let her hold me, even though she's only about half my weight. We both shade five nine and a quarter, but she's about a buck ten dripping wet, and I push the scales over one seventy-five. Don't let Theresa's frame fool you; sometimes the wiry ones are the toughest. I've worked out since I was thirteen and I've got the athlete's body, but somehow, right at this moment, I didn't feel very athletic. It's amazing how your body can take getting mutilated, getting shot, and it recovers. Sometimes your mind breaks and it's very hard to heal.

LEAVING AFGHANISTAN BEHIND

CHAPTER THREE

Theresa woke up happy as a clam. She kept trying to steal a glance at her engagement ring. No, that's not correct. She spent a lot of time simply staring right at it... and at me, smiling. Always smiling. I'm afraid I couldn't muster much of a smile in return. My night wasn't such a good one. I don't know if it was linked to what happened on the job yesterday or not and that's why I was making the appointment with Dr. Feynman. The seconds ticked slowly by, excruciatingly so, waiting for eight o'clock. With about two minutes to go, my hand was already on the receiver.

"You hovering your hand there doesn't make the time pass any quicker, babe. Just try and relax."

I heard the words, but they were empty just the same. They didn't cause me to move my hand. Theresa came and sat down on my lap, running her fingers through my short, bristly hair. She held her hand out where her new ring was showing on top and prodded me with her other hand. "Did you really carry this around for three days?"

"Yeah. I couldn't decide what kind of flowers to get, where to do it, what exactly to say, just everything."

"But you do mean it, right? You and me? Forever?" she asked, looking me square in the face with those big, bright clear eyes of hers.

"Of course I meant it. I mean, I do mean it. It just hit me last night though, no matter what happens, I always want to be able to come home to you. And only you."

"I think that should do it."

"Do what?"

"I was helping you draw out the time. Now you can call. Go ahead and pick the phone up."

"I don't deserve you, I know that, but I'm keeping you anyway."

"Well, I think I deserve you, you steroidal giant of a woman, and I intend on keeping you forever. Now make the call," she said with a giggle.

I took in a deep sigh and let it back out. "Departmental Psychiatry, this is Rachel speaking, may I help you?"

"My name is Officer Gittens from-"

"Of course, officer. The doctor has time available at eleven, twelve, and three. Do any of these times work for you?"

"I'd like to take the earliest of the three if it's possible."

"Of course. We'll see you at eleven. Do you have one of Dr. Feynman's cards?"

"Sure."

"Our address is on that card. We'll be expecting you at eleven o'clock. See you then."

I called the precinct and talked to the duty captain. I let him know that I was taking a personal day. I also let him know I'd already seen the doc once last night and I had an appointment later in the morning. He advised me to take only a half day, and show the trip to the doctor as a half day, so that I would get compensated for my time there, as well as travel time.

"I appreciate it, Captain."

"Look, Gittens, I've already glanced over the reports from last night's incident. It's just a formality. You know that. We'll have you back on the streets in just a few days. It was a good shoot. Completely clean. We just have to go through the motions. It shouldn't take more than a week, maybe a week and a half, right?"

"Right, Cap. Anyway, I was just checking in."

"Goodness knows, I'd rather have you spend a day with Liz than filing paperwork. If you need anything, call me, call your sergeant, or call your union rep, whoever you need. You hear?"

LEAVING AFGHANISTAN BEHIND

"Yes, sir," I said as I hung up. Since I wasn't going into work at all today, I decided to stay casual and got out some sweats. Of course, they were marked down the right pant leg and right sleeve, spelling out NYPD. The departmental crest was on the upper left chest. I don't think I ever wore much of anything else any more. I wondered why.

"You know, baby, one of these days I'm going to buy you a pretty bra, not another one of your fifty sports bras, just to be different. You're too beautiful to smash your boobs up like that. You need lift, separation, and support."

"You've been saying that for almost five years. How successful have you been so far?"

"Well, I got you to propose to me, didn't I? I never in a million years saw that one coming. Maybe you'll surprise me twice in one decade."

"Maybe. I've got to shove off. I want to get there plenty early."

"What you mean is, you want to go down to Prospect Park and put in a good ten mile force march getting steeled for the inquisition."

I put my palm on Theresa's face, then after a moment's hesitation, leaned in and kissed her. "I love the fact that you *get me* and I love even more that you don't try and change me."

The look on Theresa's face suddenly changed completely. Her smile vanished and all color drained out. "Please talk to the doctor. I know you never let me into the dark parts, but you have to let her in if you want her to help you, baby. Please let her help you. For my sake at least?"

"I promise. Hell, last night I told her a little bit about stuff I never even talked about with the VA."

The smile returned immediately. "That's what I want to hear." Then she dropped to a voice barely above a whisper and brushed her lips against my ear. "That's what I need to hear." I gave her a hug, grabbed my backpack, and headed out the door.

I took the bus over to the precinct, put my gear into my locker, and hit the streets running. I had on long johns, sweats, and a blue watch cap. Of course, the watch cap had our departmental logo as well. What did you expect? I ran from there to the edge of Prospect Park, then broke off on the road surrounding it. Once you get to the park itself, the road is about three-point-three miles around, just a tad longer than a five kilometer race. I didn't take it at a jog, I sprinted most of the distance. It took me about eighteen and a half minutes to finish the

- 19 -

loop. I wasn't giving the all out, since the air was pretty cold. I slowed down to a quick jog on my way back to the precinct and was jogging up the stairs when Michaels snagged me by the arm.

"That was quick. Didn't feel like going very far today?"

"Sort of."

"How far did you go?"

"Down and around Prospect Park. I have an appointment later this morning, so I couldn't go very far."

"Are you kidding me? You just ran about six miles in what? Less than thirty minutes? In the middle of winter? I got to lay off the lasagna, man!"

I laughed at him and scurried into the locker room, grabbing my backpack. It had a change of clothes, exactly what I was wearing right now. I took a quick, hot shower, trying to push some of the cold out of me. I switched to fresh clothes and decided to walk over to the doctor's office since I had time. I would slow down so that I didn't reek up the place.

I knocked on the frosted, external door, unsure of what was behind it. I needn't have. It was a regular lobby with several chairs and a couple of couches. Everything looked a little too over-upholstered. Sort of an eighteenth century French whorehouse theme, truthfully. There were two other policemen seated, a fireman, as well as two people in plainclothes whose jobs I couldn't determine. One of the policemen was another woman, all the others were men. Everybody's eyes would furtively glance around the room. Whenever two people locked eyes, both averted their gaze immediately, except for me. I don't mind staring directly at things, or into people's eyes. After all, I've stared into the face of death before, and won. There were no names used. The receptionist came out from the inner door and got the individual's attention, told them they would be seen now, then disappeared with them through the inner door. Strangely enough, nobody ever came back out. Either the building was eating people or there was a separate exit. Finally, it was time for me. The girl magically appeared from the enchanted door and explained that the doctor would see me now.

Dr. Feynman's door was shut, but there were three chairs in the hallway directly across from the doorway. I sat down and waited for what seemed like about ten minutes. Actually, it was. I know because

LEAVING AFGHANISTAN BEHIND

I kept looking at my watch. Finally, the door opened and Dr. Feynman stood to one side, showing the way in with her hand.

"Please, sit. Sorry, I'm running behind, but I won't cut into your time. Since you took the eleven o'clock and my lunch is twelve, I've blocked you for as long as we need. As I said, I hope you don't mind me eating my sandwich," she laughed. I laughed with her, even if it was only half-heartedly. "I have two. They're ham and swiss. You could have one if you liked."

I took a seat in the chair closest to her desk.

"Interesting that you should take that chair. Most people take the middle one." I just shrugged my shoulders. "That's because most people are just followers. That's all that means. Nothing too deep or secretive about that. I was just making an observation. What happened?"

"Dreams. Again."

"That's not true, is it?"

"Actually, it is."

"They weren't dreams; they were flashbacks. The question is, did it play back exactly as it happened (a true flashback), or did it change somewhat, like a modified dream?"

I thought before speaking. Finally, I ventured, "It was my first kill and it was an exact sequence of events."

"Where were you?"

"Oruzgan. Just northeast of the Kandahar province."

"Not a friendly or calm place, huh?"

"Not so much."

"And what happened?"

"Three sniper teams gave cover to clear a building that overlooked a square, so we could take control of a town and move larger numbers of troops through safely."

"Your exact role?"

"Sniper Three, which was a two-man team. Me and my observer, Ted Kowalski. The sniper and the observer take turns on the trigger. Same two always work together as a team, unless special circumstances require a change – like one of us getting shot."

"So that day, it was your first *kill* as you call it? You were successful?"

"Confirmed."

"How did you feel at that exact moment?"

"Empty. Like I'd done my job. No more. No less. No elation for having killed a human. Relief for having saved fellow soldiers. Satisfaction, I suppose, that our two wounded infantrymen would be the last taken down by this particular group of insurgents."

"What would have happened if you didn't take out your target?"

"More of my men would have been shot, wounded, or killed."

"And last night, how much of that did you re-enact during your nightmare?"

"Who said it was a nightmare?"

"First, you called me and woke me up, indicating you were in serious trouble. Secondly, after you skipped out the door today, Theresa called me. She found my card sitting on a table. We had a little talk. Nothing too deep, she's just worried about you. Just so you know, I told her up front that I couldn't discuss any particulars of your time with me. That would be up to you since you're my patient and you have full confidentiality. Second, I told her that anything she told me, I was obliged to forward on to you, again, since you are my patient."

"She's got a big mouth for such a scrawny little thing."

"She also said you asked her to marry you. She must also have a big heart for such a scrawny little thing," said the doctor.

For the first time, I actually smiled. Nothing can bring me instantaneous joy like Theresa. "I'm not ready to sign a release of information for her yet. There's still some things I have to figure out for myself. She knows I was an MP, and we've been together through two of my deployments, but that's pretty much the extent of it. At least for now."

"No problem. Now let's talk about the rat bastard that you blew completely away last night."

I froze in my chair. All of my senses shut down. I was transfixed in time, unable to move, even think.

"Officer Gittens! Look at me!"

Slowly my eyes focused. Then my fists unclenched and I began to breathe again.

"Now what we have to do is find out if yesterday's incident is really at issue, or if it is your past at issue. I mean seriously, this was one scumbag compared to between forty or fifty you've wasted overseas, right?"

"I... I... Um..."

LEAVING AFGHANISTAN BEHIND

"Okay, Amelia, relax. Slow down your breathing. That was just an exercise to let me choose a starting point." The doctor walked around her desk, took me by the hand, and made me sit on one end of her couch while she sat at the other end. She placed her hand on my knee. "Breathe. In and out. That's better."

It took me several minutes, but finally I was back in control. "Dr. Feynman-"

"The first thing we're going to work on here, is having you call me Elizabeth. I don't mind being addressed as ma'am in the least. I understand it's your professionalism, but no more Dr. Feynman. Got it?"

"Yes, ma'am."

"Tell me what went through your head when I said the things I just said. Was it from a deployment, or was it about the perp last night?"

"I don't know."

"Think. Was it feeling bad about last night's shooting, or about being deployed?"

"It was... it was... about... Afghanistan. I think if last night happened again tonight, I wouldn't do anything any differently."

"So it is PTSD. Here's the thing. I can work with you, if it's related to yesterday, for up to twelve visits before I have to refer you to a third party source. If it's all right with you, I'd like to start counting later this week as our first visit out of twelve and not include last night or today. Then after our time runs out, I have a personal friend at the VA. I'll make sure that your referral gets directly to him so we can keep this going. I'll have you sign a restricted waiver so the information will go into your VA records, but nobody can see them."

"So now what?"

"Are you currently taking any medications for this?"

"Paxil."

"I'm going to keep you on that for now instead of trying to switch it. For now anyway, but I'm going to add a sleeping pill. Take it every night, not just when you think you need it, at least for the next two months. One last thing. Do you get anxiety attacks?"

"Often."

"Have you always?"

"No."

"I'm also going to give you Lorazepam. That slows down the interactivity between sections of the brain, which will induce more relaxation. I've got to warn you on this one though, start taking it on a weekend, and take only half of the dose on the bottle for the first few times to see how it will react with you. This one you put under your tongue and it dissolves, with a very fast uptake. It works within fifteen minutes. You only take these when you have anxiety coming on, not all the time. One last thing I think you should try... although it's a bit outside my scope of practice..."

"What's that Doct... I mean, Elizabeth."

She smiled widely at me. "Thank you. I think you should stop on the way home and get Theresa some lovely flowers. She obviously cares a lot. A couple of weeks ago my partner stopped and got me flowers for no reason. Instead of the standard dozen roses, I got three dozen daisies interspersed with a dozen and a half Black-eyed Susans."

"Partner? It's probably not my place to ask, and unprofessional, not to mention a crossing-over of doctor/patient dynamic, but is this a male or female partner? I figured you for more of a picket fence woman."

"Oh, I have an apartment right here in Brooklyn. While it doesn't have a picket fence, it does have a stone fence in front and a small yard in both front and back. We have two wonderful, beautiful, little girls. See, you can have it all," she said, winking at me, "and my partner's name is Keven."

"Oh. Some people never get married these days, so it's often assumed when you say partner, you mean same sex. Of all people, I should be the one that doesn't assume. I'm terribly sorry, I meant nothing by it, ma'am."

"Okay, now you're starting to piss me off with the ma'am stuff. You're going a little overboard. And she spells her name K-E-V-E-N," Elizabeth said, with a twinkle in her eye. I smiled back at her.

"I guess I'll see you on Thursday then?"

"Amelia, believe in me and believe in yourself. There are no guarantees that we'll cure you. It's actually a guarantee that we won't ever completely do so. What we will accomplish, is to allow you to control it, and not allow it to control you. Deal?"

"Yes ma'am," I said with a huge smile.

"I said... Oh, good one. You got me. Now get out of here. See you Thursday at eleven."

LEAVING AFGHANISTAN BEHIND

CHAPTER FOUR

I decided to go home instead of going back to the precinct. I don't know why I was so compelled to go in to work anyway. I couldn't do anything and I'd already taken the day off. I guess it's because I rarely took any personal days and just wasn't used to it. Then the more I thought about it, the more I started hoping that Theresa was working from home today. She's a graphic artist and has a lot of freedom once she picks up a project. I took Elizabeth's advice and stopped at a little flower shop on the corner close to home. I even liked her idea of the daisies and Black-eyed Susans.

I picked up my phone and called Theresa.

"Hi, babe. Are you okay?"

"For the most part. Ask me again tomorrow morning. Are you at home or in your office today?"

"I'm at home. I was just getting up to get some lunch. Have you eaten yet?"

"Not yet. I was actually in the doctor's office for almost an hour and forty-five minutes. She ratted you out."

"She already told me that she was going to. I just wanted to make sure you were okay. If you want, I'll wait until you get home to eat. Oh, hang on one second. There's somebody at the door. Give me one sec…"

When Theresa opened the door, I had the flowers held up in front of my face. She practically squealed. Girls! Dang.

She grabbed me by one arm and dragged me inside. She snatched the flowers out of my hands and ran to put them on the table. After she laid them down, she spent a couple of minutes being totally picky about how they were arranged. Then suddenly, she turned to me and ran smack dab into me, throwing her arms around my neck, and giving me the most intense lip-lock.

"So does this mean you're glad to see me?"

"Always, but now so, more than ever."

"Why? Over a few posies? Maybe I should do it more often."

"No silly, this," she said holding out her ring. "I've got a fiancée. How cool is that?"

"You still sure you want to marry me after nights like last night?"

"Don't be stupid. Of course I am. Through thick and thin. You know us Italians are high-spirited. I just look at you like a wild stallion shying away from accepting a saddle for the first time. Not to break you, but so that we can take journeys together. Isn't that what we've always told each other? I would have been fine living with you forever. I just never knew how much... more, I guess is the word. It is really important after all."

"Let's make some sandwiches, and then we need to sit down and talk."

"At least I know you're not breaking up with me. You wouldn't give me a ring and then throw me to the curb the next day," she laughed.

"No, but it's pretty serious. I mean, not the end of the world. I didn't mean that to sound like it did. I mean... Let's get some food and a couple sodas, go sit down, and then I'll tell you."

"Whatever you say, babe."

We made sandwiches, got some cheese puffs and a couple of diet sodas, then went into the living room and sat on the couch. We started eating without saying much of anything. After we'd both finished about half of our sandwiches and a few cheese puffs, I put my plate down and faced Theresa.

"First off, I want you to know that I've never intentionally lied to you about anything. Ever."

"I know that."

LEAVING AFGHANISTAN BEHIND

"Please, let me finish. There is one thing that you're going to have to know about because apparently it's getting worse, not better."

"Your dreams, right?"

"Yeah. Only they're not dreams... not exactly."

"Amelia, I've been on the internet all morning, not working. You don't have to say anything. I understand."

"You may think you do, but you need to know the whole story. I'll probably see Dr. Feynman... Elizabeth... about a dozen more times. Afterward, I'm going to have to start going back to the VA."

"They never really helped you before, did they? The pills aren't working, are they?"

"What do you think you know?" I asked.

"That you have PTSD. I'm right, aren't I, babe?"

"That's part of it, but there's more. What's probably behind it, has more to do with what I did when I was on active duty."

"You were a cop, just like now. You've always been a cop."

"That's true, but that's not what I actually did."

"Oooo. Were you a top secret agent?"

"Theresa, I'm trying to be serious for a minute here. Please."

"Okay, I'll stop. So if you weren't an MP, what were you?"

"I was an MP, but in the army, they draw on many, many units for special details. Most of them, for my detail, came from infantry units, but in my case I was an embedded MP with an Infantry Division."

"Yeah, I know. 10th Mountain. I've seen all your patches and photos and everything."

"My point is, I happened to possess certain desirable skills for a particular army sub-unit."

"I'm not following you."

"Honey, I was a sniper."

"You? You were a sniper? You're kidding me. You're pulling my leg. Women don't go into battle."

"You believe that crap? Come here a minute..." I set her plate beside mine and pulled her up. I walked over to the wall that was covered with photos. "Her..."

"Vam. I know she didn't make it home. I'm sorry, babe, but I don't understand what you're getting at."

"She was in combat. She was in a platoon of about fifteen people. They mostly ran missions behind the lines. That's all she did. She was on her sixth tour. That's why I refused to re-up after my gauntlet."

"So you're serious. You were a sniper?"
"Yes."
"So you..."
"Many times."
"How many?"
"Numbers aren't important. Let's just say a lot."
"No, I mean, how many times did you go out as a sniper?"
"That's all I did for my entire deployment, all five times."
"And this is what's..."
"Probably."

Without saying anything, Theresa wrapped her arms around my neck and held on for dear life. She didn't let go for probably twenty minutes, not moving, not letting go. When she finally did, her eyes were watery.

"Why didn't you ever tell me this? Why?"
"Because I knew you'd worry. All the time. Then after I separated, there didn't seem to be much point. It was in the past."
"Obviously it's not."
"So it would seem."
"Truth. How bad have the nightmares been?"
"Not as bad lately, until yesterday. Then they came back immediately."
"What do you see in your dreams?"
"Afghanistan. And what happened there."
"Well, I can tell you right now that if I have to take you myself, you're going to be seen by a doctor regularly. For as long as it takes."
"I'm already set up."
"Really? Elizabeth really got to you, didn't she?"
"No, you really got to me. Last night. I knew that I couldn't keep doing that to you. I knew that it would start tearing you up."
"C'mon, finish your lunch. You have the day off. Let's eat and go lay down for a while. Just relax. How does that sound?"
"Good."

We finished our lunch without another word being said. After I had cleaned the dishes, we went into the bedroom and lay down on the bed, facing each other, our hands intertwined. The first words were spoken by Theresa. She pulled her left hand loose from our knot of fingers.

"Look at what my bad-ass girlfriend gave me."
"Don't you mean your fiancée?"

LEAVING AFGHANISTAN BEHIND

She giggled at me. "She's big and brave and strong and is a cop for the New York City Police Department. If you screw with me, she'll screw with you!"

"You got that shit right."

"When are we going to get married?"

"When do you want to get married?"

"I don't care. The ring itself is enough for me. We could be engaged forever for all I care."

"Wouldn't you rather actually get married?"

"Maybe. Next spring? Before it gets hot? Or next fall after it cools off? Or the next year... I don't want to push you or anything."

"What about the courthouse this month? The required wait is only twenty-four hours. Or do you want a big wedding?"

"This month? Oh, Christ, my mother would kill me. Oh what the hell! She has all her *normal* kids to do the big fancy wedding bit!" she said, cackling maniacally. "Can we at least invite them?"

"Sure. My mom and sister. Your parents. Your two older brothers. I can't see Rodolfo coming. He still doesn't accept us. And probably all of your sisters. That's still a pretty small group. You want to just do it? What the hell? That didn't sound right. There's nothing *what the hell* about marrying you. I just meant in the timing of it."

"I know what you meant, babe. Don't worry." Theresa started running her fingers up and down my bicep, slowly up and down, staring at it.

"You don't like my muscles?"

"I love your muscles. That's not what I was looking at. I love the color of your skin. It's so smooth and beautiful."

"Shut up."

"I mean it. That's what first attracted me to you..."

"And here I thought it was my boobs."

"That too," she said with a laugh. "Definitely that too. You've got some great boobs," she said giving one a squeeze.

"Harlot."

"Skank."

"Ho."

"Slag."

I started tickling her after that last comment.

"Okay, I take it back. I take it back. Stop."

"What's the matter? Can't take a little bit of tickling?"

Eventually, we fell asleep in each other's arms. It was just what I needed, at least until night came. We went to bed early, for us, without even watching the news. I felt calm and relaxed. I took my sleeping pill, like I was supposed to, and even took two Lorazepam to see how they made me feel.

"You know, Gittens, this high profile political target shit is for the birds."

"Tell me about it. Sending us fifty clicks past the end zone to take down some stupid local thug that will only be replaced by another local thug. I get tired of this."

"You think we'll make it home by Thanksgiving?"

"I hope so. I really want to see my mom and sister. I haven't seen them for almost nine months."

"You've never said. You got anybody waiting for you back home?"

"Naw. I'm not as lucky as you."

"You know we're a team, don't you? The only time I'd ever betray you is if you outright betrayed our country. And I know you ain't about to do that."

"I don't know what the fuck you're talking about, Kowalski."

"Waiting for you back home. Do you have anybody or not? Seriously. I care. Nothing you say would ever leave my lips. Not even drunk back at the compound. Oops, what am I saying? There's no liquor over here!"

"You're fucking funny, douchebag. I got nobody."

"Gittens. For fuck's sake, trust me. You're my life and death partner. We put our lives in each other's hands together."

"You know, you talk too much, ass-wipe."

"Whatever. You see movement yet?"

"Nope. If our intel is good though, they'll come around from the north side and travel down the second street, not the first one. I'm thinking we need to move over. What do you think? Theresa Biancardi."

"Who the hell is Theresa Biancardi?"

"My girlfriend, shit for brains."

"Sorry. Cool. Casual?"

"No."

"Do you love her?"

"Pretty much. We're living together. That may be it. See the black Benz?"

LEAVING AFGHANISTAN BEHIND

"Yeah. Thanks, by the way."
"For what?"
"For trusting me."
"Don't fuck with me on this one. I'll slice your nuts off and shove them down your throat."
"That's no way to talk to the man that's going to make it possible for you to make it back to a nice, warm bed tonight."
"It won't be for at least three days. It's colder than shit over here this time of year, especially up here in the mountains. And it won't be a bed, it'll be a cot."
"Yeah, that too."
"Kowalski, I think you need to uncover the scope. Let me get the range..."
"Holy shit! Where is that coming from?"
"It's starting to rain. I can't tell the direction of fire. Pull back! Pull back!"

I grabbed my gear, stuffed it in the ruck, and pulled it onto my back. I pulled my rifle up to the firing position and shoved a fragmentation grenade into the 40mm launcher under the gun barrel. Kowalski covered the scope and traded the Barrett for his Ares 16 as well. Both of our rifles had grenade launchers. We tried throwing a few out there, but without knowing exactly where the combatants were, they weren't exactly helpful. Rounds were zinging off the walls and streets every which way. We were royally fucked.

"Gittens! Back stairwell! Hump it!" Kowalski shouted at me.

We got down from the building top and out onto the back street. The bullets were hitting all around us. How in the hell were they doing that? How could they get... Shit! They had us surrounded before we started firing. What gave our position away? I instinctively turned left, Kowalski turned right, and we laid out several three-round bursts each. He pushed the back of my left arm pointing me toward a side alley. I ran ahead and turned to see him following closely behind. It was close to nightfall already, and I was praying for it to hurry up and come to give us added cover.

There weren't any more rounds coming downrange, but we could hear the insurgents coming still. Jesus, if one of my troops made that much noise around me on an op, I'd turn and shoot them myself. We made it out of town and the road flattened out for a ways. We had a choice to take the high ground, which was a longer distance by a factor of two, or run down and to the right and make cover sooner, but lose height advantage. We chose closest cover and dove downhill as fast as we could. Once we made the ravine, we ran to the north, which took us deeper into enemy territory, but got us as far away as possible, as fast as possible. I'd estimate we ran for about four or five miles.

Then the shit hit the fan again. While we were worrying what was behind us, we managed to overrun another camp of insurgents quite by accident. Kowalski and I both brought our weapons up to lay down a wall, but we were too late. We'd been seen already. The first round I took, spun me around sharply and I screamed. When I hit the ground, I was out of rounds and switched mags. I started spraying again and heard Kowalski switch his mag right after I did. I loaded a Willie Pete grenade hoping to get some backlighting for the enemy from the bright light of the white phosphorus. I had no misguided ideas that it would actually hit anybody. It worked, thanks be! There must not have been too many Afghanis in the camp because we'd already almost evened the fight. Then I took another round. I figured it probably hit the ground and ricocheted into me off a rock because it didn't have the force the first one had. Damn, it burned. I looked up at Kowalski to see how he was.

All he said was "Jesus fucking Christ, Jesus fucking Christ," over and over. Then he slumped over.

I put in my third mag and kept firing. I think I took the last fighter out with a fragmentation grenade to the chest, right as the last two bullets hit me. I managed to get on the radio and call for air support as I lay prone. I reached as far forward as I could, inching along the ground with my hand out. Finally I managed to grab hold of Kowalski, but I had no strength left in my body. None. I couldn't pull any closer to him, and I couldn't pull him to me. "You dumb bastard, don't you leave me! I've already called for a dust-off. You stay with me you motherfucker! Stay with me, do you hear me?" Then things went black.

When I woke up, I had Theresa in a choke hold. She was pinned to the floor, my other hand cocked up in a fist, and I was screaming at the top of my lungs. I didn't close down on her throat, but I had it in my hand. It scared me half to death. It took me several seconds to wake up enough to figure out where I was and what I was doing. I dropped to the floor and hugged her and rocked her and cried my eyes out for hurting my baby girl.

LEAVING AFGHANISTAN BEHIND

"Shh... It's okay, babe, it's okay. You didn't hurt me. I'm all right. Calm down. Come on, take your pills. Let's get you back up, okay?"

I couldn't move. I couldn't get up. I was so disgusted with myself! I would never lay a finger on her, ever, and here I could have done some serious damage without even knowing it. I took both the Paxil and the Lorazepam, and we got back into bed.

"Teri, Teri, Teri," I kept repeating, holding her close to me, rubbing her hair, rocking her, trying to protect her from... me? I was sobbing uncontrollably. The only time I'd ever lifted a finger in my life (from junior high school to my time in the army) was to protect somebody else.

"Do you need to call the doctor?"

Finally, I was able to respond. "I'll call her first thing in the morning and see if I can get in today instead of waiting until tomorrow," I managed. Tears were still streaming down my face non-stop and landing on Theresa's. I'm not a crier. It bothered me.

"Probably a good idea. Elizabeth told me that if you ever get too bad, I can take you to the ER and give them the information, and they can pretty much put you under. Or just this side of it, anyway, until somebody can see you."

"I'm glad my fiancée and my shrink are so tight."

"I love the way that sounds."

"What are you talking about?"

"Your fiancée..."

"Oh, Jesus, sweetie. I'm so sorry. I don't know what happened tonight that was different from any other night, especially when I came back from my last deployment and was having that bad stretch."

"I think I probably do. You were really fighting yourself. I was trying to wake you up. I was actually up on top of you, for the most part, and started shaking you."

"What the hell were you thinking? Don't *ever* do that again!"

"Yeah, I know that now, but it seemed like a good idea at the time."

"Are you nuts?"

"I refuse to answer on the grounds that it might tend to incriminate me."

"Come here, marshmallow."

We cuddled up tightly together for a little bit and just talked. "Babe, turn off the light. We don't have to go to sleep, just turn off the light. Do you mind?"

I turned off the light and eventually, Theresa fell asleep. Not me. I was still awake in the morning at seven thirty when the alarm went off. If you don't sleep, you don't have nightmares. She got dressed because she had to meet a client at her office during the morning, but promised to sneak out with her work as soon as she could. The minute she was out the door, I called Elizabeth's office.

"I'll stick my head into her office after her current appointment and see if we can get you in. I'll call you back."

"Thanks, Rach. I'll be here." Within the hour, she called back.

"Dr. Feynman can see you at twelve, under one condition. She said that you had to bring something from the deli. She said you'd know what that meant."

"I do. See you in a little while."

At lunch time, I stopped at a sandwich shop. I got two large cups of cheddar and broccoli soup and some crackers. When I finally got into her office, I laid napkins on her desk and put one of the cups of soup in front of her and one in front of me. She pulled out her sandwich as well.

"Thanks for the soup. I didn't mean you were supposed to buy me something. I just meant you were supposed to bring lunch. That way I won't feel so bad eating in front of you."

"I know. It just seemed so perfect for such a cold day."

We both ate a little bit of sandwich and sipped our soup in silence.

"So. Flashbacks. Last night's?"

"I told you sniper teams are two people, right? Last night was the night that I lost Kowalski and got shot."

"Do your wounds ever hurt, physically?"

"Sure. That's not uncommon."

"Not at all, but did they hurt you yesterday? Weather-related or something? Hurt at all? Scars irritated?"

I had to think about it for a minute. "Now that you mention it, a little bit. You think maybe it triggered that memory?"

"It's possible. When you were having flashbacks after you got back from your last deployment, how often did you have them?"

"Every few days. Not every night like now."

"I'm guessing that when you were evacuated, Kowalski was already gone."

"Yeah. I somehow knew it, even though you always hold out hope."

LEAVING AFGHANISTAN BEHIND

"How long were you in the hospital?"

"I was taken in a Blackhawk to our forward base, then MEDEVACed to Bagram where they stabilized me. At that point, they kept me for half a day, then sent me on a C-130 to Landstuhl, Germany. After three weeks, they sent me stateside to Walter Reed. Total? About five months. That was during my second deployment. Truthfully, I thought my career was over, but I guess I healed okay. They kept telling me I was going to a VA hospital. I kept telling them, "Fuck that", and asked what it would take to stay in. Every time they gave me a set of parameters they thought I would fail, I proved them wrong. Eventually, they said I had thirty days to pass the full physical with no restrictions or be discharged. I not only passed, but made first class on the PT."

"That's pretty impressive. A testament to physical stamina and mental determination... So I understand you physically grabbed Theresa, huh?"

"I was going to tell you all about that. I'm not proud of it, but I didn't know what I was doing until I finally woke up, and then I immediately let go. I feel like dog shit for that."

"Do you know why Theresa called me this morning?"

"I can imagine."

"I bet you can't. She wanted to make sure that I knew that you were completely asleep when it happened and that it started when she got on top of you and shook you. She wanted to make sure that you didn't get in trouble or get charged with anything. You ask me, she's definitely a keeper. She really cares about you and wants to help you as much as possible."

"Stupid bitch thinks she wants to marry me."

"Oh? And how do you feel?"

"Well, after I got the flowers like you suggested, I asked her if she might want to go to the courthouse this month and do it, or if she wanted a big wedding. She said the courthouse was just fine with her. She never imagined in a million years that I was going to ask her. Somehow, she didn't see me as the marrying kind. Too butch or something like that, I guess," I laughed.

"And getting married has nothing to do with being guilty about what's going on now?"

"Are you kidding? Hell no! She's the greatest chick in the world! What could be better than having her as my wife? She's totally up inside my head."

"Just making sure. Out of curiosity, what kind of flowers did you get?"

"Same ones you got."

"Yeah, Keven's pretty special. Before we quit, I want to ask you again. What do you feel about shooting the perp?"

"I don't feel anything one way or the other. That's the truth. And if you ask me about being overseas, I think my answer is the same. I have no real regrets. I just can't get the ghosts of the past to leave me alone."

"You're already set for eleven tomorrow. You think you can make it?"

"I'll try."

"If you think you can't, or if you can't get over the anxiety after a flashback, have Theresa take you to the ER. I'm going to have Rachel give you a sheet you can take with you with a diagnosis, so they won't mind treating you. It will keep them from putting you through the entire drill. They'll be able to shoot you full of Haldol or a related drug. That's the stuff that knocks horses off their feet. That's the point, you won't feel anything. And I've already told Theresa to either leave you alone until you wake up on your own, or wake you from the side at arm's length."

"Thanks, doc. I can't tell you how much I appreciate your help."

"Amelia? You know that there's no shame in this, don't you? It doesn't make you any less strong a person. It doesn't diminish you in any capacity as a person, as a woman, as a cop... It's neurological. Oh, and one other thing I forgot to mention that I really should have... Do. Not. Drink. Alcohol. None at all, for now."

"Gotcha. See you tomorrow."

I wondered how long it was going to be until tomorrow. Whether the demons would come to visit again during the night. If I could hold it all in. Or if I should even try.

I still hadn't heard from Theresa. I sort of thought she was going to come home before the end of the day, but you never knew what would pop up on her radar. The phone finally rang, showing her contact number from her office. "Hey, honey. Decide to spend the whole day in the office after all?"

LEAVING AFGHANISTAN BEHIND

"Amelia, somebody just drove by the office and shot us full of bullet holes. The police are here now. We all hit the floor, and nobody was hurt, but if they'd wanted to, they could have easily killed several people. We didn't drop until the action was pretty much done."

"At your office? Somebody did a drive-by of your office? How many cops are on the case? Are the detectives there yet? Have they blocked off the street? Give your phone to the officer in charge. I want to speak to him *now!*"

"There's about seven or eight people here. They even brought a fire department ladder truck over, and an ambulance, just in case. The ladder's actually what they're using to block off the street. The firefighters are just sort of standing around like guards."

"Give your phone to the officer in charge."

"Babe, I don't even know who *is* in charge."

"*Teri!* Just give the Goddamned phone to any one of them and let me talk to them. I'll figure this out."

"Okay, wait a minute."

"Detective Wooten, can I help you?"

"Jon. Thank goodness it's you on scene. Gittens here. What the fuck is going on over there?"

"Near as we can tell, this wasn't an attempt to hurt anybody, or there'd be bodies stacked up. They have plate glass windows and could easily see people. I think this was a warning. You're still off, pending review, right?"

"Yeah. For now."

"Get your ass down to the station, now. I want to pick your brain since your girlfriend works here. And there's one other thing, there's a slight development on your incident. Don't panic or worry, just a little twist. I can't talk over the phone, but we need you in on this one."

"I'll be there in an hour, but first I want to take Theresa to her sister's house to get her out of the way until I can get home and stay with her."

"Uh, I don't think that's such a good idea. Why don't you let us bring her back to the precinct? We'll all have a nice, cozy, little sit-down when we get there. Be there in, say, an hour. Got it?"

"10-4."

I was already going through some pretty weird shit that I didn't begin to understand, much less was able to control, and now this? What was the big secret that he couldn't talk about over the phone? I loaded up my backpack with a change of clothes for me and one for Theresa, filled up a couple of Nalgene bottles with water from our filter, and grabbed some trail bars. I added a couple chocolate bars for Theresa. How in the world she could eat pure junk, and keep so slender (and healthy), was amazing to me. She even ran about half as often as I did, and could still keep up when we went together. Finally, I headed out the door to the corner, to catch the bus.

… LEAVING AFGHANISTAN BEHIND

CHAPTER FIVE

It took me about twenty minutes to get to the precinct. Theresa was already there, along with everybody that worked with her, about fifteen people. Wooten saw me through the glass of the War Room and waved me in. Inside the *fish bowl* of a glassed-in conference room, he was standing with two suits, Theresa, and another officer in uniform that I didn't recognize. The two suits were standing with their hands on their hips, holding their coats open, vests all buttoned up, with their gold badges, and guns, hanging neatly on their trousers. Shit! 1 Police Plaza. That wasn't a good sign.

"Officer Gittens, come in, come in. Have a seat."

Theresa was sitting down, but nobody else was. For this reason, I wasn't either. "Go ahead, take a seat," he said, holding out the chair right next to Theresa for me. Gentlemanly? I scarcely thought so. Something else. I moved up behind Theresa, but continued to stand. "This is Captain Lankin, the Special Liaison with the United Nations here in the city. And this is Captain Jernick, who works with the Drug Enforcement Task Force in coordination with the DEA, the FBI, the NYBCA, and a few bits and bobs here and there."

I reached my hand out to each of the three men with Jon. Then I moved directly behind Theresa and put my hands on top of her shoulders. "Is somebody going to break out some graham crackers, chocolate, and marshmallows, or are we going to get down to why you've got everybody down here?" I asked, nodding my head to the other people in various other rooms that had been brought over from Theresa's office.

Lankin spoke first, "First and foremost, we've been following leads from the shooting of Daniel Ortega Sanchez and we've managed to come up with a lot more than you would think."

"So why are you telling *me* this, instead of Jernick?"

"Because the man you shot is the son of one of the members of the delegation from Columbia, who is here with diplomatic immunity."

Suddenly I felt sick. I sat down in the chair previously offered to me. I knew this wasn't going to go well for me. "So what you're saying is the shoot that was previously being called clean is now off the table, and I'll need to get both my union rep and an attorney?"

"No, no, nothing like that. You better listen to the whole story before you get upset. The kid that you smoked was a real bad kid. He's been arrested at least a dozen times, including twice on felonies. He's managed to slip away every time. He's a big time drug dealer and pimp. The problem is not with his dad and his station, it's with the other suspect. That man, one Emilio Cruz de la Paz, is the cousin of the man you shot. He is even worse than Sanchez. De la Paz has a record in Columbia, outstanding warrants both there and the United States, as well as in Bolivia, Columbia, and, of all places, Serbia. I guess he follows the drug trade wherever it is."

"We think today's little episode was a warning," followed Jernick, "And that means that they found out who Theresa is, found out where she works, and that she is related to your life. The question is, do they only want to put out a warning or are they going to push this?"

"I want Theresa moved out of state. I want her put under a temporary order of protection," I said.

"I don't think we need to jump quite that far that fast," said Lankin.

"And I don't remember asking you, ass wipe. They've already taken shots at her, they know who she is, they know where she is, and because of that they'll have an open range on her."

"Officer Gittens, please. Let's relax a little bit here. This meeting is to figure out exactly what we're going to need to do next, in a logical and calm manner, to make sure everybody is safe and sound and that…"

LEAVING AFGHANISTAN BEHIND

"Wooten, either Ms. Biancardi is under protection by midnight tonight, or I get out my M-24 and I deal with this on my own. I'll, of course, need some personal time."

"Officer Gittens," spoke Captain Jernick, "you grabbing a rifle and trying to deal with this as a personal problem will definitely not go well on your behalf."

"Then Jernick, you prick, do your fucking job!"

"Amelia! That's enough! Don't make me cite you for insubordination. Would you have done that when you were on active duty? Would you?"

"If somebody were threatening my fiancée, I would have. You bet your ass! Elizabeth wants to find out what's wrong with me. She wants to know if it's my incident on the force or if it's something from Afghanistan. You know what? I'll tell you the same thing I told her. I have no feelings either way about anybody I've killed. Not good, not bad, just something I've had to do. If I have to take the battle to high ground out of town and wait for them to come, for every one of those motherfuckers that I waste, I'll have a big fucking smile on my face. You got that?"

Jernick stepped back in quickly. "Officer Gittens, I couldn't clear your shooting tonight even if I wanted to. There are controls built into the system for a reason. And you couldn't protect Ms. Biancardi if you were cleared, because you're involved. You need somebody as a second party. So, I'll make sure we can get her out of town tonight, but I'm going to have to make sure you're protected here. We'll need you to assist in the investigation."

"I've no problem with that. I can do whatever we need to do."

"Amelia, no! You're going with me. That's all there is to it."

"Honey, I've gone on enough snoop and poop missions, this would just be another one. You don't have to worry about me."

"The point is, I worried about you every second of the day, and that was *before* I knew you were a sniper. I couldn't take it now. I just couldn't. They'd have to keep me sedated for the whole time."

I looked at Wooten, Jernick, and Lankin. "How much time do you think it would take for this little drama to play out, to get the CAB involved and take the whole lot of them down? To get the intel and execute warrants?"

"Best case? Six weeks. Worst case? Six months," answered Jernick.

"Fuck it. Let's rock and roll this then."

"Amelia, I'm not kidding. I'm not going to let them ship me off somewhere where I won't be able to talk to you every day. And what about my work? We can't do without the money."

"Honey, I sort of have maybe a couple of other, shall we say, lies of omission…" I said, cringing.

"Oh, great! What could *possibly* make this better than it is already?" she practically screamed.

"I've been planning on asking you to marry me for almost two years."

"You have?" she said in a quiet, demure voice."

"Yes. And to do that in the correct manner, I've been putting back a little money. I didn't have to pay taxes on my pay when I was overseas. I still got paid for maintaining my household plus I got reenlistment bonuses, deployment bonuses, and hazardous duty pay."

"So what exactly are you trying to say?"

"Until all of this went down in the last couple of days, I was going to surprise you by buying at least a row house here. Maybe even a little house with a small yard down in Queens."

"Amelia, I know it's your money, not mine…"

"No, honey. It's as much yours as it is mine. As soon as they did away with *don't ask, don't tell*, I had a JAG Corps lawyer write up my will. You're my sole beneficiary. And the answer to the question I think you're trying to ask is, somewhere in the range of about a hundred and eighty thousand."

I thought Theresa was going to faint outright. Jon smiled. Jernick and Lankin dropped their jaws simultaneously. "So, let us take care of your office. I'll put you in WITSEC instead of protective custody. That way, even if your company is really small, they have to follow all federal laws. You'll have your job for up to six months, and we'll have all this settled by then," said Jernick.

I pulled Theresa up by her hands and held her tightly. "Don't worry. It's all going to be fine."

"No, it's not. I can't stand not being around you for even hours at a time. How am I going to handle this? At least I knew when you deployed it wouldn't ever be more than a couple of weeks at the most, and we'd get to internet web conference. A Goddamned sniper! You bitch! Is there anything else you haven't told me? I mean, I would

LEAVING AFGHANISTAN BEHIND

think this would be a perfect opportunity to get everything right out on the table?"

"One thing. I'm not really gay."

She wound up and punched me straight in the bread basket. Luckily my reflexes are really quick, and I saw it coming and tightened up, so it didn't hurt at all. "Ugh! You are frustrating!"

The four men in the room were trying hard not to break out laughing. Finally, Jon just laughed out loud, unable to hold it in any longer.

"Wooten, you cocksucker, show some decorum!" I yelled.

That set everybody off. Even Theresa and I were laughing uncontrollably. Even though you couldn't really hear very well outside the fishbowl, you could vaguely hear noises and see the six of us laughing. We started picking up stares. Kettering, the other squad officer in the room with us, pointed out some of the people watching us with strange looks. That just made it even harder. We were gone. After about fifteen minutes, Jernick finally managed to straighten up and mentioned that we should probably be getting ready.

Kettering held out his hand out to Theresa. "What?"

"Your phone. I might as well take it and put it up." She reluctantly handed it over. "And your purse. And I'll take all your projects. I'll give them to somebody in your office before they leave."

I pulled out my backpack and opened it. I took out my set of sweats and left hers, also NYPD of course, along with a pair of shorts, a tank top, and a snapback NYPD cap in the pack. I handed her the pack, taking one of the water bottles for myself. "There's some trail food and chocolate in there for your trip to keep up your blood sugar. And a couple of protein bars. Don't worry, we'll get through this. We've gotten through worse."

"I'm going to miss you. Hell, I already do. I love you, you big lout."

"No, you just love my almost-British accent."

"That too, my island girl. Easter bunny!"

"I love you. Now get going so we can make sure you're safe. They'll be able to forward letters back and forth. I'll write you every day, just like my deployment. Even if you don't get them each day, you'll get one from every day. Okay?"

"Okay."

We kissed deeply, not really caring who was around us for a long time. Finally, Jon tapped me on the back and motioned me out of the room, leaving the men from 1PP to do their jobs.

"Easter egg?" he asked.

"Bunny. I'm her chocolate bunny, and she'd like to just eat me up."

"That's an HR nightmare. Now I've got dirty thoughts of one of my officers pulling a lesbian scene with her girlfriend," he laughed.

"I never saw you as a misogynist."

"I'm telling you, it's every straight man's fantasy. Say, I thought you were an MP."

"I was."

"What's this about being a sniper?"

"There isn't an MOS for being a sniper. They're chosen from many other fields and pressed into a specific duty. You can be one of three, including Eleven Bravo. I technically wasn't an infantryman, but I was part of an infantry division, so they gave me permission to try out."

"Impress the living daylights out of me, why don't you?"

"Thank you, sir."

"I can only imagine you protected your men and women like you protect your girlfriend."

"That's fiancée to you, sir," I said, throwing out an exaggerated salute.

LEAVING AFGHANISTAN BEHIND

CHAPTER SIX

Lying alone in bed was sheer torture. I missed Theresa on so many levels: as my lover, my friend, and my companion. Also as my defender against the night the last few days. I had to laugh at that one. Here I am the big tough one and she's the little wimpy one, but she had to protect me from things that went bump in the night. I know you're not supposed to do it, but I doubled up on my medications tonight. I knew they wouldn't complete the task anyway. I got dressed for bed, then I did one last thing. I got a pair of Beretta M92s out of my lock box, filled and inserted the mags, and chambered a round in each. Then I filled six more mags and put the extras mags into an elastic bandoleer. I put everything in the drawer in my bedside table. If I had to plain shit-and-git in the middle of the night, I wanted to be ready.

We had on our uniforms, but over the top we were wearing a tawb and a hijab. Unless you were right on us, you couldn't tell, and the tawbs were long enough to cover our boots, for the most part. I had a desert cammo sleeve over the Barrett. We were on a rooftop about six hundred meters past the compound. Cars kept coming about every ten to fifteen minutes. Don't these idiots have phones? It seemed every little kid on the street had a phone, and yet they weren't trying to warn anybody. My first shot had gone in at 1243. He hit the dirt like a deer in northern Minnesota taken during season. At 1259, a second car arrived. The target would never be the driver, and if there were three people, it would always be the person in the back seat. I didn't even wait for him to get out of the car. I took the shot and filled the car with brain matter and blood. The third target wandered into the field of view at 1322. Again, I took the shot with the thug in the back seat. I managed to hit him right below the neck, forcing the entirety of his chest to explode forward. The other two people got out of the car. I dropped the driver, who would always be more important than the extra rider. He had gotten about ten feet before I was able to hit him. The last car showed up exactly five minutes later. There were only two people in the car, so I trained on the passenger. They got out looking confused, then saw the carnage around them and began to panic and run. Too late. My target twisted in the wind as he went down.

"Five for five, Hondo."

"Roger that. Let's get the hell out of here," I replied. It would probably take us about six hours to extract. Movement had to be excruciatingly slow. Sudden movements would give you away quickly. Nothing to focus on, just the movement itself caught people's attention, especially street-wise people.

"Kowalski? Need to take a piss?"

"Why in the hell did you have to go and say that? Not until now. Why are you always screwing with my head?"

"You're a terrible sniper."

"Well, you're a terrible chick. A pretty cool dude, but a terrible chick."

That kind of hurt. I know he didn't know any better, but just because I was a lesbian didn't mean I was any less a woman. If only I could say something, but I knew that if I slipped up, even once, it would end my career, possibly incur jail time, heavy fines, and a dishonorable discharge. "You know, that's totally not a nice thing to say. Even if I do look a little androgynous, you know?" I whispered back to him.

"You know I was just joking, don't you? Seriously."

"'Well, I have to take it all the time. Sometimes it just gets a little old."

"I promise I'll never do it again. And when the guys are doing it, I'll jack them up. What do you say, partner?" he whispered over to me and held his fingertips out to me. I touched his fingertips with mine, which was a covert and quiet mission accomplished sign. I think I smiled, but dressed up in a uniform, body armor, a tawb, and a hijab,

LEAVING AFGHANISTAN BEHIND

in a hot afternoon sun of about one hundred and twenty degrees, it was hard to tell.

Once we were clear of that part of town, it was much safer for us to move about. We still wanted to remain concealed until we approached the compound, and then there was the problem of approaching the compound. There was almost always a fuck up. When we drew near, they were supposed to listen for a countersign from an approaching pedestrian, for people just like us, patrol units, stuff like that.

"Sea turtle."

"Stop! Ta poheegee?! Wadrega! (Stop, identify yourself)

"Sea turtle."

"Stop! Ta poheegee?! Wadrega!

"You stupid American fuck! Use the countersign! Sea turtle! Sea turtle! Use the countersign."

A Humvee approached us. Three of the four people got out, pointing their guns at us. I looked at the insignia on the point man. He was a second lieutenant and his name tag stated 'Carter'.

"Lieutenant Carter, I suggest that you first consider pointing your weapons away from me and my sergeant here, to start with. Then I suggest you get on your motherfucking radio and find out what today's motherfucking countersign is. Make sure that it is indeed sea turtle like we've been saying for the last ten fucking minutes to this moron you have posted on guard. Then check the duty logs for Kowalski and Gittens, who are motherfucking MPs, you stupid piece of shit. If you don't do that right fucking now, the sergeant and I are going to lift our rifles, which are currently loaded with 40mm frags, and unload on your stupid asses."

"Corporal, did they provide you with the countersign 'sea turtle'?"

"Why, uh, yes sir, they did, but the countersign is Orion, I believe, sir."

"That was yesterday, you moron! You almost got two soldiers shot because of your stupidity. Consider yourself on report and meet me back at the duty station in fifteen minutes as soon as your replacement has come to relieve you. Is that understood?"

"Y-y-yes, sir!"

"Sergeants, I'm terribly sorry for the mix-up. His first week of his first deployment. How many trips for you two? Obviously more than one, looking at your gear."

"Four, sir. Love to stay and chat, but we've got a debriefing at HQ if you don't mind."

"Of course not. Gentlemen…" the lieutenant said, motioning with his hand to the compound.

Kowalski actually pulled his Beretta from his webbed belt and held it up alongside the lieutenant's head. "I know it's starting to get a little dark out here, shit for brains, but does that look like a man to you? Consider your answer carefully, I suggest."

"My regrets. I meant nothing derogatory; I should have said sergeants. Please, may we give you a lift to HQ?"

"Yeah. We'd like that." The lieutenant got in the front passenger seat (the driver had never gotten out), and Kowalski and I took the two back seats. When the other two MPs started for the doors, I looked at the one on my side and very loudly said, "Where do you think you're going, double dumbass?"

They drove us to HQ and dropped us off. The lieutenant started to get out, but Kowalski turned to him and said, "We'll take it from here, sir. I think the general will handle this in private. It was an eyes only mission detail." He looked like I'd just kicked his favorite puppy. We managed to hold it together until we walked inside, and then lost it and laughed up a storm.

We were met by a major who looked at us still dressed as Arabs and chastised us for lack of decorum in the hallway, but Kowalski looked at her and said, "Ma'am, we've just gotten back from a five day mission without as much as a change of underwear. We've walked over fifty miles on foot with two rifles and a Barrett with full gear, and we've killed six people. Right now, we want to meet with the colonel, get debriefed, get a shower if it's even working, and get about two days of sleep. So if you don't mind, we'll be going in to see the colonel. Okay?" and we walked away. There was something actually liberating about belonging to one of the elite groups. You could always get away with tons of shit. The only thing I hated about being in one of those groups is that you had to smell right. For the most part that meant that taking a shower when you stood down would be followed by a week with no shower. Plus our food had to all be Afghani food, so we didn't smell like Americans. Gack! Cat on a hairball. Oh, yeah, and one other thing… no menstruating. I have to take three weeks of hormones, followed by another three weeks of hormones, with no week between. Then when I finally stand down, my cycle is about two weeks long. I

LEAVING AFGHANISTAN BEHIND

bleed like a stuck pig. And the cramps? Oh, Holy Mary, Mother of God!

At least tonight's trip wasn't a bad trip. I opened my eyes quickly, sensing something was wrong. I held perfectly still. I couldn't hear anything, which in and of itself was weird for New York. I picked up my phone and tried to dial the precinct to have them contact the patrol out front. Nothing. The signal was being jammed. I slid down to the floor and across the room. I picked up my police radio and inserted the earpiece where the noise wasn't coming out of the speaker. "168, dispatch. 168, dispatch. 10-33. 10-33. Contact squad my 10-20, verify no activity."

"Dispatch, 168, 10-4. Standby."

"Dispatch, 168, no contact with squad, your 10-20."

"168, dispatch, 10-78, handle 10-39. I say again, 10-78, handle 10-39."

"Dispatch, 168, 10-4."

"168, dispatch, advise plainclothes officer, armed, on premises."

"Dispatch, 10-4."

I slid along the floor to get a pair of sweats out and quickly get dressed, then slipped on some sneakers. I crawled back along the floor, staying low and out of sight of the window, and opened the drawer to the bedside table. I wrapped the extra mags around my neck, then pushed off the safeties to both of my Berettas. I got up close to the window and saw nothing. I couldn't see anybody sitting up in the squad where the two officers should be. If one had to go and piss in the bushes, there should still be one in the squad. I tried squinting at the squad. Shit! There was something on the glass, and something didn't look right about the window on the driver's side. I quietly moved out into the hallway, and then moved to the back of the building instead of going out the front. Now is the time I wish I lived in a single family unit. I got to the back door, quickly exited and crouched down. I normally would have my baton light to hold up for illumination and a gun rest, but this way I had both guns available for the highest concentration of gunfire.

From where I was on the side of the bushes, I couldn't see or hear much. I was going to have to move around the outside of three buildings, then work my way from the alley to the front of the street, and back down the three buildings. As soon as I started moving, I saw three figures moving in the shadows. I crawled back up into the bushes to bide my time. The three figures came up into the light a little better. I could easily see that two out of the three were carrying shotguns. I immediately knew that the officers in the squad were already dead. Probably from a silenced weapon the third man carried. I waited until they had closed the distance to about twenty feet, then I sprang up and unloaded on them. I must have shot ten rounds per clip. They were on the ground, immobile, and not making any noise whatsoever. I ran quickly to their sides and checked. Definitely carrying shotguns, and I was right about the third one. He was carrying a 45 caliber MK1911 with a silencer. I sprinted around the end of the building and up to the squad. My backup still hadn't shown up. I knew that they would quickly now, with so many shots being fired in the area. When I got to the squad, I looked at the driver's side window. It had two holes raggedly and unevenly punched through it.

Slumped over in the seats were the two officers, each with a large caliber hole in their head. I pulled the door open to check on the men and also give a little light, so whoever came on scene wouldn't be quite so inclined to shoot me. Both men were dead already. This was getting out of hand. I still felt no remorse for shooting the suspect three days ago, but people were dying due to my actions. I felt terrible now.

Just then, three squads came screaming up. They spotlighted me and I stood up straight, feet shoulder width apart, with my hands straight up in the air. My guns were on the seat of the squad and NYPD was written down my legs and sleeves. I was still approached carefully, with guns drawn, but not aimed at me. I gave them my badge number and they relaxed, but they got really agitated with the sight of the two dead cops in the car.

LEAVING AFGHANISTAN BEHIND

CHAPTER SEVEN

I told them about the men in back of the building and one of the squads went screaming around to the back. Another squad started working the front scene, calling for supervisors, and the remaining squad drove me around to the back of the building. We started going through the men's coat pockets, where I found the jammer. I pulled it out, switched it off, and then put it in an evidence bag from the squad. I went back inside my apartment and turned on all the lights. I checked the phone and it was working now. I located a saved number and dialed it.

"This is Elizabeth Feynman. May I help you?"

"Elizabeth? Hey, I know that you're probably not on call this week, but I sent Theresa out under protective detail today and got a squad to park in front of my place tonight. Three men approached my place, jammed the cell phones, and killed both officers on detail in the squad. I went out the back and ran into them. I killed all three. I think we need to talk again. I was hoping that I could talk to you instead of whoever's on call. I really hate to do that to you, but…"

"Sweetie, no. Keven is at her sister's house tonight. Let me get her back over here to watch the kids and I'll be there as quickly as I can. Stay at your house though. Don't go to the precinct. Have the officer of record work your report from there. What's your address?"

"I'll text it to you so you won't have to write it down."

"Okay. Be there in a while... Amelia?
"Yeah?"
"Are you okay? I mean, really okay?"
"I'm tired of people dying around me. Innocent people."
"Hold that thought."

LEAVING AFGHANISTAN BEHIND

CHAPTER EIGHT

I didn't even see Elizabeth come in the apartment. I was busy at the kitchen table going over the last bits of my report. "You know, Officer Gittens, you'll have to turn over your Berettas until this investigation has concluded. I know that leaves you somewhat exposed since those were personal weapons, but we have to do it."

"Fine. I also have a Colt Mk IV, a Glock 27, and my M-24." The first was for close-quarters combat, the latter for any reason to take the fight to the enemy, out to about a thousand meters. I think the reporting officer was a little irritated that I was filing my report at the same time he was. I wasn't trivializing his time, I was just maximizing the effort. It was about four in the morning when we broke it off. As he was getting up from my table and putting all his paperwork into a folder, I signed my report and handed it over. The sheer, visceral anger at my methods was evident on his face. Too bad, so sad. I didn't have time for his BS.

As I stood up, I noticed Elizabeth was laid out on the couch, her shoes kicked off, with one arm over her face, and quietly sleeping. I motioned for the sergeant to come over to me.

"When are you going to move that stupid fire apparatus and get four squads parked outside, two in front and two in back? I need to get with the doc for a while and then get her back home."

"I don't know if we can get four squads. I might be able to get one in front and one in the back, which would give you four officers. I wish I could do more tonight, but until there is some rearranging during the day tomorrow, that's all I can do."

"Is that what you're going to tell the widows of the two guys outside tonight? They're dead because the threat wasn't taken as credible?"

"I'm not going to argue with you, officer. We'll all do the best we can."

"Well, I need you to contact Capt. Jernick from 1PP to make sure he gets word to my fiancée that an incident happened and that I'm okay. If she sees this on the news and has to wonder for even one minute if I'm okay or not, someone will pay dearly. I need that done now. Am I clear on this issue?"

"Why not? I'd like nothing more than to wake up a captain and tell him how he's supposed to run his department."

I ignored him and went as quietly as I could over to Elizabeth and gently shook her arm. She pulled her arm down off her eyes, which gradually fluttered open. She smiled at me and patted the back of my arm. "Promise me you'll apologize to Keven for me personally when you see her?" I fairly begged.

"I'm sure she'll understand, especially under the circumstances," she said, sitting up. "You don't mind if I record this? It will be transcribed and the tape destroyed. I'm just too tired to keep notes tonight."

"Sure, no problem. I just wish I didn't have to get you back out. Theoretically, we don't have to talk for a day or two. We've already got an appointment for later today, but under the circumstances…"

"Don't think twice about it. Tell me, how are you, Amelia? Truthfully."

"Do you mean do I have any remorse whatsoever for those fucking bastards that killed two fine officers who never saw it coming, whose funerals will be attended by widows and fatherless children? I could give a fuck! My only regret is not having my flashback earlier, so I could have done a little preventive maintenance, so to speak, instead of finishing it."

"It looks like you were already prepared for something like this to happen."

"I was."

"And of course now they have your weapons."

LEAVING AFGHANISTAN BEHIND

"I'm still in the ready reserve, and I'm a cop. If you think that's all the armament I have, you don't know me very well, as Bugs Bunny is known to say once in a while," I said, with a wink.

"Do you feel the need to keep a small arsenal on hand to deal with problems?"

"Well, the department isn't being very effective right now."

"What was the flashback tonight? Night frights again?"

"Strangely, just a successful op. I was just the observer for this mission. We infiltrated, selectively removed some members of a meeting, and then self-extracted back to the forward base."

"You say successful. What exactly do you mean by that?"

"In, dropped five targets plus one, out, and debriefed by the OIC for the unit. Simple."

"That's six confirmed for Kowalski, then? He was your team member at that time? Or was it somebody else?"

"No, it was him."

"Hmmm."

"What?"

"I'm just wondering what woke you up in the first place. The shattering of the glass in the squad, perhaps?"

"I wish I knew."

"Sergeant, would you mind if I had my friend from the VA meet with us tomorrow for your appointment? If you'd rather not, I'd understand, but I'd like to have him get a feel for you. He's very sympathetic to veterans' problems. Working as your advocate, I have no doubt that you'll be seeing him relatively soon anyway."

"You can call me Amelia, you can call me Officer Gittens, but don't call me sergeant."

"You just said the small arms were legal for you to possess because you were in the ready reserve. You can't have it both ways. Why does it bother you to be called sergeant?"

"Because I'm not the one that should have made it home! Don't you get it? It wasn't supposed to be me!" I broke down for the first time, I mean, really broke down. I'd never cried really hard in front of Elizabeth. Tears in my eyes, whatever, but I plain broke down. Kowalski died with my hand on him. Vam wasn't supposed to be shipped stateside in a cargo plane while I was lying in a hospital and couldn't even see her being laid to rest. What a total cluster fuck that

- 55 -

whole place had turned out to be. My disillusionment was now complete!

"You know that you can't just go and shoot up the whole city of New York. You've got to let all of the teams of people do their part."

"No offense, but the team last night was supposed to do their part. Maybe they grossly underestimated the threat, and hopefully they won't do that again, but there are two men's wives and kids who will always blame me for their deaths. Was it my fault? I wonder..."

"Now we're getting to the hard questions. Do *you* think it's your fault they died? Was it poor training? Poor communication? Lack of proper threat assessment, as you say? Did you do something specifically to aid in their deaths through anything you did?"

"You know I didn't, but that doesn't make it any easier."

"Amelia, there's nothing you could have done any differently. That includes making that first apprehension and shooting the first suspect. He not only drew on you first, but he fired at you first. You had no choice."

"Now you're starting to sound like those sorry pig-fuckers in Ghaniland."

"How so?"

"They're all fatalists. If they're making explosives in their huts and they accidently blow up their own children, "It was the will of Allah." That shit, that's what I'm talking about. I know, it's the Cockpit Cascade Effect. A causes B, which in turn causes C, which would have stopped D from happening if seen soon enough, although E was misinterpreted due to the fact that F... I was supposed to be eating at that particular restaurant just two blocks away, making me the first respondent, forcing me to give chase, and the suspect turns on me, forcing me to shoot him, which causes his cousin to get really pissed off at me and track me and my girlfriend down..."

"I get it, I get it. Do you really believe that to be true? Are you a fatalist?"

"No. Sometimes shit happens."

"So why beat yourself up? You've got bigger problems going on right now."

"Bigger than somebody trying to kill me and my girlfriend? They sure as hell didn't know that Theresa wasn't home. I guarantee it. Did you hear? They're trying to kill my girlfriend. You asked me before how I felt about killing somebody. I've said it before and I'll say it

LEAVING AFGHANISTAN BEHIND

again. If you try to kill Theresa, I'll kill you first, and I'll do it with a grin on my face and mean it."

"You need to try and get some sleep. I'll only get about two hours before I have to go in. At least you won't have to get to my office until noon."

"Elizabeth?"

"Yes?"

"I just want to let you know how sorry I am to call you out tonight. And to let you know how totally grateful I am to you."

"No worries. See you in a few hours."

After she had left, everybody was starting to leave my apartment. They had managed to get three squads, one in the back and two in front. Capt. Jernick knocked and came in without waiting for an answer. "Officer Gittens, I wanted to let you know that we've gotten word to Ms. Biancardi about what happened tonight. Her detail has an encrypted NSA satellite phone for RAPID COMS. You can't use it for chit chats, but we can communicate emergency flash traffic. You've got heightened security here for the next eight hours or so. We'll transport you to Dr. Feynman's office at noon, then pick you up from there and move you to another secure location. We're going to keep you under wraps for a while until we get this sorted out."

"Cap, you send me underground and they've got no target. No way."

"At least for a week. That will give us a few days to start really beating the bushes for any intel we can use to bring this thing under control."

"Are you going to be able to bring Dr. Feynman to me wherever you take me? I doubt she'll give up her practice for one patient, for however long it takes you to do your job. Seriously, Cap. Just turn me loose on this, let me pick my own team, and I'll have it swept up in two weeks… three tops."

Jernick laughed openly at me. "In what reality do you think that would ever happen? I have to say this, officer (and I am fully aware of the implications with HR on this), but seriously, you have the biggest balls that I've ever seen on a human – male or female – and they're solid brass. No kidding. If I weren't on your side, I think I'd genuinely be afraid of you. Abject fear. I promise you, you may not like my methods, but I come with years of experience here. Please let me do my job. Okay, Amelia?"

I thought for a minute. I didn't even mean it when I preened and walked like a peacock spouting off about what I'd do with my own team. I just wanted to get my point across. I merely shrugged my shoulders, walked into my bedroom, and shut the door. I dropped my clothes on the floor right where they were, which was very unlike me. I crawled into bed in my underwear. For now, I didn't care. I just wanted rest. Sleep. My head was probably about three inches above my pillow when my brain turned completely off. I didn't stir until after nine o'clock.

"Gittens. Up and out. Grab your partner and hit Pad 17. Both of you take your rifles. We have three out of four platoons from a company pinned down over at Qalat-e Gilzay, and every time the fourth tries to pop their heads up to help, they get zingers all around them. We're going to shove you in at the south end of the village. You'll push in, look for some rooftops for high ground, and help get them out. That fourth platoon is going to cover your ground so that you can climb up a bit. You awake?"

"Yes, Ma'am. Moving, Ma'am."

I didn't have the luxury of some of the women in my barracks. I had to wear my uniform twenty-four/seven, and we couldn't use soap because we couldn't smell like westerners. I rolled out of the rack and dialed my padlock on my locker. For today's mission, we'd be using the Heckler and Koch M110 SSAS because we'd be in closer and potentially be taking many shots. I donned my body armor, loaded and holstered my Beretta, and stuck four clips of extra 9mm rounds into my jacket. I put a clip of 7.62mm into my rifle, picked out ten twenty-round clips for the rifle and stuck them in my over jacket, and put two clips in each of my trouser side pockets.

I popped my cover on quickly, followed by my Oakleys, my gloves, and my radio. I pulled back the bolt on the HK, letting it chamber a live round. "Going Hot!" I yelled through the barrack. "Hot rifle!" many of the women yelled back at me, acknowledging there was a charged weapon in a living quarters. I stopped at the next building and picked up two canteens of water with electrolytes and eight protein bars, then I double-timed it over to the helipad. The Blackhawk at station number 17 was already spun up to full speed and Kowalski was running up about twenty meters behind me. We hopped in and the crew chief clipped us in the harnesses while we hung our boots out the door, guns pointed outward, ready to drop and fight.

LEAVING AFGHANISTAN BEHIND

When we approached Qalat, we did a wide swing to the southeast. When we were on the south side of the town, we turned directly north for our insertion point. The radio chatter was going nuts. I knew they were encrypted, but you always wondered if one of the Ghanis had somehow gotten hold of one and could tell what we were doing. It would shed light on some of the inexplicable occurrences. The chopper sat down south of the last building. Actually, we didn't sit down, we just hung about six feet in the air. The crew chief cleared us of the harnesses and we dropped to the ground running. During the flight, Kowalski said he'd take the lead.

"Charlie Four Ace, Angel Team, boots wet. Show yellow streamer, say again, yellow streamer."

Immediately we saw a yellow plastic streamer thrown out of the window of the closest building. Kowalski and I ran to the back of that building and were met by four squad members of that platoon, who pulled us into the building. Their LT started shouting out a hurried briefing to us. "We've got to get a leap frog going to move you two down five blocks. It's going to be a bitch. They're lighting us up like a fucking Christmas tree. They didn't even show their little towel heads until we got halfway through the town. Everybody managed to make it into buildings, and we have zero casualties at this point, but our equipment has been shot to hell. They've got RPGs, 7.62mm, and what looks like some home-jobby looking rockets. Crude, but they've been effective as all get out. They said this was a routine repositioning of troops... Do you believe that shit?! Ready to mount?"

"Hooah!"

"Charlie Four Ace, Sierra One, go. Sierra Two, go on traverse. Sierra three, go on traverse two."

"Hold and advise. Move, move, move!"

After First Squad and Second Squad had the next two buildings, our squad moved out to get into place past those two squads. Kowalski and I moved up only two buildings to stay in the middle with Sierra Two. We kept this up for almost two hours. It was excruciatingly slow, but we made it, taking on very little fire or resistance. Finally, the LT told us to each pick a building and move up to the rooftop. Our two buildings were the tallest ones we could get to. It took us only minutes to get into place. We each had a building, next to each other, and today there would be no observer. We were both live.

"Sniper One, visual?"

"One, negative. Two?"

"Two, negative."

The wait began. It took almost forty minutes to detect some movement. I heard Kowalski come through the earpiece of my radio.

"Sniper Two... One, look... One-one-five. Make that closer to one-one-eight. Two ducks... fifth floor. Two ducks... third floor. Rooftop! Rooftop! Drop down!"

Both of us hugged the rooftop as low as we could. I moved a little closer to a section of the façade that was taller. "One, looks like the whole ground floor is littered with ducks. No major movement, but looks like a collection of ECs. A big collection. We may have found our hornet's nest. Sniper One, Charlie Four Ace, do you read?"

"Charlie Four Ace. Go ahead."

"Charlie Four Ace, Sniper One. We think we've located your little problem. Grid looks like... Stand by..." Kowalski verified our exact position with our GPS and referred to the map, verifying with a nonvisible laser rangefinder. "AFG20051204n16. Split your squads between floors and we'll start our little barbecue."

"Roger, Sniper One. Charlie One Ace, Charlie Two Ace, Charlie Three Ace, copy?"

"Charlie Two Ace, we have, uh, we have a single story. We're sort of pinned down here. We'll move out into the street when it hits the fan."

"Charlie Three Ace, same situation. Waiting for your signal and drawing fire, then will proceed on target."

"Charlie One Ace, we can't move. They're right across the street from us. We can't move, other than to retreat to the west, which would just split us up further. We're going to wait in position until clear from Charlie Four Ace."

"Sniper One, Charlie Four Ace. Advise on position and execution."

"Sniper One, stand by." It took almost five minutes of radio chatter to get everyone in position.

"Sniper One, Sniper Two, green light, say again, green light."

"Sniper One, Sniper Two. Countdown from five. On my mark... five... four... three... two... one... mark!" As I said mark, both Kowalski and I opened up. The HKs we carry have modifications to the seers allowing for fully automatic fire, but we kept them in burst mode, which fires three rounds at a time like the standard American M16M4. Instead of picking one window and clearing that room, we each

LEAVING AFGHANISTAN BEHIND

randomly chose locations so that the ECs would think that there were a lot more than two of us. At the same time as our fire broke out, everybody from Fourth Company started raining down a solid sheet of lead from the five floors below us. They carried the M4s, which only had the 5.56mm rounds, but they had two advantages that made up for their lighter weight: they had a muzzle velocity of just over 3,000 feet per second (giving a tremendous impact which tends to fragment better even though it's a hardball, fully jacketed round) and being such a small diameter, they tended to tumble when encountering any resistance.

The firefight lasted for over half an hour. "Charlie Four Ace, cease fire, cease fire, cease fire." Nobody moved for another thirty minutes. "Charlie Two Ace, move forward and fill from north end of the street. Snipers One and Two, stand ready. We don't know if this fire is truly out or not."

"Sniper One, roger."

"Sniper Two, roger."

Apparently we'd taken the fight out of the enemy. We found the five buildings down one side of the street littered with Ghanis, but we had enough sense to know that there were probably just as many that had scattered out the back side of the buildings and into the distance for now. No doubt it was only to regroup and come play another day. Now that there was no danger of casualty from friendly fire, the LT called in close air support to the east to pursue fleeing ECs. He also ordered up enough CH47s to pick up an entire battalion consisting of four companies and two snipers for extra measure, since the vehicles had been completely destroyed. By the time we hit the helipad and debarked, I was beat, Kowalski and I could barely walk. I felt for the dog faces that had been pinned down even longer than we had been.

I opened the door to the barrack and shouted out, "Man on deck! Hot rifle!" as loudly as I could. We walked over to my bunk while a couple of the women scurried to get something to cover up with, but it wouldn't have mattered, Kowalski was too damn tired to notice anything anyway. We talked about the mission. I cleared the ammo from my weapons and stowed them, locking everything up, and we began trudging over to his barrack to let him unload his gear before we went over for our debriefing.

On the way out, Corporal Welles walked up close to us and sniffed us like a dog sniffs another. "Man, you two sure stink."

"Tell me again, Cassie, how you get to sleep in a barrack full of sergeants and you're just a corporal?"

She grinned at me and pointed to her two stripes. "Hard stripes, Sergeant. None of that specialist shit for me... thanks partly to you, Sergeant. Thank you again, in case I hadn't mentioned it." Not only had I been instrumental in getting her recognized by her CO, but I got him to nominate her for a bronze star for her actions under fire. I was happy to have her move in. A real soldier's soldier.

Damn! I was hoping to sleep until the alarm went off at ten thirty, and it was only nine. I knew that I'd never get back to sleep before my appointment with Elizabeth. I might as well get up and shower. I forgot that there were two officers in my apartment besides the six outside in the squads for my protection. I dropped my underwear and walked out of the bedroom toward the bathroom. One of the officers was drinking coffee and spewed some out his nose. I hoped it wasn't too hot. Both of them were gawking at me.

"What?" I asked, holding my arms out to my sides. I figured it wasn't worth crying over spilled milk now they'd seen me in all my glory. "You've never seen a naked black woman before?"

"Actually, Officer Gittens, not white or black or anything in between with the physique that you have, but I also couldn't help notice your scars... Jesus Christ! That's some seriously wicked shit."

I had already abandoned all dignity at this point, and walked over close to the table where they could see the scars up close. They were totally mesmerized. "Touch them if you want. Just don't go touching anything else," I joked.

Both of them gently touched the tips of their fingers to one or two of the scars. "Those are big scars. What were you hit with, do you know?"

"Oh, yeah, I know. Every mother-loving Taliban was toting an AK-47. They were 30 caliber rounds. So now, if you don't mind, now that I remember I've got guests, I'll put on a little modesty, grab a robe, take a shower, and get dressed. And one last thing guys, let's not mention anything about the two of you seeing my vajayjay. My girlfriend doesn't like anybody but her and my obgyn seeing it."

Both of their jaws dropped all the way to the floor. I chuckled to myself as I made my way to the shower and the hot relief it would bring.

LEAVING AFGHANISTAN BEHIND

I stopped at the deli about four or five blocks from Elizabeth's office again. My stomach wasn't really up for any food, but I had to eat. I just got some naan and tomato pesto spread. I already had four bottles of water in my pack. I'd brought my full-size rucksack, knowing I might be out of touch for a few days. I had plenty of trail mix and protein bars, a couple of MREs, and four changes of clothes, including one pair of black jeans and a black button-down shirt. I also had my black K-Swiss shoes packed in case I needed to look better at some point. My toiletry kit was in there with a few other things and in the very bottom, I had my Mark IV 45 caliber and my Glock 27 in a 40 caliber. I didn't give a flying rat's ass what the rules were, bodies were piling up and I wasn't going in empty-handed. Lastly, I had my Second Chance folded on top.

I sat in Elizabeth's office and sucked leisurely at one of the bottles of water, trying to clear my mind. All I could think about was Theresa... how all of this had affected my baby and how I couldn't live without her, couldn't function without her around me. I had my head down and my eyes closed, but I wasn't asleep. Rachel gently touched my shoulder and whispered, "Officer Gittens, the doctor will see you now."

"You don't have to be so timid. I wasn't asleep, I was meditating." She just smiled, opened Elizabeth's door, and gestured in the direction of her office.

I dropped my ruck in the center chair and sat in the closest chair again. I pulled out my sack of flat bread and spread and starting eating, just as Elizabeth reached down into her bottom desk drawer and withdrew a bottle of tea and a couple of sandwiches. "You're traveling pretty heavy today. I hear you're about to take a little trip."

"That's funny; we used to sing a Jodie about that:C-130 rollin' down the strip

    64 Rangers on a one-way trip
    Mission Top Secret, destination unknown
    They don't even know if they're ever coming home
    When my plane gets up so high
    Paratroopers take to the skies

We weren't Rangers, but everybody in the army sings it while running. You look like shit, Doc."

"I was up late with a sick friend."

"Is that what I am? A sick friend?"

"I'd say you were a friend. Probably not a healthy relationship between a doctor and patient. Sick? Let's just say a friend in need, not a sick one."

"You're sure about that part?"

"Did you get any sleep after I left?"

"I got to sleep around six, maybe six fifteen. I woke up at nine on the nose after having another flashback."

"About what? Last night or Afghanistan?"

"Always Ghaniland."

"Don't you think that's a word that could be perceived as a little bit bigoted or prejudicial, maybe racist? I mean, you're gay and you're black... I would think you should pick up on that."

"Elizabeth, it doesn't make it right, but it's the jargon in-country. I should probably distance myself from it now that I'm home for good, but it's self-preservation when you're there." I handed Elizabeth a piece of naan with spread on it.

"Thank you. So last night was sort of different because you were fully up and awake for a few hours and then went back to sleep, but you did, in fact, have two distinctly different episodes."

"Is that what we're calling them now, episodes?"

"We're back to this again... labels. You're really hung up on labels, aren't you, Sergeant Lezbo?"

Without intending to, I immediately reacted. My shoulders went back a bit and I stiffened in my chair. I realized quickly that she was doing it on purpose, to prove a point. "Sorry, Dr. Lezbo. I get it. Chill out. Gotcha!"

"Exactly. Amelia, you have two enemies right now. I wonder if the most dangerous one isn't inside you. The other one will eventually be captured and prosecuted, if they're lucky enough not to get shot during apprehension."

"Coming from you, that's a bit intense, I'd say."

"I'm serious. We need to find a way to get you around this."

"No, I'm talking about the gang that's after me."

"Scum-sucking bastards. I'll never intentionally do harm, it's in my oath, but not giving two shits what happens to somebody because of their own despicable actions, that's altogether another thing," she giggled.

"Elizabeth, I'm scared," I said, suddenly getting very serious.

"Of what? Or whom? Or both?"

LEAVING AFGHANISTAN BEHIND

"Of not being able to see you for God knows how long. I need Theresa, and I need you. Without either of you, I'm afraid I'm going to lose it."

"Did you hear yet that Theresa's detail has an NSA phone?"

"Yeah, they told me that they got word to her."

"So problem solved... sort of."

I breathed a heavy sigh of relief finding out that bit of information.

"You better get your gear packed and downstairs. They're going to want to-"

The entire building erupted into a giant explosion. The glass panes along the entire street side of the building imploded, as well as those across the street, and all the cars up and down the street for about two hundred feet or more. I jumped over the desk without thinking about it, grabbing my ruck. I landed on top of Elizabeth and covered her. I reached into my pack, pulled out both pistols, chambered rounds in both, and put the extra clips in my pockets.

"Do. Not. Move. Okay?" She said nothing, just cowered in the corner on the floor. "Say the words. I want to hear them."

"O... okay. I hear you," she replied, shaking.

It had even broken the glass on the interoffice door to her room. I got to the side of the doorway and pulled the door open. I jumped forward into the hallway, onto my back, with both hands forward with my guns, and saw nothing. I rolled until I was facing the other end of the hall and again, saw nothing. I ran for the back stairs and cleared the second floor in the same manner. As I was going down the stairwell to the first floor, Taylor, my protective detail officer for the day, was coming up the stairway and held his service weapon up at me. We both sank down, identifying ourselves. We got up together and ran back down to the first floor. He had already cleared the hallway but not the front of the building. I waved my guns across my chest indicating I would move first. Using the barrel of the Colt, I counted out in the air - one, two, three, then yanked one of the double doors open and dropped to the floor again. As soon as I was down and angled to the left, Officer Taylor jumped through the door, standing tall, and angled to the right.

At the front desk, Rachel and the other telephone girl were both laying on the floor. They were covered in blood and there appeared to be millions of pieces of glass everywhere, including in my left side, now. Fortunately, it was safety glass. Still, it had done a pretty good

- 65 -

job of making hundreds of little cuts in my skin and through the clothing of both women.

"Call two down and backup." I rushed up to the right-hand picture window frame where about half of the glass had come from. I quickly checked the street and saw the damage from all of the buildings and cars. The unmarked car that we'd driven was parked in front of the building. It was upside down in the middle of the street with parts missing, three of the tires burning, pouring out acrid black billows of smoke. Various parts had been torn off and littered the streets. "Call it as a car bomb and roll four ladders, two pumpers, and two hoses to make sure the situation is contained in all buildings. I'd say six ambulances to make sure. I'm going back upstairs to locate casualties." Taylor nodded to me and then started barking into his radio, talking to dispatch.

"Hey, Taylor!"

"Yeah?"

"Here. Use a real gun instead of that little play toy that you fucking suits carry," I said, tossing him my Colt. After he caught that, he put his .380 in his coat pocket and I threw him three mags. He gave me the thumbs up and returned his attention to dispatch, the Active Field Sergeant, the FTO, and several other people. I figured this place was going to be crawling with about thirty responders within fifteen minutes.

I ran all the way down to the first floor and found five people, all shocky, but the worst wound was a lacerated forehead from hitting a desk drawer that was being leaned into at an inopportune time. I told everybody to stay in the hallway, bunch together in the middle, and to sit on the floor with their backs towards the wall. I ran up to the second floor as well. There were only two people there. Fortunately the rest had all been at a luncheon across town together. On the third floor, I started at the opposite end of the hall from Elizabeth. There were twelve people. I had them all line up together and wait for me while I got Elizabeth up and moving.

"Grab your purse, your laptop, and anything else you're going to need. Bring walking shoes if you have them, and a change of clothes for an emergency, if you have those. Get ready to move as soon as I come back. Make that less than two minutes." She nodded her head, but didn't move. "Elizabeth! You have to get going right this second!

LEAVING AFGHANISTAN BEHIND

Do you hear me?" She shook her head again and started getting in gear.

I moved into the hallway and got everybody started down the stairwell to two. I had everybody hold there while I stuck my head into the second hallway and motioned those two people to follow. Now I had fourteen people on the stairs. I moved everyone to the first floor and lined them up on both sides of the walls, sitting down. I told them to wait until an officer or a firefighter moved them out, not to venture out on their own. "I want to hear everybody say out loud that they understand." Everybody said they did, but many of them were still very much in shock. For the first time, I noticed that three of out of the five on the first floor had blood trickling from their ears. Their eardrums were ruptured.

I went out to the lobby where Taylor was still scanning the world outside. The first three squads had arrived, setting up perimeter about two blocks down each side of the street. I told Taylor that I was taking the doc with me and leaving the building and I would check in when we got to a safe location. He nodded his head. "Do I get to keep this sweet shot or do I have to mail it back to you when this shit dies down?"

"Oh, I'll track you down, don't worry!" I laughed. He slapped me on the arm and I bolted for the third floor to get my gear and Elizabeth. I rushed into the room. When the door whooshed open, she jumped a foot in the air. "You have everything?" She just nodded. I grabbed my ruck and fully slung it. I had my Glock in one hand and I held my other out to Elizabeth. She grabbed hold and stood up. I pulled out my Second Chance and put it on her before putting her winter coat on top. Then we went down the stairs and out the back door. We walked (well, maybe walked is putting it mildly), away from the building out the back, down two streets, then turned northwest along the avenue. I stuffed my pistol into the front pocket of my hoody. I was tempted to put it in my pack, but I wanted faster access to it. We walked about five blocks and caught our first bus. We changed buses four times to get to my bank. We went in and stood in line for customer service. It took about twenty-five minutes to see an officer.

"What can I help you two with today?" asked the older gentleman, very politely.

I laid my badge on the table. "We have an absolute emergency. I've got to get this witness out of the city now. We can't wait for

WITSEC to bring her in, even tonight is too late. I don't want my rental car to be on a credit card so I need cash. I need to withdraw twenty thousand dollars. I'll probably bring most of it back and redeposit it within fourteen days, but, as I say, we have an emergency now. Please take us to see the branch president if we are going to have a problem with the waiting period. I already know I'll have to fill out a 1099."

"I'll see to this immediately. Would you feel more at ease and less conspicuous coming upstairs and waiting in an office?"

"That would be delightful, now that you mention it."

He took us upstairs to the block of executive offices and found a conference room in which to place us. He was gone for only about fifteen minutes. When he returned, he laid some papers on the table in front of me.

"There's only one catch. Since Theresa Biancardi is the beneficiary for any amount over ten thousand dollars, we require a cosignatory even though you are listed as the primary on the account."

"Mr..."

"Randolph. Fred Randolph."

"Mr. Randolph, did you listen to anything that I said? We're wasting time here. If you can't do it, get me the branch president."

"I'm trying to explain to you, I've just spoken to him and-" I stood up and grabbed Elizabeth's hand, pulling her with me. I walked out of the conference room and asked the first person I ran into where the president's office was.

"There's a directory on the wall, right by the elevator over there."

"Please, Ms. Gittens, if you'll-"

"Fred? Shut your fucking mouth before I do something that we both regret. Go back to your desk now, if you know what's good for you."

We walked over to the elevator, looked up the office we wanted, and pushed the up button. We got out on the seventh floor and looked for seven thirty-four. As we approached the office, we could see someone seated behind the main desk and another person seated in a chair across from the desk. They were laughing and carrying on like they didn't have a care in the world. I tested the knob; it wasn't locked. We walked right into the office.

"Who's the dumbass president of this bank?"

"That would be me, Michael Sparks. And you would be?"

LEAVING AFGHANISTAN BEHIND

I slammed my badge down on the desk. Then I raised my left leg onto the desk and rolled it to the right. "You see the cuts and scrapes in my sweat bottoms? They're from fucking glass, blown out of the windows of the building we were in. The explosion was caused by the car bombing of two police officers on scene, one of them was me. I don't have time to fuck around with your chicken shit games here, and if you've got time to sit and laugh with this jack-wad," I said, with a jerk of my thumb to the person sitting across from Sparks, "then you've got time to pay attention to me. So far the entire NYPD hasn't been able to bring this thing in. So far three people are dead, several more are injured, and four blocks of the city are calling glass companies trying to get something closed in before another cold night begins. That's why I'm transporting my witness to a secure facility until we can get her proper protection. She doesn't even know where I'm taking her yet. So I guess it's all on me, huh? Now get me some traveling money... right fucking now!"

Sparks picked up the phone and talked to Fred. He directed Fred to discreetly bring up a bank bag containing twenty thousand dollars: ten thousand in hundreds, and the remainder in twenties, along with the paperwork he had already brought us.

"It will be here in a moment. Please, take a seat," he said, jerking his head toward the door for the benefit of the other occupant of the room.

It took about ten minutes to have everything sent up. I signed all the paperwork after verifying my badge number with his computer, my name and signature on my driver's license, and my NYPD ID with the signature on file.

"I'm terribly sorry that you're in this position, Officer Gittens. I wish you the best," he said, holding out his hand.

I shook his hand. "No problem, Mikey. Peace out, dude."

I had Elizabeth by the hand still. Although she understood what we were doing, she still wasn't sure how we were going to do it all, and, like I'd said, I didn't want to say out loud where I intended to go. We walked out of the bank and turned right, walking a few blocks down the street to a car dealership. I went to the service department to rent a car. I immediately asked for the manager, flashing my badge.

"Hi. I'm Magdalene Schumacher, but people call me Magpie. I understand you might need some special assistance. Always glad to help out our men - and women, of course - in blue. What can I do for you?"

"Short version? She's a witness that can't get processed into protection until tomorrow. So far, in the last twenty four hours, three people have died and about a dozen have been injured, including myself," I said, pulling up my sweat pant leg again, to show off the cuts and scrapes. "I need to get her to a secure location tout de suite. I have plenty of money on my credit cards, but I need to get where we're going without a trail. Once we're there, I'll call One Police Plaza and let them know where we are. Instead of just getting WITSEC involved, I'm going through the Department of Homeland Security as well. I've got enough cash to practically buy the car and I'll gladly put down a sizeable deposit. I want the best mileage available, but I still want a car that can plain *shit-and-git* if we need to. Can you help us out?"

"Let me see your license and NYPD ID, please."

I dropped those on the counter, along with my orange military ID from the inactive ready reserve.

"Both as a member of the police department, and for your service to our great country, ma'am, let me say thank you on behalf of our entire company here." She shook my hand. "I have two sons, both of whom are home safe and sound, thank God. One was in the 1st Armored as a gunner in an Abrahams, and his younger brother was an AIREVAC medic with the 2nd infantry. He's an RN and was a first lieutenant."

"Well, thank you very much, Ma'am, but we really need to shove off if we can. I hope you understand."

"Of course. Do you have a thousand in cash?"

"I've got more than that if we need."

"No, Officer Gittens, give me the thousand and I'll show that as a cash deposit on an open rental, with a note that it's for the NYPD. I'll put the paperwork in my desk and lock it up, then we'll settle up when you have your business taken care of. It will be *eyes only*," she said, making air quotes with her fingers.

"I can't tell you how much I appreciate it."

"Give me fifteen minutes. I'll bring you a 2014 Passat with the tires checked, windows washed, oil checked, and most importantly, a full tank."

"Thank you very much, Magpie. You're the best. Really."

LEAVING AFGHANISTAN BEHIND

"And, Ma'am," she said, looking at Elizabeth (who still didn't know why I was dragging her along), "I hope you stay safe and sound. It sounds as though if anybody can protect you, it's the sergeant here."

I could see the corners of Elizabeth's mouth curl up knowing that I hate being called by my army rank. We walked across the street to a bodega and I asked to use the telephone. They said they didn't have a payphone. I showed him my badge and told him to hand me his mobile phone. He raised his hands, informed me he had a green card, and complained this was mistreatment at the hands of the police simply because he was from southern Asia. I held the phone out to Elizabeth.

"Call Keven on her cell if you can. If she doesn't answer, leave a quick message that you're with the NYPD and will explain when you can. Tell her you might be gone for a few days, but not to worry, and you'll contact her again within twenty-four hours. After you leave that message, call her office and call home and leave the same message. Who normally picks up your kids from daycare or school or whatever?"

"Keven does three days a week, and I do two days a week."

"Whose day is today?" She thought for a minute. "Come on, everything we do from here on has to be snap, snap, snap!"

"It must be hers because I didn't take them today."

"Good. Call."

After three rings, Keven picked up. "Hi, honey. What's up? You usually don't call me until after I get home."

"Listen, I don't have but a second. Remember 'Second Wind' and don't say anything over the phone. I'm with a police officer. Don't worry about me. I love you. Talk to you tomorrow. Bye."

"Was that a movie or a book?" I asked.

"A book. Why?"

"Fewer people would know about it. You're brilliant, Doc."

"And I'm starting to not act like a *deer in the headlights* at long last."

I couldn't help but smile as I handed the phone back to the clerk, along with four sandwiches I'd picked up, four bottles of orange juice, as well as a few power bars. I paid for everything. "Thanks very much. Have a good night."

We got to the dealership, loaded our gear into the back seat, and took off. We headed north out of the City on I-81, going through Syracuse.

"Amelia, can I know yet where we're going?"

"HQ, 10th Mountain Division, 1st Brigade, 2-22 Infantry. The unit I was attached to. Fort Drum, upstate."

"That's got to be six hours out!"

"Probably, with traffic. Maybe a little less, maybe a little more." Elizabeth reached out to hit the GPS, but I held her hand away from it. "Everything electronic has a signature. Even the dealership could track us right now with the VIN if anyone knew we rented it and went to Magpie."

"Why am I here? Do you think I'm a target?"

"They took out my car at your office. Not with the quarter pound of explosives that it would take to destroy the car, but with about ten pounds that even cracked bricks in the front of the buildings, which you didn't notice since we went out the back. Their intent was to take out the building, they're just not very good and don't know enough about blast patterns. To them, quantity is quality, and it just ain't so."

"Well, you were afraid that you weren't going to be able to talk to me. I guess you got your wish, Amelia."

"Elizabeth! Believe me. Of all people, you're the one I would have spared this. If I'd only known what would happen, I would have just started going to the VA."

"You'd still have had to come to our office to be cleared for duty, and it would have been somebody else in the same building. So it's okay.

She opened the end of one of the chewy bars and handed it to me, opened another one for herself, then placed the rest between us in the seat along with the bottle of water. When she was done, she found a radio station on the satellite. She was moving her feet whimsically back and forth with the music to Adrienne Pierce's Museum. It was the first time in two days I'd really smiled and meant it.

"Hey, Ame?"

"Yeah, Liz?"

"I know a lot about PTSD with respect to cops and firemen, battered children, and to some extent, the military, but everything I know about military instances, is from books or my friends at the VA, or lectures. I'm not sure I'm the right person to help you with the military stuff," she said, still jamming to the tunes. "I'd still have to talk to you because of the stuff with the department, of course. I just want you to get the right help because, honey, you've got some serious problems. No holds barred."

LEAVING AFGHANISTAN BEHIND

"I know I do. You don't have to convince me anymore, and I won't pretend that I don't need help either. I promise. You look funny."

"What do you mean?"

"How old are you?"

"How old do you think I am?"

"Maybe thirty-four, thirty-six? You only look that old, but you seem wise beyond your years."

"I'm thirty-six. So is Keven. Why?"

"Look at your feet. You remind me of a fourteen year old girl without a care in the world. I guess it's a change from the last three days, huh?" I laughed.

She squeezed my arm and laughed, too. She took a swig from the water bottle, then handed it to me. I drank deeply from it, not realizing until now that I'd been dehydrating for about twenty-four hours now.

"How exactly are you going to get us on base? You're completely out now, right?"

"I've been thinking about that for the last three hours."

"You mean you had this planned from my office?"

"Pretty much."

"Wow. Now I know how you made your rank so quickly."

"Grade, not rank. Common mistake. Rank is time in grade. Grade is your level, as signified by symbols and pay."

"Whatever. It's still impressive. You're a pretty sharp cookie, Sarge." I quickly let go of the steering wheel and lightly slapped her, making sure our right arms remained interlocked.

"Liz, I'm really sorry about Keven. I hope this won't fuck things up for you two."

"Amelia, we've been together since our undergrad days. We were both sophomores at Columbia. We came out to our parents together, we graduated together, and although I went to medical school and she got her Ph.D. in Fine Arts, we now have two little girls. I doubt this is going to cause any serious rifts. Do you?"

"I suppose not. What does Keven do?"

"She teaches graphic design at The New School. She's already an associate professor. Not bad for only being thirty-six, huh?"

"That's where Theresa went and she's only twenty-five. She's a lot younger than me. I bet she had Keven as an instructor. When this thing is finally put to bed, we'll have to find out."

"Isn't it funny? We both feel protected by each other, and yet we're on the run, under cover, on a top secret mission, hiding, quite literally, from the law," she laughed.

"Yeah, but I bet you're doing me more good that I'm doing you. All I'm doing is dragging you through the dirt and destroying your life."

"Don't be daft. Remember our first meeting? None of this is your fault, and it's not fate. It's just that sometimes bad stuff happens to good people - those people being us and our families in this case."

"I hope Keven is holding up better than Theresa. I know Theresa's an absolute mess."

"It's because she loves you so much, you idiot. And one more thing before confession time is over. Just because we're both gay, it doesn't mean that I automatically understand everything about you. Amelia. Officer. Sergeant. You're pretty complex."

"I don't know. I think maybe you get me pretty well."

Nobody spoke after that. I looked over at Liz after another hour on the highway. She was out like a light and had been for goodness knows how long. I looked at the gas gauge. We still had plenty, but I wanted to keep it full in case of any incidents. I had pulled off the highway before we got to Syracuse, less chance for a random meeting with somebody looking for us if we were outside the city. I knew I was totally irrational, but considering the last few days, I was taking no chances. I reached down with my right hand and started shaking Liz's leg. "Hey, Doc."

"What?" she shouted, bolting upright.

"We're going to pull off, fill up the tank, and go to the bathroom here. I just wanted to give you a minute to wake up."

"Oh. I'm fine."

We pulled into the station. I topped off the tank for the second time today although we still had about a quarter of a tank left. I made Liz stay right with me instead of wandering off alone. Before I got out of the car, I put my Glock back in my hoodie. We went into the bathroom together, even though it was meant for one person. We each went, then came out. We got a couple of stares, but screw them. One woman in particular gave me the evil eye, obviously thinking that Liz and I were partners, which was funny, really, because we were both gay. I walked right up to the bitch and got in her face. I started to force the issue, but we were supposed to be flying totally under the radar, and I couldn't

LEAVING AFGHANISTAN BEHIND

afford to put any issue on my current mission. That's how I was playing this one. My current mission.

I bought a new thermos and filled it with deluxe flavored coffee. We got a bag of jerky, more protein and granola bars, four packages of meat, cheese, and crackers, and a case of bottled water. I hated buying plastic that I'd just throw away, but I didn't have the filter from my house. I made a mental note to buy a half dozen of the bottles with the filter inside so that you could go to any drinking fountain and get great water on the spot. We paid for the lot, then I turned to Liz, shielding her from the glass front of the store. "What?"

I hit the emergency help alarm on the car. It started going off, but didn't blow up. I turned the alarm off, opened the doors and closed them again, all without incident.

"Okay, we can go now."

"You're weird. I suppose that had a purpose."

"No guarantee, but we've just tested three of the four circuits that can be used to trigger a fuse."

"I think you're taking this a little too far, but just the same, it makes me feel a whole lot better when you do all these things. I sort of want to get back to Keven and Alyssa and Clarisse."

"That's the first time you've said your children's names out loud."

"Professional shield, I suppose. I will tell anybody that asks, I just don't volunteer it."

"Just the same, I feel that we're, I don't know, close?"

"If you had written down this whole story and handed it to me, with someone else's name replacing mine, my professional opinion would be that you had gotten very close to this person," Liz said, reaching out and squeezing my forearm. "Now, let's get to the base. I want to sleep. Some totally unreasonable patient had me up at two in the morning. I've had almost no sleep since, and it's almost ten at night."

I put the water in the trunk and we got into the car, setting our food on the floor, and Liz holding onto the coffee for us to share. When we were within a couple of miles of the base, I turned to Liz.

"Take your driver's license out of your purse and have it ready."

Prior to going to the gates, there are parking spaces at every entrance where you can stop if you need assistance prior to trying to gain access. I pulled into one of the spaces, pulled out my wallet, retrieving my military ID, my driver's license, my NYPD ID, and my badge. I pulled up to the only open gate and stopped even with the MP, my window already all the way down. I handed him the four IDs, which he looked at keenly, then looked at our faces, then back to our IDs again.

He immediately stood up, having recognized my previous rank, and came to attention. "How may I help you tonight, Ma'am?"

I told the Private First Class that I needed him to contact the duty section for the Charge of Quarters for the 2-22 Infantry Battalion. He told me to pull in through the gate, park in the first slot on the left, and he'd be right with me. I pulled up, put the car in park, and turned the engine off. Within two or three minutes at most, a military police pickup pulled up about thirty feet from us with its blue lights flashing. We had to wait for almost twenty minutes before two Humvees pulled up, one on the opposite side of the road, and one directly behind us. All of the occupants got out of the vehicles and moved up to talk to the MP at the gate.

I was greeted at my open window by a Sergeant First Class, my previous rank.

"Officer Gittens, I'm Sergeant First Class Hardesty. Have you driven all the way up from the city tonight?"

"That's right, Sergeant. I've got a witness who's been attacked; three dead people, including two NYPD officers, a car bombing that damaged thirty or forty cars and cracked the fronts of half a dozen or more buildings. I can't afford to wait for the proper agency to take her into protective custody and right now it's pretty apparent that there's some intel within my department that's not being properly secreted, or that the perps are incredibly well supplied with intel and or equipment. I thought, "What better place to protect her than in the middle of the 10th?" thus, we're here. I guarantee that there are at least fifty officers combing the streets for the two of us right now. My supervisor has no idea where I am and I want to keep it that way. Instead of going through my system, I want to contact WITSEC and the DHS directly. I was hoping that you good people would be warm to the idea and put us up in BOQ for a night, two at the most. Or even lockup. I've kinda thought that might be what's in store for us," I said, scratching my head.

"Stand by please, Ma'am."

The sergeant was in the gate guard's booth for over twenty or twenty-five minutes. Finally, he returned. "Could you come with me please, Ma'am?"

LEAVING AFGHANISTAN BEHIND

"Sergeant? I need to inform you at this time that I am carrying a duty weapon in the front pocket of my jacket. I am willing to surrender it so long as we are within the confines of your gate, but would expect it to be returned if we are turned away tonight. I'm going to reach very slowly across with my left hand into the right side of my pocket and extract the weapon."

"Very well, proceed, officer," he said, drawing his weapon and holding it down in front of him. I slowly removed it and held the hand grips with only my thumb and forefinger, letting it hang at an angle to the ground. He reached out and took it firmly from me, but with control. "Please exit the vehicle at this time."

I stood up out of the car and stood with my feet shoulder length apart and my arms straight out to my sides.

"Feel free to search me, Sergeant." He did so, then motioned me to the guard hut with everybody else gathered around it. The MP Humvee was still parked on the road, as was the still-occupied Humvee immediately behind our car.

"I'll tell you this much, Officer Gittens, you sure have a genuine, category five shit-storm going on down south there. I just pulled up the wires and it's everywhere. They're showing that there's a giant manhunt underway and that you two are missing. By all rights, I should call them and hold you in a cell until they arrive to get you."

"This isn't about that, Sergeant; it's about protecting an innocent civilian who is here because of my actions in the line of duty. She's not here by choice. My department's only concern is the cost. I personally don't give a flying rat's ass. My job is to protect this woman at all costs. That's why I'm here. Once we're secure, I'll give you a specific contact at 1PP and he can decide what to do with it internally, but I'm still going to get her into WITSEC on a temporary basis. Me personally. I know that you'll probably have to send this to your sergeant major tonight. If you want, you can certainly, as you said, take us to the jail and detain us, which, as I said, had previously crossed my mind. Please just get us away from here where we're pretty much open targets. Who is your sergeant major now? I've been out of your unit for over five years."

"His name is Pete Vetter."

"You mean the old sniper instructor from Benning? He was one of my old NCOs. I'll be damned. When you call him, he's going to be pissed for being bothered so late. Tell him that Raw Sugar is involved. He'll know who I am."

"Will do, Ma'am."

I returned to the car and rolled up the window. Liz was shivering since we'd been sitting with the window down for so long. I popped the trunk open and fetched her heavy coat and another jacket for me.

"If they won't take us in, I'll head south, but through Utica. It's only about forty-five or fifty miles, and we'll grab a motel there and just sleep for about a day and lay low until I can get this sorted out." Just then, Hardesty rapped on the glass with his knuckles. I rolled the window down.

"The sergeant major has given me a message to deliver specifically to you. He says that you should take your last tour bonus, buy yourself a twenty-four karat gold brick, and shove it straight up your ass!"

Liz's face melted. Mine brightened up. That was Vetter all right. We were in. I rolled up my window. Everybody from all three Humvees got mounted; the MPs headed out first. The one behind us pulled back so we could follow the MPs, and the third one pulled up the rear. We were escorted to the MP's area to park our car and then they gave us a ride over to the battalion area for the 2-22. They weren't even going to make us stay at the BOQ. They were going to completely imbed us.

"What's happening, if you don't mind me asking a stupid question?" queried Liz.

"We're going to get a shower and a bed. That's what." We finally pulled into the battalion area of the base and parked. There were technically no women in combat, so for times like this, they used one of the couple of dozen beds in some rooms in the Charge of Quarters to put us up. I was carrying everything I'd brought, and Liz brought some water, our food, and her things.

"Good evening Ma'am. Ma'am, I've been asked to assist you with anything you need for tonight and to let you know that the major will see you first thing in the morning to discuss your itinerary. Well, not first thing. For us, that's oh-four-thirty."

"I'll be running with you tomorrow. Can you get me a belt, canteen, and safety vest ready tonight? Oh, and one other thing. I hate being a pain, but my friend here wasn't expecting our little adventure today. Would you please see if the MPs will go to the infirmary and

LEAVING AFGHANISTAN BEHIND

get two pairs of scrubs, size...?" I looked at Liz, "small. I'd greatly appreciate it."

"Hooah. Give me fifteen max and I'll have them here."

"Thank you, Private Loetz," I said, reading the tag.

We walked into one of the small rooms that had two beds end to end, and a bunk bed on each of those for a section of military issue, metal frame, wire spring, heavy duty, permanent cots. I took the locks from one of the corresponding wall lockers and put all our gear in it, right down to the food (which was a violation, but I didn't care), my clothes, my extra rounds, my rangefinder scope and a small bipod, my second set of shoes, and my black pants and shirt with black K-Swiss. I locked the locker and put the keys on their ball chain around my neck. I held out my hand for Liz to indicate that she should follow suit. "Wait until they get here with your scrubs and you can put everything else in the locker, which is the rule."

"Okay," she said, as she got off her bunk and came over to sit beside me on mine.

"Are you sure this isn't reverse transference?"

"No, it's me wanting a good, close friend to have in my time of need, without my family around me." "Good answer, Liz." I held out my hand and squeezed hers.

Private Loetz rapped three times on the frame of the door, as was military courtesy, even though it was open.

Liz took the scrubs and headed for the small bathroom in the back corner to change, returning when she finished.

"I don't think I've ever seen more sexy scrubs in my life. You can tell that you're wearing either really dark blue or black underwear, and that they're lacy, because of the pattern they give to the scrub material."

"Gittens, that's inappropriate."

"As your patient, your friend, your protectorate, or just another gay gal you ran into earlier in the week?"

"Mostly as my big, strong, wise, fearless protector, I think."

I giggled. I was laying on top of the crappy little mattress, which was suspended on a stupid wire and spring basket and covered year round with two pairs of sheets and a wool blanket. Liz lay on the next bottom bunk over, with her body pointing in the opposite direction to mine, so that our heads were close together and we could talk quietly.

"Hey, Liz?"

"Yeah?"

"I'm not sure whether you felt unsafe today, but do you feel safe right now?"

"Amelia, I've been feeling so *not* safe since the explosion, I can't tell you, but I think, finally, I'm okay. I can't imagine going through this with anybody else. Anybody."

"I need to go take care of a couple of things. Stay here and try to get some sleep. I'll be back in about ten or fifteen minutes."

She raised up on her elbows to get up, then hesitated. She looked back at me, then lay back down on her pillow. As I got up, Liz called out to me.

I stepped in front of her and leaned down on one knee.

"By the time we got to the bank, I was dying. Even though over three-quarters of the trip was on buses, you weren't even sweating. You're in such good shape. I felt like I was holding us back."

"Don't be silly. I'm expected to be in shape; you're not. Not like we were humping it, anyway," I smiled.

I got up and walked into the CQ. "Runner, do you have a secure line in the office here?"

"Absolutely, Ma'am."

"I need to contact the MPs at Dix via secure phone for a relay. I need to isolate this line as the source."

"Sure, we can do that. Stand by." The PFC, who was the runner, had already been instructed to help us with whatever we needed, so he figured he didn't have to get permission. Not quite true, but luckily he didn't question it.

"This is Lieutenant Rowell, 200th MP Command, 744th MP Battalion, 343rd MP Detachment, Fort Dix. How may I help you?"

"Lieutenant Rowell, have you heard anything on the news today or tonight about a car bombing and a missing doctor and police officer?"

"Yes I have, Ma'am. And your connection to this would be?"

"My name is Officer Gittens, and I'm the missing cop. I have the doctor safe with me at another installation. I needed a relay so that there would be no possible link to our current location. I need you to please contact Capt. Jernick, that's spelled J-E-R-N-I-C-K, at the NYPD, at One Police Plaza. I want you to pass along the information that we're being protected by an infantry division and they can call off the manhunt. I'll contact him tomorrow after I get my witness into truly safe protection. For proof of contact, tell him I said he was an ass wipe. He'll understand, and that will confirm my identity."

"I understand, Officer, and I will relay that information immediately I get off the phone with you." "Lieutenant?"

"Officer?"

"Please don't trace this call back and please don't let him know where we are. So far, two agencies haven't been able to protect anybody. I don't want to take any chances."

"Will do, Ma'am. Have a good night."

Finally, I could sleep. I checked Liz first. She was almost curled in a ball, which I thought was funny. I reached down and stroked her forehead for a moment. She didn't even stir. I got into my bunk, quietly, after first laying out my clean set of sweats for the morning run. I would relish the exercise. Usually when I work out it forces whatever demons I'm facing to retreat, at least for the moment. I fell asleep almost instantly, but the nightmares came almost instantly as well.

CHAPTER NINE

I was walking down the street by Theresa's office, late in the afternoon. I could see several people working with their heads focused on their large, wide screen monitors, working on projects. The front glass suddenly exploded! I saw one of the girls in the office drop down on her desktop as a bullet flew out of the back of her head. Then a man behind her was hit in the center of his forehead, causing him to be thrown out of his chair and onto the floor. Then two more. Suddenly I saw Theresa, and she was looking up from her computer and out the window like she saw me. I try to scream out for her to find cover, but she can't hear me. I'm scanning the street from my position, with my Leopold scope with BORS ranging system, and I am unable to find any shooter. I'm scanning desperately, desperately, for anything, anybody out of order. I can find nothing.

Theresa keeps looking around, not able to comprehend what is happening. I keep yelling for her to find cover, but she can't hear me. Finally, in order to draw fire away from her, I jump up screaming and waving my rifle and arms in the air. "Here I am. Take me. Take me instead. Leave her alone!" The next thing I saw was a round explode through her chest, making her fall backward like a rag doll over the desk behind her. It's at that moment that I feel the searing pain shooting through my lower left abdomen. And again. And again. And again. I'm lying on the ground and Kowalski is lying beside me, holding my coat in his hands, shaking me. "Why didn't you protect her? Why did you let her go, like you let me go? What is your problem, Gittens? How could you let this happen again?"

I felt somebody gently nudge my shoulder right then. "Officer Gittens, we're falling out for morning PT if you still want to accompany us." That was the first nightmare that was invented in my mind, not just a replay of something that actually happened, and my little Italian hunny bunny had been the one in danger.

"Mph. Uh... Yeah, give me a second." I rubbed my eyes for a quick second, then remembering that I was back in an army unit, sprang out of my bunk. I pulled my shoes on quickly, threw on my safety vest and canteen belt, and sprinted out to the CQ office. "Let Liz sleep as long as she can. Keep the door shut if you can. And if it wouldn't be asking too much to give her a little grub when she does wake up, that would be greatly appreciated, along with everything else you're doing for us, Corporal."

"Officer Gittens, after showers when you return, the major is set to go into conference with you. And one last item: after your call off base last night, we got a return call from the MPs at Dix with the message "Showing green smoke." They said you'd know what that meant, Ma'am." Jernick knew that I was retired army and that the color green, when used strictly as a talking point, was used to signal friendlies. While the color always rotated, this was his way of giving me the green light.

"Thanks." Yes, I did know. It meant that they'd contacted Theresa and that they were handling the manhunt for us, as they saw fit. They may have called it off, they may not have called it off, or they may be spinning the media however they saw best, but I now had permission from on high to handle this one from my end as I so desired.

I went outside to the pavement where the platoons were all lining up. I chose the one closest to me. Just on the outside of the first rank, or row of four-wide troops, was the company Guidon, who carried the colors, or streamer flags, for a platoon or a company. Standing just behind that person was the person in charge of the troop movement at the time. It could be an officer or an enlisted man. If the enlisted NCO were moving the troops, the officer would stand directly behind them. Additional NCOs would accompany at various points in the column. Senior officials, such as division, brigade, battalion, and company

LEAVING AFGHANISTAN BEHIND

officers and senior enlisted would run directly ahead of the largest group that they represented.

My company was being run today by a Staff Sergeant, with the Sergeant First Class and the first lieutenant lined up as the first rank. I fell into the first rank, remaining quiet. The Lieutenant spoke to me.

"Glad to have somebody from the NYPD running with us this morning, Ma'am. We should be going about eight or nine miles, maybe a little less. Are you up to the challenge?"

"LT, waiting for a doctor's appointment within the last few days, I took a quick run out to and around Prospect Park in the city. About six miles in about twenty-eight minutes. I think I can probably handle your muster."

"Outstanding! Welcome."

Finally, they started calling each of the components to attention. Starting the whole thing moving was sort of like getting sheep to start herding, but once it started it was a smooth and beautiful thing. Call me crazy, but this is one of the things I missed about being on active duty. I found myself humming to myself at about the three mile mark, which was picked up by my running mates.

"You in a good mood this morning, Officer?" asked the Sergeant First Class.

"Hooah! Never better. Never better." I know I was supposed to lay low, blend in, and make sure that nobody knew my name, but that morning I did the first totally stupid thing I'd done in days. I was overtaken by an endorphin rush I guess. I started sprinting to the head of the column from roughly just behind the middle of the length. Realizing that, in time, I dropped back and settled in with the second platoon in the column, keeping my heels cooled. If I were still overseas, it would be a rookie mistake like that, that could get people injured, or worse yet, killed.

Finally, we made it back to the assembly point and were all released to our smallest units. First everybody got a quick shower then went to chow. After I had showered, I looked over, and Liz was still out like a light. I figured I'd load up a tray of food with a bit of everything (since I didn't know what she ate) and bring it back for her after I ate. I knew she wasn't a vegetarian or kosher because she'd eaten ham sandwiches and beef jerky. As a Unit guest, it would have been perfectly acceptable to fall in at the officer's table, but instead I chose to sit with the NCOs in what's called the Snake Pit: NCOs only, no officers, no junior enlisted. I was pretty famished and finished a quick couple of trays of food. Afterward, I took my tray back and loaded it up with a little of everything. I had a glass of OJ on the tray, knowing there'd be coffee back at the CQ. By the time I got back and opened the door to our four-bed bay, Liz was sitting up in bed, scratching one of her arms, with her long hair going every which direction. I set the tray on the floor, just off to one side of her.

"Oh, you're a saint. An absolute saint."

"You know, Liz, I think you're an incredibly beautiful woman."

"What do you want?" she laughed.

"No, you are. I mean it. But... I was... er... going to ask you if you wanted me to grab your purse so you could brush that mop of yours before anybody else saw it." Now it was my turn to laugh.

Her hands went immediately up to the top of her head where she started feeling around. "Shit. Hurry up!"

When she was finished, I got on the floor on my knees between her legs. I had my hands on her hips.

"Now. Much better. Even without fresh makeup, you look marvelous. And speaking of marvelous, I have news that everything has been approved and we're in the clear. I know it's going to be hard hanging out for who knows how long, but it's for the best."

Liz leaned over to me, put her arms around my neck, her head on my shoulder, and sighed. "I just can't stand being away from my girls. All three of them."

I walked across the room to retrieve a chair. I placed it in front of Liz sideways to make a table, and then put her tray on that. The way she dug in, I was afraid that if I tried to reach in, she'd bite my arm off by mistake. There was a knock on the door, so I opened it.

"Hi. My name is Captain Sigourney Fleischman. I'm on the medical staff here. I heard you needed the scrubs last night so I decided to come by today to take you ladies to issuance and get you both some ACUs, a cover, and a pair of boots. The usual stuff."

"That's very kind of you, Captain, but we should be shoving off here within twenty-four hours."

"I don't think so. I don't know what your situation is, why you're here, or even who the two of you are. All I know is that the 2-22 CQ called while you were out on PT this morning and you've been given the order to stand fast. Looks like you may be here longer than you expected. Anyway, as soon as you're finished eating your breakfast,

LEAVING AFGHANISTAN BEHIND

Ma'am, I'll be waiting outside, and we'll go over and get that done," she said, as she left the room, closing the door behind her.

"What does that mean, Ame?"

"Not sure yet, but I figure it means that we're being supported here for a few days. Don't worry though, the very reason I chose this place is that we're on an Advanced Infantry base, with 13,000 members and civilian support staff, and we have over one hundred thousand acres to hide out in. We're well-armed. It doesn't get any better than this. What we do have to do is make sure that we don't get called by our names. They're going to start talking all over the base as it is. Human mentality. You finished with breakfast?"

"Pretty much," she said pushing the chair back. I went over to the door and pushed it and locked it. "Go ahead and get changed."

"Thank you."

Liz dropped her scrubs but was still in her black underwear. It was a stark contrast to her pale skin. She didn't turn away from me when she started putting her clothes from yesterday back on.

"Can I say something without offending you, Doc?"

"At this point, I'd think we could talk about pretty much anything," she laughed at me.

"If I went for blondes, which I don't, and if I went for pale skin, which I don't... well... I think you'd definitely be the one to do it for me. You are some kind of hot. I mean smokin'. I don't know why I never noticed how much before."

"That's so sweet of you to say. I'm guessing that what floats your boat is chocolate hair over grey eyes and olive skin."

"You were at the precinct when Theresa was there, weren't you? How can I not? But you weren't there then, I don't think..."

Liz had just finished lacing up her running shoes that she kept with her in her office. She walked up to me at the door, moved up right in front of me, almost nose to nose.

"I saw pictures of her and of the two of you together, at your place when I came over yesterday morning. Christ, has that been less than twenty-four hours? It seems like forever. For me, I do the blonde over blue, hence Keven looking more like my sister than my partner. We get mistaken all the time. But if olive or dark skin did it for me, I'd be totally happy with either you or Theresa. I think you're both incredibly beautiful women," she said patting me on my side.

I winced slightly when she did. "Oh, God, your scars. I didn't think. I'm so sorry."

"No, not the scars, the glass all over your floor in the lobby," I laughed.

"Well, you know what they say, 'just because you're paranoid doesn't mean there isn't somebody out to get you,' " she said, laughing. "Have I told you how much safer I feel with you watching me instead of somebody else? You're incredibly strong, both physically and mentally." I tickled her sides for a second, causing her to jerk and laugh.

"Ready to go join the army, Sergeant First Class Smith?"

"What?"

"You're getting a grade and a change of name. You'll fit in better on base. And I'll have to teach you how to put your hair up in a military bob. It's cool, though. You can take it out at the end of the day and your hair's all back where it was at the beginning of the day. You don't have to do a dyke cut."

I pulled the door open and showed her the way. As soon as we walked out into the battalion offices, the first sergeant himself met us. "As soon as the two of you get back from issuance, the command sergeant major has requested you get a ride over to the 2-22 HQ building. You'll be meeting the XO to discuss your future arrangements and to coordinate with your unit at home. Welcome to Fort Drum, Sergeant."

"Thank you, Sergeant."

"Ready, kids?" Captain Fleishman beamed at us. "You'll both be happy to know that we're one of the four bases chosen to test the new female ACUs. A much better fit... for the body armor as well. Not for the infantry, scouts, and artillery, of course, but the air force has a unit here, the Coast Guard has a unit here, and the medical staff, as well as administrative staff for the entire Division, including the ones in Colorado are here."

"What are ACUs," asked Liz.

"Army Combat Uniforms. What you see all the soldiers in these days. The new camouflage material," I answered.

We followed her outside where she had a Humvee already running and warm, which was great. It came complete with driver. I loved this morning's run, but it was seriously cold out, and I didn't have all of my normal gear. We got to issuance and were fitted for four uniforms plus

LEAVING AFGHANISTAN BEHIND

long underwear, winter coats with liners, ponchos, rucksack, web belt, 2-22 patches, and a patrol cap. Each of us was given SFC insignias for our ACU jacket, our body armor, and our cover, as well as unit insignias for the 10th, and SAPPER indicators. Qualifying for a SAPPER is a real chore and it would let people admire us from a distance without bothering us too much. They made name tags for us on-site, with me getting Plummer and Liz getting Sutton. Lastly, we were fitted for boots, socks, and sole liners.

"Go change while they're making our name tags, Sergeant Sutton. Put your civvies in the bottom of your pack. You'll need your tennies once in a while, so keep those up top. And put the body armor on one side so it's easy to get out when necessary. Lastly, the helmet goes on the very top."

"Jesus! I can barely lift this shit!" Liz shouted.

"Sgt. Sutton, it doesn't inspire the troops when you're so negative!" I said, slapping her on the ass (out of sight of everybody else).

"I'll try and remember that, Sgt. Plummer," she giggled at me. She really did put an effort into it though, and managed to manhandle her gear around enough to get herself loaded up. We met Capt. Fleischman again and were taken to battalion headquarters.

I leaned over close to her ear, curling my first finger up over and over, signaling her to move in tight. "What?" she whispered.

"You've got a seriously nice ass," I winked at her. She smiled, but you could tell she was trying not to.

As soon as we left the building, we passed a Lt. Colonel, who was going into issuance. The captain and I saluted, but Liz didn't. I jammed my arm into her side, she looked around, and then pulled up a very weak and sloppy-looking salute. After the situation had passed, I told the captain that I'd be spending part of the next day giving her a little bit of instruction on how to *act properly* in public. That made the Cap laugh pretty hard.

"I still don't know what the two of you are doing here, but it must be pretty important, that's all I know. And as for you, Little Miss NYPD, if I can believe your other clothes, all I want to know is what your MOS was. It's pretty evident."

"Thirty-one Bravo, Ma'am. Right here in the 10th. Attached to the 2-22 as a sniper."

"Impressive. Yet another example of women in combat when we weren't supposed to be. I was at Agram and Kandahar. Both tours ended up being fifteen months, and both times more than half my time was spent at forward operating facilities in trauma. But was I in a combat job? Hell no. Do I have a Purple Heart? Two of them. Makes me laugh. How much time did you spend over?"

"I did a gauntlet. Shortest was four months, longest was fifteen."

"Can I ask you a personal question, Captain?" asked Liz.

"Sure. We're all one big happy family here."

"You're a doctor, right? M.D.?"

"That's right."

"I thought you automatically were a captain if you are a physician. How is it that you've been overseas twice and you're still a captain? I guess I don't understand this whole thing…"

"PMS. Prior Military Service. At least that's what I'm guessing, right Cap?" I answered.

"Correctamundo! I was a master sergeant. Started as a lowly Private E-1. I was originally a medical aide, then a MEDEVAC. The army paid for me to go to RN school for fifteen months, where I managed to fast burn a two year program big time. Then, through correspondence, I got my BSN. I didn't apply for the job as an RN because I wanted to keep my high grade. Then I decided I wanted Med School. This time they said they'd pay, but I had to take the promotion to an officer. By that time, I'd decided I really wanted to be a doctor when I retired, so I said I'd do it. I hate being a lowly captain and being forty-seven years old, but I'm set for life. I could retire next year with seventy-five percent pay, and I'm making just over sixty-seven hundred a month right now. That's less than a thousand a month over my pay as a Master. Low man, remember. Well, one more stop. We need to go to CBPO and get you two IDs made."

That was a yawnathon. It took only about forty-five minutes waiting for a photo, since all of our *official* paperwork was completed beforehand. After taking the photos, it took another thirty minutes to get our cards, but we were now officially soldiers and were on our way back to the battalion area.

"Well, I do appreciate your help today, Captain. I wish I could tell you what our situation is and can't begin to express our gratitude."

"Glad to help. I wasn't even supposed to be the one to help, but it was absolutely *dead* today and I was bored. I hope you get what you came for. Have a nice time back here at your old home, Sergeant."

LEAVING AFGHANISTAN BEHIND

I saluted the captain again, sharply, and this time Liz picked up on it. Fleischman returned our salute and we snapped back down. I'll give you this, Liz is observant. She is one sharp cookie. We were driving back to the battalion at the moment, our driver at the wheel and both of us seated in the back of the Humvee.

"So, Liz, do you ever run?"

"I used to, a lot. Not so much now that we have kids."

"How old are they?"

"Alyssa is four and Clarisse is two."

"What kind of distances did you run?"

"Five-K, ten-K, a couple of half marathons a year. I've run one marathon. I sucked at it, but I finished."

"How long did it take you to finish a half?"

"Two hours."

"That's pretty fast. You feel like running with us tomorrow?"

"What if I can't keep up? I'm supposed to be a sergeant. Can I get driven to the ER to see if I've got appendicitis?"

"Maybe," I laughed.

As soon as we got back, we stowed our gear quickly and locked it up, then made our way to the Division HQ for our meet and greet with the major. As we walked into the Division HQ, I had to bump Liz's arm and nod at her patrol cap to remind her to always take it off indoors.

"Sorry."

"Never apologize; it's a sign of weakness."

"Oh. Sorry."

I glared at her and she started to laugh, but managed to keep it in pretty well.

I walked up to the desk and spoke to a specialist. "We're here to see Major Leitner. He's expecting us."

"Not a problem Sgt. Plummer, Sgt. Sutton. One moment." He returned within thirty seconds and ushered us down a short hallway and into a doorway with a huge plaque on it reading 'Major Leitner, Executive Officer, 2-22 Division, 10th CBT, 10th Mountain. The Spec opened the door and we walked into the office. I stood at attention at the front of the major's desk and Liz followed my lead. I saluted, followed quickly by Liz, mimicking my every move.

Leitner finished reading his current report, signed it, placed it at the right front corner of his desk, and then turned his attention to us. He rose out of his chair and returned our salutes, standing there for a moment.

"You know, Gittens, I'm sure as fuck glad you're on our side and not theirs. Were you always this much of a fucking pain in the ass when you were active?"

"That's what I'm told, sir."

"So. You're Raw Sugar. You know, I heard of you before this whole debacle that's transpiring. You were a legend." He turned to Liz. "Doctor, the last part of sniper school, you have to land some tough shots on a target without being detected by an entire team. She eats energy bars all the time, right? Well, back then she used to have short pieces of raw sugar cane and chew on them. Every time the observers thought they had her spotted, all they would find was sugar cane with chewed up ends from where she *had* been. Crazy. So, I understand you girls are seriously fucked and you need our help. Gittens, only you would have thought to hide out in the middle of an infantry division, especially the 10th Mountain. Balls of steel, chica. Balls of steel. Well anyway, I talked to Jernick directly today, using an encrypted phone of course. He thought your idea was a flash of fucking brilliance. He's going to keep you here for at least another two weeks while they do some routine street intel gathering. From there, they'll decide what to do next. They still have you listed to the media as missing and being searched for, to keep the hornet's nest stirred up. They're going to try and put all the resources that can be shoved interagency to find out who knows what in the city. Meanwhile, kick back and enjoy the morning run. Our food is definitely better than an MRE, unless we're bivouacking, and there're movies on base you can go to every weekend."

"It's good to hear, after all these years, somebody thinks I have a brain."

"That's a good one. Oh, and two other notes: Doctor, your three girls are A-Okay and know just enough about what's going on to keep them from being in danger. And there are highly increased patrols around your house. Highly! Gittens, word is getting to your girlfriend daily as far as an update, and starting tonight we'll give you an encrypted computer link for burst traffic. No real time, but at least you'll be able to send letters back and forth every night. Apparently she's not just watching TV. They've got her set up with a work station and she's still doing graphics design work while she's there."

LEAVING AFGHANISTAN BEHIND

"There must be some sort of misunderstanding, Major."

"Oh? How is that?"

"I don't have a girlfriend."

"Oh, sorry. No offense meant. I'm just reading the message."

I smiled a big shit-eating grin. "As of three days ago, she's my fiancée."

"Oh, a smart ass too, huh?" He looked Liz right in the eye. "You can take the girl out of the country... not that you need my approval, but that whole *don't ask don't tell* was pure crap. I did an exchange tour with Danish troops. Dedicated sons-a-bitches. Doesn't change the work ethic or efficiency at all. Pure bullshit."

"Major, did they say anything other than my three girls?"

"That's all I have in the memo."

"Two of them are my daughters. The third one is my life partner. I'm gay too. Apparently it *is* contagious..."

Everybody had a quick laugh.

"Officer Gittens... Excuse me, Sergeant Plummer, from the moment you leave my office, you two are Diana Plummer and Sharon Sutton. No questions. Just like WITSEC, right here on base. If you hear your name, don't react! Plummer, I'll expect you to teach Sutton common military courtesies she may need in dealing with people. And you'll each get a new patch that's not easily identifiable to anybody here, so they won't be able to ask questions about you. If anybody, and I mean anybody, including General Davies, questions you, offer to let them take you to a holding area and have them talk to me or Vetter or the CO. There are only six or seven people that know who and what you are. Let's keep it that way."

"Hooah," I said, standing up and saluting the major. Liz and I left the office and were escorted back to our battalion. It was almost time for lunch by now, and I wanted to give Liz some tips and knowledge before we had to go mingle with a variety of personnel.

LEAVING AFGHANISTAN BEHIND

CHAPTER TEN

I led the way over to the chow hall. The area was absolutely crawling with people. Liz did a great job of knowing who to address and how. She actually beat me to the salute for a few officers, maybe because I was less impressive. We got inside and walked up to the food line. We went through and got our food without saying anything that wasn't necessary, such as requesting a particular food. When we got over to the Snake Pit, we sat on the very corner, away from all other people. Unfortunately, a couple of friendly types came up and sat near us.

"Ladies... I'm Taggert, and this is Bowers. We're in charge of recurrent small arms training for pretty much all kinds of armament for the battalion. New here? Haven't seen you around before today."

"In transit," I offered in return, and nothing else.

"How do you like our little nest up in the mountains? It's actually a lot nicer in the spring and fall. Winters, like now, are bitter, and summers will let you fry eggs on the sidewalk."

I just nodded my head in acknowledgment. The two other sergeants talked between themselves, totally relaxed, not about business, but just life in general.

"How long are you two ladies going to be with us before you get your transit?"

"Not sure. Working on logistics."

"Cool."

Taggert and Bowers kept talking periodically between themselves, but Liz and I never said a word. I made a motion to Liz by making a circle with my fork to get her to hurry up and eat. She caught it immediately and washed down the bite in her mouth with some water, then took another quickly. Completely out of the blue, Liz turned toward me. "An gceapann tú go beidh orainn a fháil ár n-orduithe leis an dhá nó trí lá a?"

"Nidya?" I replied. I got up and Liz followed suit. "Gentlemen. Hooah!"

"Hooah," they both responded in kind.

Liz and I walked back to our room at the CQ. Once we were inside with the door shut, Liz started laughing. "What was that last little bit? What does Hooah mean?"

"It means anything and everything, except for the words no or negative. Don't ask, just accept it. It's easier. Speaking of *what the fuck was that*…What did you say in there, and in what language?"

"I said, 'Do you think we'll get our orders within the next two or three days?' in Irish Gaelic. I studied it as an undergrad just because I was interested in Irish culture. What did you say?"

"I had no idea what you said so I just made up a word."

We laughed our asses off. It may have been the first relaxed moment we'd had for the last thirty-six hours. There was a knock on the door a few minutes later.

"Come!"

A specialist poked his head in the door. He was carrying a laptop case.

"Sergeant, here is your laptop. It's a burst mode, satellite link connection. You can't stream videos or chat or anything like that. Not only would it not work due to the methodology of the connection, but it's firmly locked down in the policy and privileges of the image. The power supply is with it. You'll find that you can use spreadsheets and doc files, but you have to create the file first, then save and encrypt it. After that, you'll be able to use it. If you fail to save the file before you close it, it will be scrubbed from the drive. Same if you don't encrypt it. It exists only on this drive and can't be transmitted unless the laptop is hooked into the DOD/INSQ network.

"The other thing is, the only websites you'll be able to access are the ones that are already in the favorites. There are news sites, a few

LEAVING AFGHANISTAN BEHIND

general sites. We've created email accounts for each of you. The names and initial passwords are on a paper inside the case. Change the password at first login. Your partners will have identical PCs issued by the end of today. You'll find their addresses, without passphrases of course, and they will have yours. By this evening, you will be able to communicate, but I must tell you emphatically, this is still not to be used for open communications. Say hi, I love you, be home soon. No details, no specifics... well, you get it."

"What group do you work for, Spec?" I asked.

"I hang out under the 10th Sustainment Brigade Special Troops. Mostly various tasks as needed to support the regulars, on a project by project basis, but most of us Chipheads have a couple of build benches and server rooms over there, separate from the base infrastructure."

"Chipheads? I like it. Thanks for the lifeline, Spec."

"Don't mention it, Ma'ams. Glad to help. You have a nice afternoon now."

"Me first, me first," Liz shouted, as she jumped up and reached for the bag. I couldn't help but laugh out loud at her.

I handed her the case and swung up onto my bunk, laying down and covering my eyes with my arm. I drifted off. About an hour later I felt something in front of me. I moved my arm and Liz's face was about six inches in front of mine.

"Can I help you with something?" I asked.

"We're so totally screwed up as doctor and patient at this time, I figure why bother."

"So you're not going to help me anymore?"

"I'm going to do everything I can to help you still, but I want something in return. Whether I deserve it or not is in question, but it's still something I want."

"What do you want?"

"I... I want you to be my sister. Forever. I want you and Theresa and your kids to come to me and Keven's and hang with the kids. I don't want to take you away from your families, but maybe the day before or after a holiday, you could come over. Or maybe you could even bring your families over to our place, if you'd like. Maybe I'm being stupid because of the circumstances. Oh hell, forget I said anything. Go back to sleep and ignore me. I'm rambling because I've been scared and tired and…"

I reached up and grabbed her and pulled her to me, kissed her on the cheek, and hugged her like a little girl hugging a toy doll hard enough to push the stuffing all to one end. "I wouldn't have it any other way, sweetie."

Liz returned my hug even harder. This is the kind of bond that I'd formed with certain people that I'd gone into battle with, and come out alive. We stay in touch with emails all the time, and always will, but we're spread to the four winds. Liz's and my families lived within minutes of each other.

I pushed Liz up off me, then got up out of my bunk. She'd taken off her ACU jacket and was in an olive tee. I made her put my Second Chance on and put her ACU jacket over it, to cover it up.

Overboard? Definitely. Paranoid? No doubt. But I was taking no chances whatever.

Since Liz had finished sending an email to her girls, I sent an email to Theresa. Then I checked in with Jernick. I asked him what he wanted us to do for the next couple of days. I put up the PC and then we watched TV for a couple of hours before I made Liz get up and help me GI the room.

"You're kidding. It's clean."

"No, it's filthy. It's dusty. You'll be amazed how much we'll pick up from the tiles and surfaces."

And she was amazed. We cleaned for about two hours, including the latrine, the floors, the racks for the bunks, the locker surfaces, and the windows. We wiped the walls, everything. After we were done, I got the laptop out and checked email. I'd already gotten a message back from both Jernick and Theresa. Theresa mostly went on about how much she missed me and how she was going to punish my ass for the *lies of omission* when we got back together, but the way it was written, it was obvious she was joking.

Then I opened Jernick's email. He told me to do absolutely nothing for the next week. In their first day, they'd run across a gang from Cuba that had been under surveillance for almost five months. They'd been caught in a sting, holding seven kilos of black tar heroin and ten kilos of cocaine. They were two-strikers and were looking at going down the river for the rest of eternity. During interrogation, one of them said that they knew something about the missing cop and doctor, and who might have something to do with it. They were already talking about deals and giving up information and everything. The one

LEAVING AFGHANISTAN BEHIND

thing they were told was, no matter what else could be worked out, some verifiable details would have to be presented within two hours or no deal.

The Cubans gave up the Columbians in a heartbeat, and now the hard, old-fashioned police work was on. That was a pure miracle, one that couldn't even have been granted by St. Francis. He asked that I trust him to do the work he was so well trained to do and begged me for patience. I responded to his email letting him know that subsequent smoke would be orange. I also let him know that I was very apologetic for my behavior in his office, but I was highly stressed and didn't feel like I had any power to do anything. After I sent the message, I walked out to the desk at the CQ and asked to speak to the SGM. I was told that I could go back to our quarters and he'd come let us know when he'd heard. It was only about fifteen minutes, maybe less, and he led us down the hall to the office. Once we were inside, Vetter held his hand out to get us to sit down. He stared at us for several minutes with a shit-eating grin on his face. "You know, Sgt. Plummer, I still have egg on my face from your little low blood sugar episodes, you ball buster." He broke open with a huge smile and stuck his meaty paw out to me. We shook for a long time. He then turned to Liz and shook her arm practically out of its socket. "Yes sir, Sgt. Sutton, she pulled some serious 'hey, let's make them all look like dickheads' sort of shit all the time. And the worst part? Technically, she couldn't even be there! So, I got the word on who you work for now, Plummer. I would have thought you'd be somewhere in the Caribbean checking out your roots. Hanging out. Doing not much of anything."

"Me? Retire? I'm only thirty-six. I fucking wish, SGM!" We both laughed. Liz just sat there smiling, somewhat nervously. You could tell we were in the presence of strong character here, and Vetter was definitely intimidating.

"You know, Pete, there's something I've always wanted to say to you, but was never in the right situation where I could…"

"What's that, Raw Sugar?"

"I don't know if you'd suck a dick or not, but I know you'd hold one in your mouth for a while!"

I thought Pete was going to have a heart attack he laughed so long and so hard. Every once in a while he stopped for a few seconds, then he'd start back up. He was seriously not getting oxygen, and his skin was turning a brilliant scarlet. I got up and went around the back of his desk and started pounding him on the back. He had his face on his desk pounding it with his fist. It took nearly twenty minutes to get him to stop. By this time, even Liz was totally wasted, all three of us were.

"Goddamn! If you think I thought that was funny, wait until I tell my wife tonight." He looked at Liz. "Even Marianne knows of Raw Sugar. That's what a legend she was. She'll get more of a kick out of somebody wanting to mouth off to the instructor than I did! I swear she will. Here I actually thought she was a *don't ask, don't tell*, and then to hear her tell that joke!"

"Actually, Pete, I am gay, but that didn't keep me from hurling curses at you as my instructor. You know everybody does it inside their mind. I just have a better class of curses."

"That you do, that you do. So you really are, huh? Well, times have changed. It's too bad we hadn't changed the rules already, back when you were in. I don't know if I agree with it or not, I'm maybe too old school, but the law of the land is the law of the land, and I'll do what they tell me. Whatever I am or am not, I'm a good soldier and will follow orders."

Pete hung low over his desk and got very quiet, motioning us closer.

"I understand this whole operation was your idea. I heard you personally wasted four people in the line, even though it's cost you a lot personally. I thought you were the ablest, most professional soldier when we had you, and it's obvious you haven't changed one bit, Amelia. I just want you to know how proud we were of you, and how proud we are of you now. You're one helluva veteran, both as a soldier and as a cop." Then he turned to Liz. "Doc, no matter what happens until this is over, you stick with Amelia and do exactly what she says, and you'll be fine. Trust her more than anybody you ever have," he said, giving the thumbs up sign.

"Good to know, Pete. Good to know."

Pete sat back up in his chair and raised his voice to a normal level. "Sgt. Plummer, what can I do for you and Sutton today?"

"I need two Berettas and a thousand rounds of ammo."

"Oh, is that all?"

"No, I need them until we leave."

"Couldn't you ask for something a little easier to get, like your own Humvee and driver?"

"And one of those too. Seriously. One of those."

LEAVING AFGHANISTAN BEHIND

"Christ almighty. Give me time to get some paperwork filled out for you and make a couple of calls. Sorry you don't still have a military driver's license, or I'd just give you something. Wouldn't make sense to train you up and then you run away right off. Would a staff car be good enough? For that you don't have to have anything but a state issued DL."

"Does it have GPS and know every point on the base?"

"Right. One Humvee and a driver. Go back to your quarters, and I'll send a runner for you." Liz and I stood up and came to attention in front of the SGM.

"Plummer, leave the door open when you leave."

"Hooah."

Liz and I went back to our quarters. I checked the email again. There was a note from Jernick stating they had more information and he'd take the time at the end of the day to give me a few details. I also had an email from Theresa. *"You know my great uncle is a direct immigrant from Sicily. He's connected. If you ever do this to me, to us, again, I'll have him get his friends and come kick your ass! You better get this cleared up. You have three weeks and five days left. Then I'm getting married whether you're there or not! I can only close my eyes and try to feel your arms around me, holding me. The look of the flowers up in front of your face is still vivid in my mind, in spite of everything that's happened. It's too bad they're going to be dead before I get home. It doesn't matter, of course. We'll have a lifetime to buy flowers and put flowers in our children's hair. I've been picturing that in my mind. We've always talked about liking children, and I can only imagine that you want to have children with me. I hope you do. I want so much for us, but for now I'd settle for being able to snuggle up to you in bed at night and smell your body wash. Nights are the hard part here, when the lights are out and it's quiet. They let me give them a play list of music. They pushed a bunch of music to my NSA laptop already and are going to do more every day. Listen to me go on and on about nothing in particular. Just know that I love you so much and can't wait until we can put this whole ugly thing behind us."*

"Teri, you're not rambling, no more than I will be now that I'm writing you back. I don't know if they told you or not, but there is some information already coming in. Who would have thought, so quickly?

By the way, I've adopted a sister. Officially. You and I both. We've adopted Liz and Keven. I guess that means that since they're now our sisters, their two little girls are our nieces. Family, you ask? We already have one. We just haven't met them all yet. Haha. About your question: of course I want children. You know, because of my wounds, the possibility of me getting pregnant is slim to none, but we can get you pregnant whenever you want. We can do it when we get home. We can give it a few months. We can wait a couple to four years to have some time alone before them. So much to talk about when we get home. Just so long as you still want to marry me. Your loving fiancée, Amelia."

Liz checked her email again, and like me, she had a short note from Keven. She answered and then shut the PC down.

"Get your web belt and holster out along with your two canteens," I said, as I opened my locker and pulled mine out. She followed me out into the CQ where we went to one of the water dispensers that had added electrolytes. We filled all four canteens and reattached them to our respective belts. As we were finishing up, the CQ Runner came up to us with a clipboard.

"Sergeant, if you would sign here... and here, this will give you a Humvee with a driver. Thank you, here's your copy. Take these papers to the armory, which will allow you to check out your weapons and receive your ammo. Good afternoon, Ma'am."

"Thank you."

Liz and I headed outside the building, where our Humvee was running, with our driver waiting. We got into the back seat and directed him to the armory. He asked which one and in response I just handed him the order.

"Yes, Ma'am. That's the one here in the battalion. We'll be there in five minutes unless we run into PT traffic."

"PT traffic?" Liz asked, quietly leaning over to me.

"Physical Training. People out running."

"Ah."

"Here you go, Ma'am. Do you know what time you'll be done here?"

"No idea at all, Corporal. How do we contact you?" He gave me a handheld radio.

"Just jump on and ask for the motor pool. Ask for Corporal Blevins, and I'll come running."

"Very good. It will probably be a couple of hours at least. Maybe three. Depends on how long we can last."

LEAVING AFGHANISTAN BEHIND

"I'll be waiting, Ma'am."

We went up to the front cage and were met by an armor. "What can I do for you sergeants today?"

I pushed our papers through the cage to him. "We need two 9mms and a thousand rounds of fodder."

"Jesus, how many days are you going to be here?"

"Maybe a few."

"So you know, you will have to turn in all unused ammo at the end of the day each day. It will be stored separately from all the other, then you can pick it up the next morning."

"If you read our orders carefully, you'll see that it's signed by both Major Leitner and SGM Vetter, as issued to us, without restriction. If you'd care to call the major or the SGM, I'm sure they'll be glad to talk to you about it."

"One moment." He picked up the order for distribution and dialed the phone. It had to be Pete on the other end. I could hear bits and pieces of it from where we stood. "If you'll wait for just a moment, I'll be right back." He went to a computer and generated two sheets, went back with the papers to one of several room-sized safes, and came back pushing a cart. On it were two Berettas and a thousand rounds. He had us sign for the equipment.

"One last thing, I need to get six extra clips for each weapon for match practice and two web belts with holsters."

"The orders don't mention that."

"Please go make another phone call."

He pondered this a minute, then shrugged his shoulders and left to go get twelve clips. Meanwhile, Liz and I picked up our weapons and pulled the metal cartridge boxes closer to us. After the armor had given us the clips and holsters, we put the web belts on and holstered the weapons, and put the clips in our pants pockets, we each grabbed a box of ammo and headed for the door. We walked down the footpath about a hundred yards and came to the first firing line, which we had been told would be operational for the day, but had no one scheduled. We talked to the range master and told him we'd be doing tons of practice and needed a spotting scope and assistance from downrange. He picked up the field phone and got an observer to go down the tunnel to the slit trench in front of the target for spotting and correcting.

"Let's get to it, babe. You're in the army now!" I first showed Liz how to remove a slide and spring to clear a jam. Then I taught her how to the use the safety and the steps the bullet took through the gun along with the theory of the blowback design. I explained that with the first pull of the trigger, if the slide hadn't been racked and doesn't have a bullet in the chamber, no fire will belch out of the pistol. And I stressed what precautions need to be taken, especially if there *is* a bullet in the chamber. The last bit of training on the pistol itself, was the simple fact that whether or not it actually was, the gun was *always* treated *as if it was loaded*!

Then I walked her through breathing and sight techniques to use on the targets. Since she was a beginner and there wasn't anybody else on this range, we moved up to the twenty-five foot line to start with. Eye and ear protection on, then *fire at will*. Liz was thrilled that out of her fifteen rounds, ten hit the target. I gave her initial instructions, but said nothing until she finished her first complete clip. I showed her what she was doing wrong and how to correct the errors. With the second clip, she put all fifteen rounds on the paper. With the third clip, all of the rounds were in the black. By the fourth round, I had her putting all the rounds inside the seven ring.

"Is this always easy for people to learn?"

"Women do better because they have a lower center of gravity, for one."

"You're saying I have fat hips and a big ass."

"No, you said that, not me. You know what I mean, anyway. The second thing is that women tend to listen to instruction better than men."

"Really? You think I'd know that, being a psychiatrist. You know, this whole adventure is going to be really helpful to me, if we get out of it alive."

"That's the plan. Now, next clip. Holster the weapon... get your breathing under control... then draw your weapon and empty the clip as quickly as you can."

"Ooo. Matt Dillon."

"C'mon, shoot. Quit screwing around."

"Yes, Sergeant." Then suddenly, she drew and emptied the clip. I was pretty impressed. Minimal instruction, virtually no experience, and in rapid fire mode she still put twelve of fifteen on the paper.

I held my hand out to have her give me her weapon. I put a fresh clip in it and made sure that both of my weapons were on safety with a round in the chamber. I stuck them in the web belt, not in my holster. I

LEAVING AFGHANISTAN BEHIND

drew, clicked the safeties off, and emptied thirty rounds in my target in under seven seconds. All but two rounds were inside the ten ring, the other two were inside the nine ring. I smiled at Liz.

"Show off."

"No, experienced, and at only twenty-five feet. Let's back up some," I said, as we moved back to fifty feet. We shot for hours, yet we still had ammo left. Liz listened intently and took her newfound training seriously, although she still cracked jokes here and there. Eventually it was time to return to the battalion area. I got on the radio and called for Corporal Blevins to come pick us up. I had Liz load one last clip and put it in the gun. We got back to the battalion area just in time for evening chow. We put the ammo in the lockers, but kept the pistols on, as we would throughout our stay.

As we were going to the chow hall, the CQ yelled at me that Liz and I had something that had been brought in. I picked up the envelope and we went back into our room and shut the door. I opened the envelope. It contained two unit-specific patches for our left shoulders, along with a new insignia to be worn above it.

"What do these mean?"

"If I'm not mistaken, and I don't think I am, they mean jack squat. Just like the word I made up to answer your Gaelic. They're new, an original design, they mean nothing, and they can't be traced to any unit," I said as I replaced our old unit patches with the new ones.

"For so much of life being screwed up right now, I'm having the thrill of a lifetime. I feel so guilty about my little girls. They're missing mommy while she's off playing Girl Scout and having fun."

"I have to admit, I know what you mean. I really miss it," I said with a grin.

"It shows, Amelia. It really does. You're so... professional about it. Now I get your answers."

"What answers?"

"When I ask you what you feel. No joy, no remorse, no grieving, no satisfaction, and yet nothing like being a cold-blooded killer... a professional soldier."

"Thanks for understanding."

Liz walked up to me, put her arms around my neck, and squeezed, not letting go. With not much else to do, I hugged her back.

"I want to tell you something, which blows even me away."

"What?" I queried.

- 105 -

"I'm *in* love with Keven, but I do love you."

"Me too. I know exactly how you feel."

Liz kissed me on the cheek, then we opened the door and went to chow. We were about halfway through the allotted chow time when we entered the mess hall. We moved through the line, again only speaking as much as was necessary to get our food, and headed for the Snake Pit. We had no sooner sat down than up strolled Sergeants Taggert and Bowers. Crap. As they sat down, I preemptively gave the thumbs up sign to the both of them.

"Well, to look at your sleeves, you got your transit orders," offered Bowers. His forehead was screwed up, sort of like he was trying to figure out what our insignias meant. Win number one for the home team. You could tell he was itching to know, but being in for as many years as he had been, he knew better than to question things that didn't concern him. It's like the old World War II expression, *Loose Lips Sink Ships.*

"How long before you take off?"

I just shrugged my shoulders. Liz and I ate quickly while Bowers and Taggert took a more leisurely approach. They talked to each other about their day's activities in the field with their troops, pretty businesslike, but at a relaxed pace. Liz and I both finished eating at exactly the same time, drank the rest of our water, and rose from the table. Both of the other sergeants' eyes opened a little bit wider when they saw we were under arms. We walked quickly back to our room at the CQ.

"Draw your weapon, take out the clip, clear the round from your chamber, and load it into the clip. Next put the clip back in. When you're done, re-holster your weapon. Safety first," I told her.

"Okay, you said to always treat it as if it's loaded, but we don't have any rounds chambered. Does that mean to pull the clip, pull the slide back, and verify it's empty, then go back to treating it like it's loaded?"

"Full marks!"

For never having held a gun before today, she was brilliant.

"Before we go to sleep, we'll chamber a round and hang the web belts on the post of the top rack. That way, they'll be right there and ready to go."

"Even though we're here and you think we're perfectly safe surrounded by an infantry division?"

LEAVING AFGHANISTAN BEHIND

"Look, I know it was only one squad car, and they really had no idea the level of the threat, but two cops died outside my doorstep. Semper vigilans, ever vigilant."

"Sure."

Of course, even though it had realistically only been a few minutes, Liz jumped on the laptop. She had another quick note waiting from Keven. *"I miss you so much. I'm sad. Thankfully our little babies don't quite understand and although they miss their other mommy, they're satisfied with the thought she'll be home very soon. As for me, I'm not satisfied. I got the book out again to read, to help me fully remember every detail, and hopefully understand what's going on. What could have possibly been the trigger? I pretty much know, but still. Know this, my sweet darling: I worry about you every single second of every single day. This is the first time in our sixteen years together that I've had to go through this. It's as if it's somebody else's life and I'm watching through a one-way glass. Please be safe and hurry home to us. KayKay."*

"You want on?"

"No. I'll check it in a couple of hours. Still planning on running with us tomorrow?"

"Actually, having stayed busy all day, not sitting at my desk like usual, I was surprised that I have more energy than I have had in a long time. It's a reminder that I'm going to start spending more time exercising, but yeah, I think I got it."

"Sharon, go to the desk and ask for a safety vest so you'll be ready."

Liz walked up to me and stuck her face right in mine. "It's so totally James Bond. I'm scared to death, but at the same time it's a total fucking adrenaline rush! Back in a sec, Diana," she said with a smile, then opened the door to our room and disappeared for a few minutes. "I already drew water and electrolytes for the morning. You might want to do that, too," she said, putting her folded safety vest on the top rack above her.

"Yeah, good idea. I'll do that in a few minutes." I looked at my watch and it was already 1710. "Hey! Grab your cap and come with me if you wanna take in something über-cool!" I went running out of the building with Liz right behind me, pulling our caps out as we passed the doorway. When we were outside, I moved off to one side of the sidewalk, directly in front of the building. "When you hear the music, face the flag directly and salute until it stops. Pay attention to all the people around you, but without moving your head, just your eyes."

Less than two minutes later, Tattoo came over the loudspeakers across the entire base. For everybody, outside every building, life came to a standstill. Civilians stood still and either put their right hand over their heart, or if they had a hat, held it in their right hand over their heart. All personnel in uniform came to attention, pirouetted to face the flag, and saluted. There must have been seventy-five or so people in our area. We hadn't had time to grab our winter coats, so we were both shivering by that point. At least Liz had on my vest, so that gave her some extra warmth.

"That was *amazing*!"

"I know. That's called Tattoo. I never got used to that. Every day I wasn't deployed, and was at home, for my entire time in, it gave me shivers. Now let's get inside and get our coats on so we don't freeze."

"There's more?"

"A little bit." We got inside and put on our coats then went back out to be ready for 1730. "Same thing when you hear the music." By this time though, there were probably more than a hundred and fifty people moving along the road. They were going between training and quarters and overnight duties and what not, not to mention an entire company marching off to an overnight bivouac on the base. The music started wafting in, and everybody came to attention and saluted. Taps played slow and steady, marking the ceremonial end of the day. When everybody came to, Liz dropped her salute, but stayed perfectly still. She wasn't moving a muscle and had a very sad look on her face.

"Hey, are you okay? I thought you'd like it."

"I did. It was wonderful. It just reminded me of my father's funeral. I was only six. He was part of the peacekeeping force in Lebanon. He was actually killed in a motor vehicle accident, but it was on active military duty and deployed in a foreign country. I still have his flag. All my mother got was that flag, thirty-seven thousand dollars in life insurance, and that song. That day they played Echo Taps. I... I need to go inside," she said, as she turned and passed me on the way back into our room, fairly knocking me to one side in her haste.

As I entered our room, she was sitting on her bunk, with her face hidden in her hands. I shut the door behind me and walked over to her. I stood in front of her and put my hand on her shoulder. She brought up one hand and placed it on top of mine.

LEAVING AFGHANISTAN BEHIND

"I'm just a psychiatrist. Who am I kidding? I think I was making it exciting to avoid the reality of it all. My entire life has been turned upside down in less than forty-eight hours. I don't know how you do it, Amelia. You're so strong. I know you're having some serious problems that I'm trying to help you with, but that's only exorcising your demons. You, you're physically, mentally, just so... so..."

"Everybody has something they're good at. Here. Let's get your coat off." I pulled her up off the bunk by her hands. Her eyes were wet, but she didn't have any tears streaming. That was good. She was still in control. I helped her take off her coat and hang it up on the other end post of her bed.

Then I took her locker key off her neck and took out a complete change of uniform from her pack and set them on the bed. I unlaced her boots and had her take her feet out. I undressed her completely, then held her hand and walked her over to the small latrine with the shower stall in the corner of our room. "Make the water as hot as you can stand it. You'll need it. It will keep you loose for tomorrow morning." She took a shower. While she did that, I folded all her dirty clothes, put them in her open weave laundry sack, and put them in her pack. I locked up her locker and put her key in my pocket. When she came out, she was all dried off, but with her hair still wet. I dressed her, finally finishing with re-lacing her boots. "Go blow-dry your hair and we'll put it back up. Okay?" She merely nodded her head and went through the motions of completing the task I'd given her. When she came back in, I had her sit on the bed and handed her the laptop. "Go ahead and send her a note. It'll help." I took her locker key and put it back around her neck.

I got out a fresh uniform from my locker and took my shower. When I got back in the room, Liz hadn't moved.

"Have you opened your email yet?"

"No. Not yet."

"You better do it pretty quick. We'll have to hit lights out. We get up at 0400 in the morning."

"Yeah."

"*My dearest KayKay. I'm seriously losing it. At first I tried convincing myself I could do this, but I can't. Then I thought of what I'd tell one of my patients, but that didn't help. It could still be weeks. I'm dying here. I don't want to burden you because I know it just makes you worry more, but I had to reach out to you and tell you* what's in my heart. I was eating in a mess hall with about fifteen hundred other people, all in uniform. The other sergeant was the only other female there. Everybody stared at us for being armed. Usually, you only have guns when they're issued at the armory for a specific exercise. The infantrymen that have them all the time, have them in a gun locker in their barracks. Okay, so there actually are a couple of cool things going on here. We went target shooting today for almost two and a half hours. I'm not bad for a beginner, but then, no one was shooting back. I couldn't help but think of how excited Alyssa would be watching all the soldiers. Maybe not, who knows, but I wanted her on my lap while I ate. I have to tell you, having my friend here is the only thing maintaining my sanity at all. That and knowing that you're waiting for me. Please don't give up on me... even if it's a long wait. Okay? I love you lots and lots. Your Lizard Breath."

"You need on?"

"Yeah. I need to check on my brass and see what's up." I took the laptop from her and opened my mail. There were two messages. One from Theresa and another from Jernick with an *important* icon beside it. I read the one from Theresa first.

"*I wish I could play with your boobs. Love you. Miss you. Dying here without you. Please let this be over soon. PWA.*"

Then I opened the one from Jernick.

"*Located friends of incarcerated informant. Will get last of intel as soon as relocated out of state for protection. Expect two day delay. Anticipating location of targets immediately thereafter. Hang on.*"

I shut down the laptop. Hang on...

"*Let's get one thing straight, asshole. I'm not your fucking friend. I'm your partner. That's all I want. Don't try and bond or any of that other male ego bullshit with me,*" I nearly shouted. "Did I say anything?"

"*Just letting you know.*"

"Fine. Out of the blue, after sitting behind this wall in the sand in the middle of bumfuck, you want to tell me that?"

"Whatever."

"Gittens, this is our third time on trail. What is your major malfunction?"

"Okay, you want to know what the hell is on my mind? My old partner and I were together for years. You understand that. And he died on my last patrol on my last deployment. So I don't want to go

LEAVING AFGHANISTAN BEHIND

through again what I went through getting over him. No, that's not right. I'm still not over him. I never will be. And no, we didn't have a 'thing', I'm just talking about sniper/observer team. That's all. So shut the fuck up."

"Zero one eight degrees... What's that?" he interrupted quickly."

"Not sure. Seems to come and go."

"Maybe just heat."

"I don't know. I think you might have picked up on something. Maybe too far out."

"We'll just keep an eye out. Keep watching the whole azimuth though."

"You think I don't know that, you dumb shit?"

"Look, all I want to do is my job and get back home safe to my girl and my kid. So quit being so fucking full of yourself, Gittens. You do your job, just like you say, and you better do it pretty Goddamned good."

I put my head down. He was right. Our first two patrols were known to be empty and precautionary in nature, but this was a live one. I needed to get my shit together, in one bag, and behind me. I scanned slowly and methodically left to right, right to left, high, low, low, high... I kept coming back though.

"Change to zero one four. It's most definitely man-made, and it's most definitely on the move."

"Yeah. Been watching that."

"Hey, Washington..."

"Yeah?"

"Sorry. I'm usually not that full of myself. I'm just having some adjustment problems."

"I know about your scars. Are you sure you're going to be able to do this?"

"I'm sure."

"'That's good enough for me."

"Besides, you couldn't be all that bad. You're black, too." I laughed.

"Yeah, but you have some sort of fucked up accent. Where are you from, anyway?"

"Bermuda."

"You could be out on a beach instead of here, and you actually chose here? Are you totally nuts?"

"You're only about the fourth or fifth dozen person to ask me that. Everybody's got to be someplace."

"One one zero. Something's definitely up. I don't want your opinion of what it looks like to you. I want you to tell me what it feels like to you, Gittens. I've got one tour; you're on your fourth. What do you think?"

"Truthfully? Given range and speed... I think those bastards are a pair or two pairs of people doing exactly what we're doing, toting a couple of SV-98s. Ain't it great? Our new 'friends', the Russians, are supplying the enemy, just like the old days. Fuckers."

"That's sort of what I was thinking. I vote we wait it out here until dark and then pull back to that ridge we passed a few hours ago. Go up to the top of it and sit it out there tomorrow. Then if we don't see any action, we can either hoof it or get an extraction from there tomorrow."

"Roger."

We waited four hours without seeing anything other than the movement, from right to left, of the other ECs. One thing was certain after watching them for the next couple of hours: they were getting closer.

"Right back, latrine break," I said. I scooted down the wall just enough to keep the piss from running back to us, since it was so flat. I'd just about finished when I noticed Washington glancing my way.

"You saw a vagina before, meat?"

"No. I can't see anything anyway. I was just thinking about the no women in combat rule and how you're getting around it. I don't see any difference in you and me. You're actually faster than me. I can lift more than you, and out here with no cover we both gotta squat to pee to keep from getting shot. What's the big deal? That's all."

"Good man. Somebody that gets it." I moved back over into position.

"When we get back, can I see your wounds? I mean, if you don't mind? All I've ever had was a wall of a building fall on me and break about half of my ribs."

"Shit, man, that's enough isn't it?"

"I guess it is at that."

We kept a solid vigil. Everything seemed to be okay after dark, so we moved back and up to higher ground. We ate some energy bars for breakfast and were in place before sunup. Another long day of waiting,

LEAVING AFGHANISTAN BEHIND

except today, just before 1130 hours, a shot hit the embankment about three meters to the left of us, with the sound coming in about a second and a half later. That meant a quarter mile away. Shit. We both ducked. For this type of mission, we both carried a rifle.

"You ever see Rooster Cogburn?"

"You ask me now?"

"Like John Wayne said, 'prepare to meet your maker!' " I shouted, as I peered up over the embankment. I didn't see any movement, but God was definitely on my side today: I caught the micro-momentary glint of light off glass. His scope! I did a quick breath control, then fired as close as I could to the light. Moments later, there was another glint, except this was a protracted reflection. It was the sunlight off the front of the shooter's scope as the gun was falling backward to the earth!

"I don't know how many of them there are, but there's one down." Just then, the embankment immediately in front of me exploded. The EC had hit a rock in front of me while I was scanning for additional movement. A stupid mistake! I should have moved down ten meters one way or the other instead of straight back up. I was trying to save time. The rock pieces scattered and one large piece, about a half an inch or so, hit my upper right arm, missing my body armor by less than two inches. Dammit!

"Fuck. Washington, I got a small problem here," I said, as I fell back into the ravine. "I need you to wrap this for me, I think."

I had no idea that I was bleeding heavily. Washington immediately broke out a first aid kit and wrapped me, but I was still bleeding. Suddenly more rounds started coming in, more and more and more. This wasn't a sniper rifle; this was from AKs. Washington got out my kit and wrapped around the first compression. It helped, but it still didn't stop the bleeding completely. While he was working on me, he called for close air support.

"Snake-One-Seven, Snake-One-Seven, mayday, mayday, mayday. Requesting immediate Charlie Alfa Sierra, on my position from radio, all directions, under direct enemy fire, cover entire grid, say again, cover entire grid from south to southwest, thirty meters from my coordinate. Broadcasting coordinates from two radios for confirmation." Washington put my good hand up on my radio and forced me to key the mic.

"So you wimp out on me on our third date, is that it? Over one little rock? Okay, so it was traveling at twice the speed of sound, but that's no excuse. You got me? You got me, Gittens?"

"Yeah, I'm good."

"Stay awake. And keep your fucking head down. We need to roll you over. In a half a minute or so, we're going to be right in the middle of a shit storm here."

"I sort of thought we already were," I laughed over the noise of the battle. We laughed together, but his eyes were serious.

The intensity of the gunfire was increasing; obviously they were getting closer. Washington had our Barretts stowed and our Ares out and ready. He checked both weapons, then put my sling over my body on my right side. "Put your hand up in the trigger housing. Hooah?"

I made sure that I didn't have any impediment in my right hand and fingers, that all of my problems were with my left arm. "Hooah." Washington charged my weapon and screamed almost in my face, "Weapons hot, motherfuckers!"

"Snake-One-Seven, Snake-One-Seven, request time on target, say again, request time on target. It's really starting to heat up down here."

"Snake-One-Seven, Snake-One-Seven, STARS Two-Niner," came the woman's voice back on the radio. The Air Force Command and Control Joint Stars were on this one for us. That made me feel a little bit better. "Expected time on target is six minutes, say again, six minutes."

"Snake-One-Seven, STARS Two-Niner, negative, negative. Need assistance zero time. Assistance zero time."

"Snake-One-Seven, STARS Two-Niner, understand, nearest CAS is now four, say again, four minutes. Now three minutes, say again, three minutes."

"Snake-One-Seven, STARS Two-Niner, adjust support zone ten meters, say again, adjust support zone ten meters. All directions. All directions."

"Snake-One-Seven, STARS Two-Niner, confirm, support zone is now ten meters, confirm, support zone is now ten meters."

"Snake-One-Seven, STARS Two-Niner, affirmative, affirmative. Ten meters."

Washington picked up our gear and had me by the neck of my armor. He moved us about twenty meters north in the ravine. He faced

LEAVING AFGHANISTAN BEHIND

me south to cover both the top of the embankment and the ravine in that direction. He reached into my cover jacket and pulled out all but two of my clips. He laid them on the ground next to me.

"I changed my mind." He unslung my rifle, then took the clips and sat down back to back with me, facing north to cover the opposite direction. "When you need a reload, yell at me. I'll just switch out rifles and load since you've only got one arm. Hooah?"

"Hooah."

I'll give you this, in all my years in the army, I think Washington was the best I'd seen yet. Maybe even better than Kowalski, as a general soldier.

The first of the rounds started whizzing down into the ravine a little bit, instead of all hitting the top of the opposite embankment. It was starting to get a little too real.

"Snake-One-Seven, STARS Two-Niner, time on target."

"Snake-One-Seven, STARS Two-Niner, expected time on target, one minute. Say again, one minute." "Goddamn it! We may not have a minute. We are in a ravine, recessed two meters, alter zone to zero meters, say again, alter zone to zero meters. Do not shoot into the ravine. Do you fucking understand me?"

"Snake-One-Seven, STARS, Two-Niner, time on target less than thirty seconds, less than thirty seconds, understand two meter depression, keep gunfire out of depression and alter support zone to zero meters, confirm."

"Snake-One-Seven, you got it! Get here now!"

Without warning the entire theater exploded. I rolled over on my side to get low and I felt Washington cover me for more protection. You could hear the GAUs from the A-10s ripping up the earth. There must have been four of them, from the sound of it. Normally they traveled in pairs; we got lucky. There were barely two seconds between passes, as they set up a round-robin circling pattern over us, one run after another. I don't know how long it lasted; all I remember is that beautiful sound, hearing the Gatlings firing spray after spray into the air around us. When it stopped, we were virtually buried in a layer of about three or four inches of dirt and dust and debris.

"Gittens, you okay?"

"Yeah, you?"

"I think so. Let me recon and make sure we're clear..."

That was the last thing I heard.

"Sergeant? Can you hear me?"

"Yeah. Where the fuck am I?"

"You're in the field hospital," the nurse said to me.

"You stitch me back up and give me my rifle. You're not sending me back to Germany."

"No, don't worry about that," he laughed. "Apparently the round hit a rock that fractured, hitting you with one big piece and several small pieces. While you were already under, they cleaned it up and in a few days you should be good as new. Your duty may take three or four weeks, but at least you'll be back in your unit."

"I can't believe you're getting your second Heart for somebody throwing a damn rock at you!" said Washington, who had been sitting in a chair off to one side.

"If you ever keep up higher to shield me again, you prick, I'll find a bigger rock and personally shove it up your ass!"

"Well, I'll leave you two lovebirds to sort this out. We just gave you some pain meds so you should be good for another four to six hours, Sergeant. If you need anything, let me know," he said, as he walked through the curtain surrounding my bed.

"Thanks, Lieutenant."

"Washington, forget what I said. We're tight, right?"

"You know it, girl. Ain't nuttin' but a thang!" he said, giving me some dap.

"Amelia, can you hear me? If you can hear me, tell me what you're seeing…"

I reached out and Liz was holding one of my hands between hers. I opened my eyes a little bit, fluttering them, gradually coming back to reality.

"Quickly, while it's still fresh, what happened? What did you see?"

"The day my second team member and I got overrun. That's when I got wounded the second time."

"Tell me what happened. Think, tell me what happened in your flashback, not how you think you remember it."

"We found a target and figured out that there were EC snipers moving opposite our scouting direction. I saw a sundog on a scope, and from the second sun flash, I thought the rifle was dropping. I think I dropped him. Then they started shooting back. I did something stupid. A freshman mistake. Instead of moving down about ten or twenty meters and popping back up to locate other ECs, I was trying to

LEAVING AFGHANISTAN BEHIND

save time and went straight back up. They had me. They shot the berm right in front of me and a rock broke into fragments. I took one in the arm."

"You made it through okay, right?"

"Sure."

"What about your team member? Did he get hurt?"

"No, he pretty much handled the whole situation. He turned out to be the best, most professional soldier I'd ever meet my entire career."

"Did he make it home?"

"Yeah. He's a firefighter for the Poughkeepsie Fire Department. He did our tour together and one more before getting out. He and his girlfriend already had a little boy and they're now married and have a little girl, too."

"You say he handled everything. What happened?"

"He dressed my wound. It turned out it needed quite a bit of attention. He was constantly calling in for support and updates with Command and Control. In addition to the snipers, apparently there were a butt-load of Taliban fighters. It was starting to sound like a bag of popcorn in the microwave. They were close. Eventually, Washington got us both down and back to back to cover both directions and we waited. By the time the air support got there, they were within yards. We altered what's called our support zone, from thirty meters down to zero. That's where you basically hide behind a rock or a tree and you call down an airstrike on your own position."

"Do you know how many of the enemy was killed?"

"I heard later it was somewhere around forty or so."

I looked at my watch. It was 0200. "Liz, get back to sleep. We have to get up in two hours and then run ten miles. You'll need your sleep."

"Are you going back to sleep?"

"Probably not."

"I think you blame yourself for things that happened that were not under your control. You obviously blame yourself for Kowalski's death. I think you blame yourself for not being able to be a full half of the team once you got under fire and also for forgetting to move before you stood back up. This was triggered by your shooting in the department. It doesn't mean, in the case of the police department, you blame yourself for that, but it triggered suppressed feelings and unresolved issues from the past. Then you blame yourself for the attack on Theresa and for her being in danger. You especially blame yourself for the death of the two police officers on your protective detail. I think you blame yourself for me being in danger. I don't think you're just protecting me. At least, I hope it's more than that…"

I sighed deeply and she patted my arm.

"Amelia, the army is a dangerous place. You were in a combat zone for a total of over seven years. You had friends that didn't make it home, while you somehow managed it. You can't be perfect. Nobody can. Nobody! Honey, you've got to let it go. We need to get through this thing we're in now and move on. That's my professional opinion."

You know, getting to play doctor to you has actually helped me calm down a lot. Just so you know, I'm sorry about last night. I don't know what happened. I mean, we're perfectly safe right here, and things are going so smoothly."

"A secret? No matter what you think you know, whether you're an officer or enlisted, the first few days of being in and around the military totally screw with everything you used to think was normal. It doesn't make any difference how many times you've watched 'Officer and a Gentleman'. Did you ever think you'd be sleeping with a loaded gun hanging on top of your four poster bed?"

"Ugh. I don't like guns at all, but right at this moment, I'm glad I have one. You know, for a plain little old beat cop, as you call yourself, you sure get a lot done. You pull off miracles."

"Time will be the judge of that." We lay there for the next hour and a half, neither one of us moving at all, neither saying a word. Finally, we heard the rapping on the door frame, one, two, three times.

"Sergeants? Formation."

"Thank you, Runner."

We quickly popped up, put on our boots, our web belts, our winter coats, and lastly, our safety vests. We both went in and skipped brushing our teeth until after morning chow, instead swishing a capful of mouthwash and spitting it in the sink.

"After you, Sergeant Sutton," I said, putting my hand out in front of us.

We formed up with our platoon, waiting for the complete assembly. Thankfully we were in the assembly before half of the actual army troops. We greeted the major and SGM.

"Glad to see you running with us this morning, Sgt. Sutton."

"What a beautiful day to be running, Major."

LEAVING AFGHANISTAN BEHIND

"Outstanding!"

"Major, since we fill out more than our rank this morning, would you mind if Sgt. Sutton and I fell back behind the Guidon?"

"I think he'd love the company, Sergeant. Go ahead. My compliments."

"'Morning, Sgt. Hardesty. What a fine morning for a run!"

"Happy to have two extra troops to extend our wonderful family to look at Mother Nature's beauty. Nice to see you here in the daylight instead of at the front gate in the middle of the night!"

Finally everybody was at attention and the troops were gradually put in motion. I kept looking at Liz, hoping she'd be okay. At about the six mile point, I decided to go ahead and address her.

"Sgt. Sutton, how's that appendix of yours doing?" I looked at Hardesty. "Chronic. Usually not a problem, but can't be too careful."

"Couldn't be better this morning, Sgt. Plummer. No pain whatsoever. Hooah!"

"Hooah!" both Hardesty and I shouted out together. Then he shouted out clearly and loud enough to be heard all the way back to the City, even over the yelling of the cadences, "Hooah?" Several hundred troops responded with a huge roar, "Hooah!" I'm sure even the major and the colonel shouted along with everybody else. That gave Liz the biggest smile I think I've ever seen on a human being. We finally finished up back in the battalion area, grabbed a shower, and a uniform change.

"Ready for chow?" I asked Liz.

"Are you kidding me? I could eat a side of pork right now. Sausage, bacon, more bacon, maybe a breakfast pork chop... and I would kill for a donut. Don't ask me why. I never eat them."

I had to laugh at her. While we still had the door closed and locked, I brought her close to me and hugged her tightly. "Thanks. I'm better now. And this morning was great. I can't tell you how cathartic that run was. I have to start running again. Maybe going out during lunch or even just one day on the weekends." She leaned up to me and kissed me on the cheek. "I've got my partner and I've got my wonderful children, but I always wanted a sister. I'm so glad I have one now." I smiled at her and ran my fingers along her cheek.

"Let's get going. By the time we get back, we might have some email."

Waiting for us in the mess hall, was a bit of a hiccup. Our CO and XO weren't dining with us this morning, and they had the SGM with them. Those were the three people which we'd need available at any given time to explain our circumstance. In addition to this aberration of daily routine, we had a visitor to the 2-22 this morning, who was going to be participating in a Field Training Exercise. Coincidentally, this was the reason our leadership was missing. They were having morning chow with a Brigadier General and the Base Commander, who was a two star or a Major General, discussing the upcoming FTX. A bird colonel walked up to Liz and me at one of the chow lines. He was looking at our belts, our arms, and our patches. Being a full colonel, he'd obviously been in for well over twenty years and knew a lot.

"Good morning, Sergeants."

"Good morning, sir."

"I couldn't help but notice you're under arms in a battalion area, in a mess hall."

"That's correct, sir."

"Mm-hmm... and I'm looking at your unit insignias. I don't know that I've ever seen them before. What outfit are you with?"

"It's a relatively new unit, sir. It's currently forming up. If you have any questions, we've been asked to direct you to our CO, XO, or SGM."

"Well now, I happen to be here to work with them for a few days and I'm aware that they're with the general this morning. So we'll have to work around that for the moment, won't we?"

"Sir, we've been specifically given direct orders to have all inquiries go through one of those three people."

"I see. What unit are you assigned to, Sergeant?"

"Sir, I've been directed at this time to offer to be detained until all this is sorted out, but all information has to come from one of those three people."

"Buffalo chips! You two come with me back to CQ. We'll by God get this squared away, and we'll get it squared away by God NOW!"

"Yes, sir." We led the way back to the CQ. I was more irritated that I was hungry and my blood sugar was dropping a little. Liz, on the other hand, was scared shitless.

Once we were in the CQ, the Colonel asked the runner for an office. We were led back to a room with a huge table and about a dozen chairs around it. Before sitting down, I pulled out my military ID card.

LEAVING AFGHANISTAN BEHIND

"Sharon, you might want to get yours out too," I said, handing mine to the Colonel. Liz followed my lead and offered hers as well.

"I'll be right back," said the Colonel, and left the room.

"Oh, we're screwed. I just know I'm going to jail now," said Liz.

"No, you're not going anywhere. Not today. Trust me."

"How can you be so calm? This is serious!"

"Of course it's serious. And trust me, it's not very often a bird colonel gets it broken off in his ass! Just sit back and watch the show…" Liz rolled her eyes at me, wringing her hands under the table.

We waited for almost twenty minutes. I was hungry, Liz was scared. I was relaxed, Liz... was not. Suddenly the door was opened by a captain. He came into the room and held the door open for the two star general, who was followed by a command sergeant major, his personal top enlisted man. They were all followed closely by Colonel Bremer, who was followed by Major Leitner, Colonel Xavier, the traveling ass wipe, and our SGM Vetter. After everybody was in the room and had stood silently for a couple of minutes, General Taubman started, "Do you have any idea who in the fuck just pulled me out of a working breakfast a few minutes ago? I got a call from the Pentagon. From the Goddamn Pentagon! It wasn't from an aide. It wasn't from an admin. It was from Lieutenant General Norwich himself. In person! Calling me! Wanting to know who on God's green acre had upset the fucking applecart and started this cluster fuck. Colonel, did Sgt. Plummer, or did Sgt. Plummer not, tell you that she was instructed, no, ordered, to direct any inquiries to one of three people?"

"Yes, sir, that is…"

"You even mentioned to her that you knew where those three people were this morning, is that correct as well?"

"If I may, sir…"

"And you chose not to even attempt to contact one of the three of us? She even offered to be put in detention until this was straightened out, did she not?"

"Yes, sir."

"How the fuck did you ever make it to full colonel? That's what I want to know. Sgt. Plummer, Sgt. Sutton, I hope that our drawing attention to your presence has been minimal enough so as to not jeopardize your impending activities and/or mission."

"Thank you, sir. I don't believe it has, at least not at this point. But the farther under the radar we fly from here on out, the better. The idea was not to tell people to leave us alone, but to just mix in while we are here waiting for all of our arrangements to be completed."

"So this is settled, right, gentlemen?"

"Right," was the chorus.

"Right, Colonel Xavier?"

"Right, sir."

"Out-fucking-standing! Colonel Xavier, you will stand down for the remainder of this exercise and replace yourself with your XO or request another battalion commander from your brigade. Understood? Out-fucking-standing!" He moved toward the door and the captain held it open while the room emptied. Only Vetter and Leitner stayed behind. We all gave it about a thirty count to make sure everybody was out of earshot before we lost it. Everybody but Liz. She was still in shock.

"I'd have paid for a ticket to that. I used to work for Xavier's command a while back. What a pompous ass," said Vetter. "I wonder how they got wind of it that quickly?"

"NSA. Don't forget, this whole thing is being overseen by them at this point. My idea, their project. As soon as there was a request made by Xavier on a computer, it flagged them. It initiated a paced sequence. Once it's triggered, the rest is automatic."

"I'm sorry we lost you. You would have made one of the best lifers I've ever met."

"Hey, Sharon, breathe before you pass out!" It took Liz a moment to remember I was talking to her. She managed a short, stifled laugh, then you could see her lungs expand way out and then back down. "Pete, as much fun as that was (at least for some of us)," I said, punching Liz in the arm, "would you mind getting us a ride over to the base chow hall. They'll still be open for a few hours for breakfast, for those slimy civilians, and to tell you the truth, we're a little hungry now."

"How 'bout I give you ladies a lift myself. My chow was interrupted too and they have some killer biscuits and gravy over there. After you…" he said holding his hand out. Liz was sitting up front with Pete.

"Liz, do you have any idea the equivalent of power Lt. General Norwich has? He's the commander of half of the active duty troops and bases in the US mainland. He's like a governor or a US senator.

LEAVING AFGHANISTAN BEHIND

He called from the Pentagon... To talk to us, here at little ol' Fort Drum. Priceless!" he said, laughing his butt off.

"I'm guessing that looking back in the years to come, I'll tell this story to my children and friends, huh?" she asked. I reached my hand up from behind her and put it on her shoulder and patted her.

CHAPTER ELEVEN

When we got back to our room and whipped out the laptop, I jumped on first, to look for directions for the day from Jernick. Again, I had two messages, one from Theresa, and one from Jernick, marked important. Of course, I went straight for Theresa's.

"*My protective detail is made up of a couple of pretty cool guys. We're in this executive suite sort of thing at a private apartment building. Wish I could tell you where. I also wish I could experience some of where I am. Looking back, if somebody asks me if I've ever been here, I'll honestly have to answer 'not really'. I have a bedroom and they have a bedroom. One of them is in the main lounge area at all times. There're two couches in there and a desk where I work. I work a lot and watch a lot of movies. Thank goodness for Netflix and aliases. I'm trying to be strong for you because I know you're strong doing what you're doing. I did get a short briefing yesterday, although no locations or specifics. Baby, you're brilliant. How could I ever have hoped to have such a wonderful fiancée?*" She went on for practically three pages, saying so much, without ever being able to say anything at all. I was the one that was lucky, not her. I made up my mind that when we were all home, I'd marry her within a week.

Then I opened the email from Jernick. "*Passengers identified, travel arrangements made, destinations will be reached within seventy-two hours. Patience.*"

"They've got the Cubans that are locked up all identified and have gotten them new locations out of state. Now it's going to be about a three day total wait for the Department of Justice to get them transferred to prisons out of state for safety. Then they'll give up the information they have on the Columbians." Just as I was getting ready to close the email, the laptop beeped at me. There was a new email. It was from Jernick. *"Xavier is a cock-sucker,"* was all it said. I had to laugh. I waved my hand at Liz to get her to come look at the last email. She laughed.

"Yup. Something to look back on down the line and laugh with the family and kids," she said.

I handed the machine off to her and she read what must have been volumes of writing from Keven. I lay back on my bunk, thinking of what we should do today. More time back on the firing range. I decided to try something. I stood up quickly and pointed at the doorway, then from a crouching position I practically shouted "Draw your weapon!"

Liz dropped the laptop on the mattress, almost letting it hit the floor, and quickly drew her Beretta, pointing it toward the door. Not the cleanest execution, for a beginner, but I'd take her on as a partner any day. "That was amazing! You rock, chick!"

"Wow. I can't believe I just did that. Maybe not up to your level of proficiency, but I did it. Who would have thought?"

There were three raps on the door frame. "Sgt. Sutton? Sgt. Plummer? Is everything all right in there? Ma'ams?"

I crossed the floor quickly, telling Liz to holster her gun, and then unlocked and opened the door. "Couldn't be better, Runner. Thank you for asking. Just doing a little training. Sorry. I should have warned you so that you wouldn't have been jumpy."

"No problem, Ma'am. Just wanted to make sure everybody was okay. Have a great day."

"You too. Hey, Runner, would you happen to have a computerized list of training exercises and activities for the entire base today? I figure almost everything's computerized now…"

"Oh, yes indeed, Ma'am. What in particular are you looking for? Maybe I can help or suggest something."

"Any arty?"

"No, Sgt. At the moment, they're deployed for a week at Fort Dix for a joint training due to some fire direction control upgrades. There is

LEAVING AFGHANISTAN BEHIND

a mortar live fire exercise this afternoon at 1345 if you want to hear noise, up north of Dixon Road. It's a pretty good little hump up there, though. Even with a driver, you'd have to leave immediately after lunch to get set up to get a good view of what's going on."

"Perfect. Get us a pair of tickets from the fifty yard line, and make sure that the major or the SGM talks to their people to make sure they don't mind us watching. We don't want to play with their toys, we just want to watch. And make sure we get there early. Instead of the mess hall, give us three MRE's to take along, with about a dozen protein bars, would you?"

"Hooah," the runner said and returned to the CQ desk.

"MREs?" quizzed Liz.

"Meals, Ready to Eat. It's the modern version of c-rations, the individual field meals. Except now they're much better, and they have a little heater in them, like a hand warmer that's chemically induced so that the meals aren't all cold. And they don't taste like potted meat anymore. I'm sure he'll be nice and get three good ones. You doing all right today? Worried about patients... other than the totally crazy chick standing in front of you?"

"I'm actually pretty lucky. The vast majority of my patients are short term. I do have several long term ones though, and I worry about them. It hasn't been a big deal so far, but it's only been a couple of days."

"Don't get too bogged down in it. Remember, while we're here, we're safe. Which means your patients get their doc back, doesn't it? Do you like fireworks?"

"Love them. Always have. Kev and I take the girls. Even as young as they are, they love them."

"You like war movies?"

"Sure. Why?"

"I guarandamntee you that this afternoon will give you a woody." Liz laughed at that.

"I'm sure you mean metaphorically..."

"I don't know. It might actually be metaphysically. Wait until you experience it, then you tell me," I said, winking at her.

Liz went back to her novel to Keven, and I did a power nap on the bunk. I woke up after about fifteen minutes. "Is the safety on your gun on or off?"

"I think it's on," Liz replied.

"You mean you don't know? Check it."

"Sure, it's on," she said putting her gun back in its place.

"Is it loaded?"

"Yes."

"Does it have one in the chamber?"

"Yes," she said after a moment's hesitation.

"Yes it does, or yes you always consider it chambered for safety's sake?"

"Both."

"Good girl. Wake me in forty-five minutes if I'm not already up."

"Okie-dokie."

The explosion rocked the entire compound and spread shrapnel and debris over a thousand square meter area, if not larger. Even with the blast deflector walls, there are breaches in order to get in and out of the inner circles. Outside the blast walls there was more compound that's just controlled by gates and soldiers with guns. There was screaming everywhere. People hurt, people screaming orders, sirens going off, utter mayhem. The first thing I did was hit the dirt. Then I saw the robe coming through the gate. Without thinking, I pulled out my Beretta, the only thing I had on me, and fired at the person. He stopped, reaching inside his robe. Shit! He was looking for a detonator. I fired six or seven times, with at least two rounds going into his head. Right behind him were two more people. I dropped them as well. Instinctively, I reached up to my over jacket and grabbed my only other clip. I clutched it in my left fist, using that hand to steady my shots. I scanned the area around me and there were two air force personnel hunkered down behind a deuce-and-a-half, which would protect them from things blowing up, but not bullets. I ran behind their truck.

"How many clips do you guys have?" The first one checked and pulled out five, the second had just one. I took four from the first, and left each one with the clip in their pistol and one extra. "Stay down!" I turned and crossed the area, ducking behind one thing at a time: a truck, a storage container, a wall, whatever I could find. I now had a better line of site of the breach into the red box, the inner zone of our forward base. This way, I could see farther down the street when people were coming. I moved along the northern wall as quickly as I could, staying pinned up against the wall, occasionally moving my head out for a better glance down the street. I heard some noise

LEAVING AFGHANISTAN BEHIND

behind me and immediately crouched and turned, ready to fire. There were four other soldiers with M4s following behind me, all moving to seal the breach as I was.

We made our way to the northeast opening to the entry alley. Three of us went left and the other two went right. There was a car that careened toward us, in my direction. The soldier nearest me unloaded an entire clip into the car where the driver would sit, then we three turned and ran because it still could have been loaded with explosives and remotely detonated by another EC. The five of us ran in the other direction and kept going. At about thirty meters, we were met with gunfire. I guessed about fifteen or twenty ECs were firing on our position. We moved against the buildings on our side of the street and began lighting it up. I felt, more than saw, movement behind me. A sixth sense. I put the barrel of my Beretta up to the window and fired twice, knocking the EC down to the floor. I moved back to the door and entered the room. I picked up the AK from the dead man and found several clips of ammo on him. I figured it'd do in a pinch.

We stopped at the end of the street, looking around. No more shots were coming our way and we were getting too far from the entry to the red zone. I pointed at two of the others, then pointed up and across the street at the rooftop. I pointed at the soldiers that had been with me, then pointed at the rooftop on our side of the street. Everybody nodded assent. I shoved my hand out indicating move out and we entered the buildings and made our way to the tops. Fortunately, in both buildings we were able to get to the roof and fortunately, over here, almost all the buildings are built contiguously with a common wall. Once you were on a roof you could go a long way. This could be a blessing or a curse, depending on your particular situation and who was firing at whom.

We got to the point where the car was motionless. The driver's arm was hanging out the window. After scanning, I signaled to the two across the street and waved forward indicating we should move down farther. They returned a similar sign in assent. No more had we started, than the car exploded. When it did, the two buildings practically collapsed, bringing all three floors of brick and all five soldiers down to the street in two big piles. We were frantically trying to dig ourselves out, helping each other, when a handful of Ghanis started firing and running our way. We unloaded. To tell the truth, they may have known how to shoot a gun, but they obviously had no *real military training. The five of us took them down in nothing flat. We continued up the street, to the outer ring past the intersection. The whole side of the green zone wall was like a soccer field with ECs running around in circles with no particular cohesion, just firing at everything. There was some fire from the northwest side where our boys were starting to get organized. Fuck this. I wasn't waiting. I got the other four behind me in a fighting vee, spread out over a twenty meter arc, and we moved forward. Within about ten minutes, twenty-three additional ECs were dead on the ground. Within seconds of the end of the firefight, over sixty infantrymen swarmed in around us.*

In one swift motion, I went from a deep sleep to being completely upright on the floor, wide awake, panting, in a crouch, and both hands out in front of me for protection. When I finally cleared my head, I saw Liz standing about six feet in front of me; she had her feet set shoulders width apart and her fists firmly on her hips.

"Spill it. Exactly…"

"No big deal. My third Star."

"Amelia, they don't give out Bronze Stars for holding the door open for little old ladies. You had to be under fire, and for a V you have to perform an act of heroism. Was this one an oak leaf, a V, or both? Before you answer, I already looked it up. I know the difference."

"Both. I and four other infantrymen were at a forward operating base that had gotten hit by two car bombs. I managed to neutralize three ECs, then I met up with four infantrymen. We did a sweep one direction and coming back somebody detonated a car bomb remotely. We basically got buried in the debris and the rubble and dug ourselves out. We pursued the fight further and got into a hornet's nest. We pulled a standard combat formation and cleared the outer zone. Immediately after that the area was secured by an Infantry Company."

"I see. And how many ECs did the four of you neutralize?"

"I'm not sure exactly, but I think the number was somewhere around thirty-four."

"So you didn't tell me about this earlier when we were talking numbers, did you? Error of omission?"

"No, we were talking about sniper hits. You never asked me about total battle kills."

"I'm going to ask you this one time, and one time only. Don't bullshit me. How many *total* kills did you get? At least an estimate."

"Maybe eighty-seven?"

LEAVING AFGHANISTAN BEHIND

"Oh, Amelia, Amelia..." she said, stepping toward me and wrapping me up in her arms. She put her mouth against my ear. "Sweetie, I can't help you if you don't completely open up to me. I need to know everything that's going on so I can try and formulate a plan to alleviate what's going wrong. Okay?"

I just nodded my head. It felt good, being held. I wished at that very second it was Theresa, but truthfully, Liz and I had gotten incredibly close. "Go wash your face and hands and try to freshen up. It will make you feel better," she said. So I did.

I didn't feel better. I felt cleaner, but not better.

Fortunately, I was saved by the knocking at the door.

"Sgt. Plummer? Your driver is here."

"Thank you, Runner. We'll be right there." Liz put her hand behind my head and kissed my cheek.

"C'mon, sis, we're going on an adventure. Put on a smile."

We were way early at the firing range. We were pulled off the road, completely past the debarking point for the unit, where the trucks would come in with troops and material. I showed Liz how we use our MREs, and we ate along with the driver. He sort of smiled when he realized that Liz was new to MREs, as if to say, "What rock have you been living under all these years?", but said nothing.

"So, Corporal. When you're not driving people around, what do you do with your time?"

"I mostly spend time either watching movies or at the base carpentry shop. I make furniture."

"That's way cool," said Liz.

"Yeah, I used to play games like almost everybody else, but I totally got burned out. Then I was home on leave and had to fix a couple of chairs for my grandma. When I got back to the base, I wanted to make her an entryway bench. You know, you can store stuff under it, like your winter boots during the summer. It's five feet wide, has three cushions, and you can sit down and take off your shoes or your boots or whatever. You could set down things you've just brought in the door until you get your car unloaded, then just shut the door and take everything you've brought in and put it up."

"I bet it's lovely. What a great thing to do for your grandmother. She must be so proud of you, Corporal!" Liz followed.

"Yeah, I guess she is at that. When she came to my graduation at basic, she came in her old pastel church skirt with matching jacket, pill box hat, the whole ball of yarn. She's very much old school. Doesn't have a cell phone and still thinks a man in uniform is the best thing since sliced bread."

"My significant other thinks that too. Except, there's always the slight worry of danger..." I didn't want to go too far into detail, even with the new rules.

While we were chatting, the trucks started rolling in. They'd pull just past the point where they wanted to park, and then back in off the road onto the gravel. There must have been forty trucks.

"There should be two or three teams each from about seven of the brigades showing up today. They don't all come at once; it would be a total cluster, if you don't mind my language, Ma'am." I laughed as I shook my head. "And tube has three members…"

"Hold the details until the show starts and forget anything you hear here today, got it? We're in a different sort of business than infantry and we've got a different skill set, so this is sort of a new thing for Sgt. Sutton."

"Hooah!"

All of the troops started unloading gear and hiking up into the woods. About fifteen minutes later, I reached into my pack, pulled out two bottles of water, a few protein bars, two pairs of huge observer's binoculars, and a radio with an earpiece. I gave half of everything to Liz.

"Put your radio around your neck, flip this switch, and put the earpiece in. When you hear it start, scan the area with your binoculars."

"When what starts?"

"Just listen." Immediately the radio chatter started coming in from everywhere. Liz had a mixed look: confusion, delight, wonder, amazement, anticipation... and more.

Then the first call for a single round downrange for mark came. You could hear the sound of the mortar rounds sailing through the air, followed by a loud explosion as each hit the ground. Today wasn't practice, it was live fire. They were shooting high explosive rounds.

"Don't you love that sound, Corporal? They must be using 81mm today, huh?"

"That's affirmative. On both counts," he grinned. Liz's jaw just dropped. Again there was a call for a mark, then after the second

LEAVING AFGHANISTAN BEHIND

rounds had all gone off, a command of "fire for effect" was given, so that a predetermined number of projectiles would be hurled downrange.

"Fireworks! I get it now!" shouted Liz, practically jumping up and down on her knees.

"Ain't it a kick?"

After spending a couple of hours watching this wonderful FTX, I had the driver take us over to the main part of the base. It was the same place where we'd eaten breakfast, and where Liz and I went to the NCO Club.

"You do drink, don't you?"

"Usually wine, but a beer would do wonders for me right now."

"Good. Wine is sort of sissy crap here. They have it, but you get funny looks." We walked up to the bar and I held up two fingers. "Dark."

"You got it," said the bartender as he turned around to pour us a couple off the tap.

"So, cowboy, you got any other way cool tricks up your sleeve?"

"Maybe one. I'll have to wait and see. It may be a little trickier to arrange."

We had chatted up for a couple of hours before we headed to the civilian mess. Truthfully, the battalion mess was better, believe it or not! It was only 1645 and we went to AFEES to check out the store. I convinced Liz to get a couple of souvenirs displaying "My Mommy is in the Army" and "My Wife is a Soldier". We charged them to the AFEES ID cards we'd gotten processing in; the new ID cards have a smart chip in them.

"Hey, want to check out what movies are playing next door? Nada going on tonight, so it might be cool," I suggested.

"Sure, why not."

There were two action/adventure movies playing and one of them didn't look too bad. Liz looked at her watch.

"It doesn't start for a little while. Can we go outside?"

"It's kind of chilly," I replied.

"I don't mind. I want to catch Tattoo and Taps again. I know I kind of lost it, but I really want to hear them both again, especially Tattoo."

"Sure."

We turned and walked outside. Liz put her hands in her pockets several times. I kept having to remind her that it was a no-no. She said it was just something to do with her hands, she wasn't cold.

- 133 -

"That's not what I heard…"

"You bitch! That was mean," she laughed. Suddenly the loudspeakers started the music for Tattoo, and we saluted. We waited the fifteen minutes after that and listened to Taps. Fortunately, tonight Liz was fine with it. We hustled into the theater after that, where it was warm, and got some popcorn and a couple of drinks. We got a seat way early, even though there weren't many people there that night. It was still a half hour before the movie. "I wish I had the laptop with us now."

"Patience is a virtue," I told Liz.

"Up yours. You're not the doctor. Stop trying to give me advice. Anyway, have you thought any more about tomorrow's activities, or are we just going to lie around the room all day?"

"Oh, I came up with something hours ago; I just have to set it in motion. I'll be able to do that tomorrow after PT. I have to say, you did really well today."

"Tell that to my legs. I still hurt. I can barely walk."

"It'll get easier."

"I don't want to be here long enough for it to get easier. Can I ask you something?"

"Sure," I said.

"Is it just me, or is it bloody hot in here."

"You're wearing my vest under everything."

"Oh, I keep forgetting I have it on. How can you wear these things all summer? Don't you just burn up?"

"As opposed to having a bullet rip through your body and render you basically lifeless? Remember, it's not magical. If you get shot in the neck or head, you'll die. If you get shot in the arm and it hits an artery, you'll die. If you get shot from one side and it goes down through your shoulder tunneling downward, you'll die."

"Thank you for that encouraging lecture, Professor Gittens."

"No problem."

The movie came on at that time. It turned out it was not very good after all. It was really cheesy, but it killed a couple of hours. Instead of getting a driver, we just got a base cab to take us back to the battalion area. We both emptied and refilled our canteens on the way into our room. We quickly got the laptop out. Liz read through her email from Keven. There were four from her throughout the day, including a long one at the end of the day from home. I had an update from Jernick and

LEAVING AFGHANISTAN BEHIND

decided to read it quickly. No news, just a status. Then I opened the one from Theresa. It was about six pages worth of typing. She really poured her heart out. I choked up badly, wanting to be with her, hold her, protect her, all of which I knew I was incapable of at the moment. Before I even got to the end, I had to shut it down. I'd try to finish reading it and reply later, I just couldn't right now.

I stripped my CDU coat and started doing push-ups and sit-ups in reps. I also held the wooden chairs by the very top and fully extended my arms out to the side for resistive weight. I did this for about forty minutes while Liz watched, and read bits and pieces of her various emails from today's deliveries from Keven. It was too bad, I thought, as I was pushing through a set of fifty sit-ups, that we couldn't send or receive photos of any kind. Those were the rules. Finally I laid flat on my back on the hard floor, panting, trying to catch my breath.

"How do you do that?"

I didn't even answer her. I just took a shower, putting on my same uniform, since it wasn't particularly worn. I climbed into the bunk and Liz handed me the laptop.

"I saw you. You weren't finished reading. You stopped and gave it to me. Why don't you go ahead and read the rest? It might just do you some good."

I said nothing, but took the laptop and opened the email as she'd suggested. I could barely read for the tears. I'd put Theresa in this position. I thought about all the time she'd lived in Watertown in a dump, working strictly from home, and rarely venturing out of doors. That was during the "don't ask, don't tell" days. We couldn't be caught. I'd made life rough for her, but she stuck to me faithfully, and this is how I repay her? I'd really let her down. I rapidly shot a note to both her and Jernick.

"Forty-eight hour walkabout. Belongamick. No worries." I showed it to Liz, told her to send the exact same message to Keven, then I put the laptop on the bed.

"Penny for your thoughts?" asked Liz.

"Just thinking about tomorrow."

"You're a terrible liar, sweetie."

"Whatever. When was the last time you went camping?" I asked her.

"God, it was a couple of years before Kev and I had the girls."

"Say, which one of you had the girls, or are they adopted?"

"We each had one. Mama KayKay delivered Alyssa. Clarisse was delivered by me, Mama Lizzy."

"So, any regrets?"

"Oh, God no! Our little angels are the most wonderful thing that's ever happened to us."

"Actually, I was talking about taking me on as a patient."

"None. Unequivocally. Hell, I'll probably be able to get published in an American Psychiatric Association Journal," she giggled.

"Now I know I *am* totally fucked up."

Liz reached out and put her hand on mine. "Sweetie, considering what you've been through? You've taken more than any five people ought to have to take in a single lifetime. You do your job and get us home safely, and I'll do my job and get you better. I'm not giving you back to the VA. I want to get Josh involved (Dr. Turner) for his help and experience, but I'm going to take care of you for as long as it takes. Don't you think by now we're inextricably linked?"

I stood up and walked over to Liz's bunk, holding my hands out to pull her up. She gave me her hands and let me hoist her to standing. Without saying a word, I reached out and lightly squeezed her.

Liz gave me a giant hug. "I suspect there's no longer any normal boundaries."

"You know, your sense of humor through all this has really kept me going. So, are you and Theresa going for kids?"

"Theresa definitely. I don't know about me. Maybe, but physically I don't think I can pull it off. I'm okay either way. Just as long as we have them together. Live birth, adoption, whatever. She's white, I'm black. I figure we need a baby from Nepal or Mongolia. Well, I need to step out to the CQ desk and check some scheduling, back in a few." I unlocked our door and approached the Duty Spec. He jumped up quickly, but I told him to relax. It was a quiet evening and I wanted to keep it that way.

"What can I do for you, Sergeant?"

"We've got some gear we need to take to the field tomorrow and put through a test run. I need to find a grid that's a go with nobody, and I mean *nobody*, on it."

"You should be in pretty good shape. From what I understand, most of the troops are running a lot of classroom time to catch up with some modifications that have come through now that the budgeting bullshit has been settled. Oh, sorry for my language, Ma'am."

LEAVING AFGHANISTAN BEHIND

"I've heard worse from kindergartners. Don't sweat it."

"Yes, Ma'am. How large a piece of land are you talking about?"

"Four hundred hectares?"

"Oh, that's no problem." He pulled out some flat charts with grids laid out of the base. "See these up here, the two big ones? You can probably stay out of sight here with no trouble. Both of them are about four or five thousand hectares. That will give you plenty of extra room."

"One last thing I need. I know it's short notice, but I need to get word to the Division CSGM and 1SGT's offices tonight, so it's waiting on them in the morning. If everything goes as expected, I'll need an extraction and dust-off pair day after tomorrow, as part of our simulation. Remember this is a *simulation*. It would be sort of cool if the dust-off bird were shooting powder only, no bullets, eh? Think you can get that done?"

"Oh, yes, Ma'am! Is there anything else I can get for the two of you sergeants?"

"As a matter of fact, check me out a couple of AN/PSQ-20s and a drop-off close to the area. We're getting a little bit of a late start. I also want to make sure this is marked as a covert operation. Are we absolutely clear on this particular issue, Specialist Brown?"

"Hooah!"

"We'll be ready to roll out in fifteen. Have everything ready."

"Hooah!"

I went back into our room and locked the door.

"Empty your pack completely. Quickly."

"What are we doing?"

"Just do it as we go!"

We emptied our packs and started with a change of socks, lots of protein bars, and four MREs each. We already had our canteens, but I added four bottles of water to each pack. I loaded our binoculars, some grid maps I'd gotten yesterday, a handheld GPS, a pair of tactical radios, one yellow and one green smoke grenade, and our ponchos. We donned our body armor, our winter coats, and our tactical vests over that, which left only our gloves to be put on. I pulled out a cammo kit and smeared Liz's face, then did mine. I could do my own in my sleep and get it perfect. I pointed to the latrine and Liz went and looked at her war paint. She was as giddy as a kid in a toy store before Christmas.

I held her gloves out to her and we walked to the CQ desk. "What's the word, Spec?"

"Five minutes, Ma'am."

"Outstanding."

We moved outside to wait for the driver because wearing all our cold weather gear inside, we were sweltering. Finally, our driver pulled up. We both got in the back seat. He turned out to be an S1C like the two of us.

"First we need to swing by the armory, if you would."

"No problem."

We walked into the armory, unannounced and without permission, yet somehow I think everybody working in that building already knew who we were on the food chain, anyway. "What can I do for you tonight?" asked a Staff Sgt. behind the cage.

"I need two M4s and ten clips of blank rounds. Make sure the rifles have BFAs on them… but of course you know that."

"Your cards, please?"

We both shoved our IDs across the counter at him and when he saw our names, his eyes grew noticeably bigger.

"Wait one," he said, disappearing. He came back with two rifles, ten clips, and two sign-out sheets. "Hope you have a good night out in the woods. At least at this time of the year you won't have to worry about tics, only the rattlesnakes," he laughed.

"Goody, goody, gumdrops! If we can get a snake or two, I can make some damned good breakfast tortillas!" I said, smiling.

He turned and walked away to file the paperwork, shaking his head. "Breakfast tortillas... that's funny," he said to no one in particular, shaking his head. I'm glad he was amused. We got back in our vehicle and got driven out to the trail head.

LEAVING AFGHANISTAN BEHIND

CHAPTER TWELVE

"Thanks, driver. We'll take it from here."
"You bet. Good luck and have fun."
"How could we not on such a fine army night?"
"Hooah!"
I stopped and put the night vision on Liz first, then mounted mine.
"Watch me and my rifle. Put on the safety here. Then take out one of the clips from your tactical vest, give the back of it three or four solid taps against your boot heel to seat the rounds, and shove it in the receiver, here," I said, pointing to it for her. "Slam it up and home, just like you did your Beretta, but harder. Good. Hold the rifle in your left hand on the forearm guard, right here. Yeah, just like that. Now this rectangle-looking thing? That's the charging handle. On a rifle, you call chambering a round, charging it. Pull it back as far as you can, and then let go of it as quickly as you can, so that it slams the round into the chamber. Excellent. One last thing. See this?" I said, pointing toward the select. "If you set it up here, where it is, it fires one shot at a time. If you set it here, when you pull the trigger it fires three round bursts. No more fully automatic in this type of rifle, like the Vietnam days. So, you ready for this?"
"Hooah!"
"Out-fucking-standing!" We smiled at each other. I took the lead because even though we both had on night vision, until you got used to

it, it was still way too easy to step wrong and mangle your ankle or your knee. We'd been walking for an hour or so when I turned around to Liz. "Need to rest?"

"Not me, I'm good to go."

"Ugh! Good to go is a Marine term. Make sure you don't use it around here or you'll definitely get some icy glares."

"Oopsies!"

"More than you know." We kept trudging and didn't stop to sit down until we'd been hiking for about two and a half hours. I pulled up onto a stump and patted it, indicating Liz should sit down. I pulled two bottles of water and two protein bars out of her pack, one for each of us.

"Why don't we just drink out of the canteens?"

"Conserving the electrolytes for tomorrow during the day. Oh, did I mention? Think about the message to Keven."

"Yeah, I got the reference to Crocodile Dundee."

"You know what Belongamick is then?"

"Yeah, Mick's place. Your place. Sort of like, this place is for... Holy shit! We're going to be out here for two days?"

"Better than sitting around being bored, isn't it?"

"Shouldn't I have brought a roll of toilet paper?"

"No way to dispose of it, and besides, we've got leaves everywhere."

"Okay, you may have just lost me. Swiping my kootchiepop with dead oak leaves is just plain unsettling."

"Oh, you big baby. You'll do just fine." We hiked in for about three more hours total, until I was pretty sure that we were smack in the middle of the desired grid. I stopped and told Liz to offload all her gear.

She unslung her rifle and dropped it on the ground. "Never do that. Find something to lay it up against, or sit on the ground and prop it on your lap if you have to. Find something. It'll get too dirty if you don't, and then it won't fire."

We got our ponchos out for ground liners, laying the rifles on them beside us. We used our packs for pillows, drank more water, ate more protein bars, and had our night vision flipped up where they'd be out of the way, but we could quickly drop them back down at a moment's notice. We lay there and just chatted for a while, although when I checked my watch it was well after 0200.

LEAVING AFGHANISTAN BEHIND

"Ame?"

"Yeah?"

"I know it's not very army-like, but would you hold me?"

I laughed at her. It was a lot to take in for two days. I got it.

"Sure, come on over," I said, holding my arm out so that she could lie over it and put her head with mine on my pack. It put our noses tip to tip.

"So, how is it that we're about the same age, but you're my way older sister? Is it like the American Indian tribes where seniority is based on a mix of experience and wisdom?"

"I can be your younger sister if you want. Just as long as we're together for all the holidays, like you said."

Suddenly I felt Liz's lips against mine. Not a lover's kiss, but not a sister's kiss. Somewhere in between, and lasting somewhere in between time-wise.

"I can't believe I'm lying here in the middle of the forest and low-lying mountains, staring up at a billion stars on a moonless, cloudless night. My breath is coming out icy and in clouds. I'm dressed in an army combat uniform, carrying a rifle, wearing a loaded 9mm pistol, having walked about eight miles cross country in complete darkness with night vision goggles and camping without a tent. This is some *serious* shit!" she yelled out into the night so that if anybody had been within a mile of us, she'd have given away her position.

"Okay, Girl Scout, now quiet down and don't tell anybody else where we are, just in case somebody was wrong and there really is somebody out here."

"Sorry," Liz whispered. She snuggled up against my chest, putting one of her legs across one of mine. I had my arm wrapped around her as both of us drifted off to sleep.

Washington was on the south end of the village. I was on the north end of the village. We were covering a small troop movement below. There were supposed to be about a dozen ECs with AKs in the area. There's always some crazy fucking towelhead that's carrying an RPG stolen from Russian troops years ago, most of which didn't work very well due to bad firing circuits. They happened to show up with about twelve of them, and there were actually more like three dozen ECs. Washington and I were giving covering fire with our M110s. We were prepared that day. Not only were our tactical vests completely full, so were our side pockets. We each had a bandolier carrying an additional twelve clips as well, but it proved not to be enough. We were spraying the streets constantly. We had American troops mostly, but a few British troops smattered in among them. We managed to get all of our troops safely to cover, but we were firing and firing and firing and firing to keep the EC's heads down. It was the first time I'd ever carried that much ammo to a fight and I had one clip left. One.

"Snake-One, Snake-Two..."

"Snake-Two, go ahead."

"Snake-One, I have one folder in the cabinet."

"Snake-Two, I have two folders in the cabinet."

"Snake-One, split and rendezvous at point Delta."

"Snake-Two, on the move. See you at Delta. Out."

I was pretty much stuck until dark. That was a given. So was Washington. When it was dark, though, and I mean really good and dark, I got back on the radio one last time.

"Snake-One. Go! Go! Go! Out."

We both took off in opposite directions. I had been running for about half an hour, when I called for an extraction. I got no answer. Low bid fucking radios. I ran for another half an hour. I stopped to rest for a minute. I couldn't see or hear anything around me. I had gotten out my night vision about fifteen minutes back while I was still on the move. After resting five minutes and getting some fluids, I checked my digital compass and took off again. I kept running and running and running. I had been running almost two and a half hours. Not trotting or jogging, but running. I was deep in enemy territory and my backup had decided not to go drinking with me that night, but to stand me up instead. I ran and ran and ran. When I stopped the last time, before getting back to the forward operating base, I'd been running about six and a half hours.

I had nothing left in my legs, they were wobbling all over the place. I started throwing up every ten or fifteen feet. People were steering clear of me. I moved immediately to the CP within the compound. Once inside, a first lieutenant walked up to me and asked if I'd been injured or was a casualty.

"What are you talking about?"

"Sergeant, you're bleeding from your back." They unslung my 110 and laid it on a table. Then they started taking off my gear. Apparently the blood was from where the sling had rubbed against my neck above the protective line of my armor.

LEAVING AFGHANISTAN BEHIND

My current XO walked into the briefing room and wanted to know what went wrong with my mission. He seemed pissed.

"Your counterpart seemed to make it back fine. We were seriously beginning to wonder about you!"

"With all due respect, sir, what is this particular waypoint on the mission grid?"

"Here? It's Delta, of course. How is it that you didn't make it back with everybody else?"

"Because I was on the north end of the village. I had to go ten miles north and then turn to the east, completely skirt the village, then go south to be picked up at Bravo. Tell me somebody got my signal."

"We got a signal, but there's no way you could have been at that point. You wouldn't have possibly been able to get there that fast. Impossible."

"Did you get my signal from Charlie?"

"By that time we figured the mission had been compromised and somebody had gotten your radio, or another one perhaps. But still, that was thirty-two miles away from the village. There's no way that you could have made Charlie in that time. What I want to know is, how you got back here and by what road. You're in some deep shit, Gittens."

"Couldn't have made it in time? Is that what you just said to me?"

"You heard me, Sergeant."

I pulled my Beretta and held it up directly to his mouth, forcing it hard enough to make him open his lips around it and bang against his teeth. I actually chipped the tip of his lower right center tooth. "You stupid fuck! I'm a Goddamned double marathon runner. I just ran over fifty miles tonight to keep from getting killed out in the desert. You understand me? I just ran over fifty fucking miles. You ever doubt me, you come out with me and see how far I can run. You want to ride in a Humvee while I'm running, that's okay too. But if you ever abandon me out there again, you better make sure that somebody finishes the job, because as sure as God makes little green apples, I will hunt you down and I will fucking kill you, motherfucker! I will personally splatter your fucking brains on the walls! I don't care if I go to jail for life, or get executed for doing it in a combat zone. You will never, ever, leave me behind again, especially when you get a radio signal for extraction! And if I ever hear about you doing it to anybody else, the same goes. I will hunt you down and I will personally kill you.

You motherfucking cocksucker! You hear me? I said, do you hear me?"

I still had my Beretta in his mouth and he was nodding his head. Two of the other three sergeants were starting to move in closer to disarm me, but the pistol was in too tight. For added effect, I pulled the hammer back so it would fire in single action mode, taking little effort to discharge it.

Apparently when I started stirring, I'd rolled Liz off me. Fortunately, I didn't hurt her or get violent like the night I grabbed Theresa.

"Hey, hey, hey, soldier. Having a "memory" of sorts?"

"You might say that."

"Want to talk."

"Might as well." I related the entire story to her.

"I'm no dummy. That's pretty much Hollywood stuff. Cop pulls a gun on another cop, soldier pulls a gun on another soldier. There are consequences... serious consequences."

"I got lucky. That was his third strike. He should never have been made a major. He should *definitely* never have been given a battle command. And, like I said, he made more mistakes than me. He filed charges against me. They came and put me in the stockade and word got back to Division, then to HQ, and at HQ somebody brought it to the attention of General Floyd. Floyd was enlisted for ten years before he got an appointment to go to West Point. Real old school, and he really hated the way they were "hanging me out to dry", but in the end, they looked at my record. For that, the incident was completely expunged. Completely! You could go to the NSA and to the Defense Department and there'd be no record of it. Thanks completely to Floyd and his connections as the major general in charge of the entire Afghanistan battle theater."

"Amelia... would you have shot him?"

"If he did it again, probably."

"That's not good, you know. That's not in the line of duty, exactly."

"You don't understand. He put soldiers at risk. Constantly. He had a reputation for doing that. He had complaints up the chain of command and nothing was ever done because they were too afraid to admit putting him there was a mistake. I just had the courage to do what everybody else should have been doing."

LEAVING AFGHANISTAN BEHIND

"And that made what you did okay?"
"No comment."
"Think you can get back to sleep?"
"Maybe."
"Try."
"Okay."

At the very first suggestion of indigo, I shook Liz and told her we needed to get up and get moving.

"Ugh. I want a cup of coffee and I need to pee."

"You'll have to squat to pee, and don't forget to line your feet up across sloping ground so that as the ground drops down in front of you, the pee will run away from you and not all over your boots."

"Keven and I never went camping quite to this extreme!"

"C'mon. Get ready and I'll make us some breakfast. Nice warm eggs and sausage."

"MREs?"

"Yup. Pretty decent, too."

After we'd eaten and I had all the trash secured in my pack, we went forward, looking for the densest thicket I could find to put up a forward observation post, if you will. We made ourselves as comfortable as possible, while taking a few small branches and covering them with dried leaves for a better camouflage.

"Today you're going to be genuinely bored."

"How so?"

"Today, we do nothing at all. We're going to move around and look at wildlife, if we can find any. That's pretty much it. We have no camera or phone or satellite laptop. We have radios for communication, but only if there's an emergency. Didn't you ever sit in your office and say to yourself, 'If only I could just have one day to do nothing?' Well, today's the day you've been waiting for."

I sat on a log that I'd covered with leaves to cushion it somewhat, then pulled Liz down onto my lap sideways, putting one arm over her legs and rubbing up and down her back with my other... well, up and down her body armor anyway.

"You said your parents had both passed. What about Keven's?"

"Both her parents are alive and well. She has three sisters. Two of the girls are gay. Well, one of them is bisexual and currently partnered with a male, although that changes all the time. The third is a borderline homophobe. Her parents are great though, absolutely supportive. What about you and Theresa?"

"My dad died before I finished high school. Something that always makes me sad is thinking about how proud and happy my dad would have been if he'd seen me graduate from basic training at Fort Leonard Wood in Missouri. My mom and sister, Cheryll Anne, both live in New York as well.

Theresa has three brothers and five sisters, nine kids total - good Roman Catholics. Her parents are both alive and still married, a miracle. Theresa is the youngest of all the kids. Everybody but the oldest brother have accepted both Theresa and me with open arms. It's wonderful, really. Would you believe that Theresa was a blind date? Neither of us wanted to go through with it, but when we met for the first time, we both knew right then that this was the woman for us. It was magical. It was a total Disney moment," I laughed.

"I've talked to her twice and I already know that she cares very, very deeply for you. Is she a good lover?"

"That's sort of personal, isn't it?"

"You mean like the kind of question a little sister would ask her older sister about the girl she's dating?" I had to laugh at that. "You're funny, Liz. How'd we ever get here? Who would have imagined in a million years? You know people in Hollywood can't dream up shit like this, yet here we are. I think the two of us should co-write a book when this is all over. What do you think?"

"Might not be a bad idea at that."

"Except for one thing. Well, a few things... The Department of Homeland Defense, the Federal Bureau of Investigation, the Federal Witness Protection Program, the National Security Council, the Department of Defense, the Department of the Army, the City of New York Police Department, the New York State Criminal Apprehension Bureau, and the New York City Gang Violence Investigation Unit. I think that pretty much covers it. If I've... Oh, and the New York City Police Department liaison to the United Nations. There. Now I think I'm done."

We stayed pretty much in close to our area during the day. Not that we were afraid of anything happening, or even being discovered by another army unit. It was just a way for me to keep Liz entertained while keeping her safe. Two things I wouldn't let go of, though: she was always wearing my Second Chance bulletproof vest under

LEAVING AFGHANISTAN BEHIND

everything, even though she also had on body armor, and the fact that she and I both carried loaded Berettas.

We spent another night and I stayed awake.

"What's up tonight?"

"Nothing. I just thought I heard a noise. No dream."

"That's some small wonder. Go back to sleep."

I listened for a minute. There it was again. I snapped on my night vision. I quickly put my hand over Liz's mouth so she'd get the picture. I got her goggles on too, so she could see. I handed her rifle to her, made sure she had everything packed up in her rucker, and made her pull her pack up on her back like I had.

"This is where it gets fun as hell. There's a little wash up about a mile to the east by northeast. How fast do you think you can run there if you have to?" I whispered in a very hushed tone.

"I guess as fast as I have to," she whispered back.

"Put your selector on burst mode." I pointed out with my hand shaped like a knife over in one direction. "Do you see those infantrymen moving through the bush? They've also got on night vision, but they have no idea we're here. They're on an FTX. They think they're on a lone patrol. I'm going to turn this into a game of 'Capture the Flag'. Know what that is?" Liz nodded her head at me. "They are almost certainly a single unit out for training, as opposed to *us against them* type of training, since they don't have any laser vests on. Just the same, we're going to start lighting them up with noise. This is going to fuck with them so bad! Keep moving forward so they won't get a fix on our muzzle flashes, and just keep moving forward. They're going to figure they've all been killed. Then you and I are going to start out slowly and quietly, gradually picking up speed, until we're sprinting up to the wash, where we'll hole up for the night. Then tomorrow, an extra special surprise."

"Amelia, how in the *world* do you know all this? I know you were in the army for a while, but seriously... does everybody know all this shit?"

"In my opinion? Not really. I think faster on my feet than most of them, even the career guys. In my opinion, the only group of guys that are smarter than me are Marine Corps officers. Now that is one smart bunch of dudes. Crazy as all fuck, but with the exception of scientists, you'll never find a more eclectic, intelligent group of individuals." I adjusted Liz's pack, then mine.

"Check your tactical vest for your clips, so you'll know exactly where they are," I whispered. She felt her vest. "Start from the front of the column and work backward. They'll hear the noise coming in and it will actually sound more like they've stumbled on another patrol and gotten wiped out. Ready to rock?"

I felt Liz's hand come out and squeeze my forearm for a moment, then she turned around. She was actually the one to get off the first shots. We lit up the night sky.

"You Goddamned motherfuckers. Who in the fuck set this up? This was supposed to be a patrol, not an FTX!" We kept firing and running and firing. "Jesus, where are they? They've got to be everywhere. They had to have known we were coming. This is total bullshit!"

"Christ, I just ran through a briar. I think it cut my leg open."

"Down, down, down. Follow the flare. See if you can pick anybody up on the night scopes!" It went on and on. By that time, we'd put about sixty rounds downrange with our blanks and were hotfooting it up to the wash. We finally made it up to the wash. There was a sand deposit up the left side that went up into the tree line. We ran all the way up into the trees where I stopped and turned around, but Liz didn't. She barreled right through me, knocking me to the ground. She straddled me, pushing my hand up above my head, knocking the rifle out of my hands. For the moment, she was showing tremendous strength, just through adrenaline alone. She was cackling.

"We did it! This little girl from the city, with no training or experience, just kicked some army ass! And they're in the 10th Mountain! Whooooo!"

"Okay, I'm both proud and happy. Secondly, never, ever knock a gun out of anybody's hands… especially not mine! I'll let it slide this time, and this time only. Lastly, keep your voice down. The idea is not to be caught! Now let's get moved up into cover where we can wait for tomorrow's surprise."

Maybe it was a good thing for me, too. I slept completely through the night. Of course, even having come on base, I'd been taking my sleeping pills, my anti-depressants, and my anxiety medication. I let Liz sleep while I made breakfast. I started kicking her with the toe of my boot when it was ready.

"Sgt. Sutton. Get your ass up, you lazy tub of lard!"

"What?"

LEAVING AFGHANISTAN BEHIND

"Sutton. Up!"

Liz scrambled to get up, but she was still grinning from ear to ear after last night's little game. It took us just ten minutes to eat and police the area. We got everything packed up, then I made Liz drink a bottle of water and eat a protein bar.

"You ready for today's big event?"

"Is it way cool?"

"It's going to be the biggest one yet. I promise."

"Better than last night?"

"Yup." I put my radio in my ear and turned it on. I keyed the mic. "Tiger Shark One, Tiger Shark

One, this is Blue Mountain Twelve."

"Blue Mountain Twelve, this is Tiger Shark One, go ahead."

"Tiger Shark One, Blue Mountain Twelve, are you reading my GPS at this time, over?"

"Blue Mountain Twelve, that is affirmative, reading your relayed signal five by five."

"Blue Mountain Twelve, requesting extraction from six meter grid location at this time. Undisclosed EC activity in the area, requesting overflight by Six Shooter."

"Six Shooter Seven, roger, in formation with Tiger Shark, inbound Charlie Alfa Sierra. Link in five minutes, say again, five minutes."

"Blue Mountain Twelve, approach green smoke, say again, approach green smoke.

"Six Shooter Seven, understand, green smoke."

"Okay now, Liz, here are two smoke grenades. To make it generate smoke, grab it in your right hand, and with a good hard grip, pull the pin loose with your left hand. Then throw it as hard as you can away from you. Don't wind up like it's a softball. Keep your arm fully extended and hurl it. If it doesn't travel very far, back upwind. It doesn't blow up or anything, as suggested by its name, don't worry, it's just like a smoke bomb from some little kid's fireworks. It's just intimidating. Got it?"

Liz nodded her head. "Grab, pull, throw. Got it."

Now, when I give you the thumbs up, you take the yellow grenade, pull the pin, and then throw it."

"But didn't you say green on the radio?" she said, worriedly.

I grinned widely. "And let the fun begin! Got it?"

Liz looked positively defeated. "Okay. If you say so, Sarge."

About three minutes later the choppers were right on top of us.

"Tiger Shark One, request smoke, expecting green smoke."

"Blue Mountain Twelve, stand by for green smoke." I held my hand out with my gloved hand, thumbs up. Liz did as she was told. She pulled the ring on the yellow smoke and threw it as hard as she could. Within seconds, Six Shooter Seven had opened up and was pouring it on with a similar gun to that of the A-10. Liz jumped up from where she was and if I had been sitting down she would have been up in my lap. I couldn't stop laughing. You don't really get the full effect, since there are no fifty caliber bullets hitting the ground at the rate of five thousand rounds a minute, but it is still way cool. And crazy loud! They sprayed for four passes, before dropping back.

"Six Shooter Seven, Blue Mountain Twelve, suppressing fire on yellow smoke. Do you wish secondary extraction at this time? Over."

"Blue Mountain Twelve, continue extraction, expect green smoke."

"Tiger Shark One, expecting green smoke."

"Okay, Liz, throw the green can now."

She did as instructed, and the AH-60 Black Hawk settled down about four feet above the ground in the wash. I grabbed her hand and broke out in a dead run. We hit the edge of the bay, threw our gear in the aircraft, and grabbed the hands of the air crew, who hauled us aboard. We wheeled into the sky back in the opposite direction, and I looked out our ship to the left. I nudged Liz, then made a motion in that direction so she could see it.

The GAU electrically-operated, high rate of fire machine gun was mounted in the nose of Six Shooter Seven, an AH-64 Apache. She couldn't help but smile. I touched the shoulder of the Crew chief, and with my hands stacked on top of each other, made a flapping motion away from my wrists. He nodded at me and spoke into his helmet mike to the pilot. Seconds later, Six Shooter opened up a five second sky burst of blanks just for effect. Liz broke out into a huge grin. Even though I couldn't hear due to the noise, I could tell she was laughing her ass off. Within fifteen minutes, we'd made a wide sweep up to the north and circled around to the helicopter pads and landed. We got our gear and debarked the helo.

"That was a great little simulation you had going there this morning. I want you two sergeants to know that we really enjoy getting to mix up things with something different every once in a while," he said, as he stuck his hand out and shook with both of us.

LEAVING AFGHANISTAN BEHIND

"That sure means a lot coming from you, Captain."

"Anytime, ladies. Anytime. By the way, we heard what you did to that patrol last night. I'd sure as shit hate to come across you two in the middle of God knows where without my thinking cap on," he laughed.

Liz started to salute him, but I grabbed her hand.

"Never salute on a flight line. Always pay more attention to the aircraft, the mechanics, and the trucks. It's a safety issue."

"Gotcha."

"So, how was this morning?"

"I think I have an erection! You were right after all. Both metaphorically and metaphysically!"

"Ain't it though! Let's go get some chow, get cleaned up after two days in the boonies, and we'll check in with the families."

"Sounds good, Sergeant."

"After you, Sergeant," I said, putting my hand in front of me.

Our driver took us back to the armory where we turned in the A4s, along with all clips and unused ammunition. After we finished, we got taken back to battalion area. We were too late for chow, but there were always some sandwich materials, as well as breakfast MREs. Liz and I were still pretty stoked from the last two days' events, when we ran smack dab into SGM Vetter.

"In my Goddamned office, *now*!" We were still in full CDUs, including our ACH helmets, even though you're not supposed to have any type of headgear on indoors. Since we were in full CDUs, it was considered an exception to the rule. We lost our smiles, but strode cockily, nonetheless, back into his office. We waited in front of his desk, at ease, for about half an hour before his return. He slammed the door with some ferocity, then walked around behind his desk, standing with his hands on hips, saying nothing at first. "What the *fuck* would you have done if that was a live fire FTX and you'd started spraying into the crowd, who thought you were live? What the *fuck* would you have done then?"

"I already had their intel. It was Charlie Company of the 4-31, performing a night acuity mission. Personally, I feel they're the ones that should be getting an ass-eating right now. Obviously they're not very good at it. Certainly not up to the 10th's reputation."

Vetter grabbed a whole stack of things from the front of his desk and launched them in no general direction. "You two are restricted to battalion area! After you check your rifles into the armory, you will go out on morning runs, you will go to chow, and other than that, you will remain in your room. Is that understood? You come to me with a request, a favor, and this is how you repay me?"

"SGM, by tomorrow morning, you'll be legendary. Two special ops ghosts with no particular unit, assignment, or identities, wasted an entire company of Opposing OpFor. Goddamned heroes, I tell you. I know we did wrong, but in the end, it will be good. Trust me on this one."

"Restricted! Do you fucking hear me?"

"Can we go across base and watch a movie?"

Vetter hunched over his desk with his hands holding his upper body up, shaking his head. He stayed like that for over fifteen minutes.

"So, Liz. How did you like playing army for a couple of days?"

"As I told Ame, I think I *still* have an erection."

For the first time, SGM started relaxing and laughed. "I've got about five or six more years in *This Man's Army* before retirement, if they don't downsize me out. I still want to run an entire brigade. But the day after I leave, I'm going to tell people about this. They won't believe me, but I'm going to tell them.

Clear your little asses out of here before I go getting all pissed again."

Both Liz and I came back into character immediately, stood at attention, and said, "Yes, SGM," spinning on our heels, and beating a retreat.

Just as we were entering our room, the CQ jumped up and came over to us.

"Sgts? I was told to inform you that as soon as you return, you need to read through your dispatches ASAP."

"Thank you, Spec. Will do."

After we got inside and the door was locked, I turned to Liz.

"Did I disappoint?"

Even though we were both in full gear, she launched herself into me.

"In the last two days, I've peed in the leaves, slept under the stars on a plastic sheet, seen a dozen types of wild animals, learned the names of three dozen plants, seen through the night with special goggles like it was daylight, and hunted down and killed an entire company of some of the most highly-trained soldiers our country has. I made an attack helicopter come out of nowhere and give off the most highly shit-

LEAVING AFGHANISTAN BEHIND

kicking sound you've ever heard in your life, then got the right airship down to pick us up and give us a ride back with our boots hanging out over the empty space below. And to finish, I got screamed at for doing a spectacular job. What a fucking kick! I'm just a lowly psychiatrist. I'll be writing papers on *myself* for goodness sake. Whooohoooooo!" she yelled.

"Well, I'm sorry you're so wishy-washy about this one. Could go either way, huh? You go take a shower and get clean ones and I'll check in with Big Brother. Then you can see how many thousands of love letters KayKay has written you."

Liz opened her locker, got out clean ACUs, dropped her pack in unsorted, and picked up a couple of protein bars and held them in her teeth. She then put her web belt over the top post, removed her Beretta, removed the clip, removed the round in the chamber, put the round into the clip, and replaced the clip, flipping the safety off, then back on, to make sure it was securely in place. She winked at me on the way into the latrine. She'd learned a lot in four days, and learned it well. I pulled out the laptop and uplinked.

"*Two transfers waiting, completed by COB today. More info to come.*"

I looked at the time stamp. Yesterday. That would mean that all the Cuban prisoners would be in different prisons out of state by this time, and our team would get the information they needed to pinpoint de la Paz and the other Columbians. That should have already been underway as I was reading, at the very least, during the day today.

"*BCA dropping the hammer at 0530 this morning. Yellow smoke.*"
I looked at the time stamp on this one. 0430 this morning, just before we were getting ready for our extraction.

There was one last item.

"*Heavy resistance from delegation. Execution not, say again, not delayed. Resulting network may be untouchable for short time, but all will end well.*"

After that business had been taken care of, I moved onto Theresa's email.

"*My darling Amelia. This reminds me so much of when you were deployed. No direct information. Sending mail every day, but waiting until it finally caught up with you and you could return it. Just like then, I'll write at least twice a day. Oh, and the food is much better here. I manage to work through the days, watch movies or read during* the evenings, but I still cry myself to sleep every night. I suppose I'm nowhere near as brave as you are, but I can't help it. I worry about you so much. I just want you back to me, so that we can get married. I've been thinking, when this is all over, if we need to for safety, let's just move cities. It will be hard, but we'll get by. Whatever it takes to make it work will be fine with me. Just come back safe to me. Oh, and one more thing, I want a list. I want you to tell me every other lie of omission you've ever told me. Ever. Time to come clean with me, you. I don't want any more surprises.

You hear me? Your most treasured love, Teri-berry."

There were six more from Theresa, pretty much all saying the same thing. Liz had just gotten her hair blown dry and come out into the bay area of our room. I turned the laptop around and let her read the first email from Theresa.

"Teri-berry?"

"KayKay?"

We both laughed. After she had gotten dressed, Liz took the laptop for a while.

"I always used to think I was this laid-back artist, a sort of mix of old hippie with modern influence. I thought that I was young and invincible, being the youngest associate professor at The New School, in any department, much less Graphic Arts. Oh, and after watching the news, I had T in my classes. She was, and I'm sure still is, absolutely brilliant. Anyway, this whole thing about how the two of us, ordinary people, got dragged into the most bizarre of circumstances, and were put under such a tremendous spotlight, not to mention possible danger, has really changed me, in more ways than I ever could have imagined. Our little angels already share both our names. That part doesn't bother me. We'll still probably keep our professional names, just for ease. I know, in our distant past, it's been mostly me that's stressed that it's never been important, that a piece of paper doesn't make us what we are or aren't to each other, but I've changed my mind. I want you to marry me. I need you to marry me. If you can't, or simply don't want to, for whatever reason, I'll understand, and I'll never bring it up again. I just want to do the ultimate thing I can to show you my love, and I understand now that a commitment of marriage is that very thing. Let me take you and the girls to the courthouse when you get back and marry me. Let me be your wife and you be mine. Your KayKay."

LEAVING AFGHANISTAN BEHIND

Liz set the laptop on my legs and went into the latrine to get some TP to use to keep the tears back. She came back and sat on my bunk alongside me, and started to really cry. I put my arm around her to try and comfort her.

"Two or three more days and this will all be a painful memory. Heck, they won't have even gotten the permanent rework done on your offices yet. You'll be ahead of the game."

"Officer Gittens, tell me about the first day you were in Afghanistan. Not in battle, just the first day you got off the aircraft."

"Whoa. That's sort of formal. Well, Doc, it was 2012, early spring. I had already been in the army for three, maybe four years. I'd also been through sniper school, so I was already acting in that capacity. My group was flown to Yemen via C-17s and offloaded. The 10th is a light force. They're made to be mobile. So the first forces were all flown in by CH-27 Chinooks. That's how I got my boots wet — put in-country. From there we started building up from scratch until we gradually had local airstrips under control and flew in large amounts of equipment for all regimental divisions."

"How long were you in Afghanistan before you were doing your job?"

"Maybe two hours, but initially, you have to figure that was only as an Angel. That's what the people are called that sit at really high points and just keep an eye on everybody. Long, boring duty."

"And how long before you'd gone out on your first mission, per se."

"Fifteen days."

"How long after your first mission until you had your first kill?"

"It was that mission."

"So you were twenty-one, no, twenty-two years old, in a foreign country for two weeks, and faced down death."

"Don't get me wrong, Liz, there were people way worse off than me. Death and destruction was all around. You have to remember that the casualty rate in those days was really high."

"Yes, and you were mixed up in it during all that time. See the point I'm trying to make here?"

"I guess... but, no, not really."

"Every flashback, with one exception, was about Afghanistan, not your life back in the city. And your actions in trying to protect, what did she call herself, Teri-berry? And me? All done in a military fashion."

"Why, oh why, did I ever let you read that email?"

We both laughed.

"Because it shared a walled-off side of you. You did it as a show of trust, at least that's my professional opinion."

"And if I just wanted to show it to my little sister?"

"Well, don't you trust your sister?" she asked smiling.

We chatted until noon chow about little bits and pieces, here and there, but always doing a dance around the ghosts and demons, skirting widely around them.

"Say, after we get back and the weather warms up, would you and Theresa consider coming on a camping trip with the four of us?"

"It won't be the same. No night vision, no weapons, lots of food and a camp stove to cook it on. Plus tents to sleep in... You sure you still want to?"

"Heck, yeah, I want to. I told you I've been before, I just somehow let life take me over, and I don't want to do that anymore. I want to live again. I want Keven and me to do some of the spontaneous things we used to do, but I want the girls there. Truthfully, I want you and Theresa there too, at least some of the time."

"Sure. We'd love to-"

There were three raps on the doorframe. "Sgt. Plummer? Sgt. Sutton? Major Leitner has sent over a runner to accompany you to his office." Liz and I looked at each other.

"I think I may have gone too far this time. Remember, don't say a word, and remain at attention the whole time. Even though we're temporary, decorum is expected." Liz just nodded her head. I got up, put on my web belt, and chambered a round in the Beretta. Liz followed my actions and fell into step behind me. There was a runner and a P-2 (Private Two), ready to take us over to the major's office. It was a short walk. I figured maybe we'd be called into the captain's office in our building, but then we'd already seen the SGM. We were led into the main battalion offices. We stood at parade rest along one wall. Our arms were folded behind us, our feet shoulder width apart, with our caps in the side pockets of our trousers. I guessed we waited for almost twenty minutes.

"Ladies, come in, come in. Liz, Amelia."

Whoa, he used our real names and was being incredibly nice. Either there was good news or we were getting prematurely kicked off the

LEAVING AFGHANISTAN BEHIND

base. We followed the major into his office; he whistled a tune the whole while. He walked around to his desk and immediately sat down.

"Please, take your seats and relax." He took out a folder, opened it, and withdrew three or four pages of information. "This morning at 1122 hours, one Emilio Cruz de la Paz, his brother Juan Fidelio de la Paz, and six of their closest friends and play buddies, were taken into custody in Yonkers, New York, in a single family dwelling, by a joint city, state, and federal task force. Within five minutes of that, give or take, the remaining twelve members of their little crew were taken from various locations in the Bronx. This just came across my desk moments ago. I got a call first, then this was faxed. It looks like you girls are going home! And before I even got to yell at you about your little *night romp*," he laughed.

"I can't tell you what a relief that is, Major. Do you mind if we eat a little of that great chow you've been handing out the last few days before we hit the road back to the city?"

"No problem at all. It's that time right now. In fact, if you left now, it would put you there late in the day, fighting the worst of the traffic, probably adding an hour and a half to your trip. I would suggest that you stay the night, boring as all this is, go running with us in the morning, eat morning chow, and then go back. Hell, I'll even take you over to the PX and personally buy you some sweats and long johns so you can run like the wind, independent and proud."

I looked at Liz. We both shrugged our shoulders at the same time.

"What the fuck. Why not, if you don't mind putting up with us? We can go back over and watch a movie tonight. I think they changed them yesterday."

"Gittens, you're only 32 and you've already made SFC. You could get back in, you know. You could stay out of the fray and train other soldiers at any base you wanted in CONUS. Why don't you consider it?"

"Sorry, but I don't think my fiancée would go for that. She has her sights set on a little row house in Bensonhurst, where all her family live, especially now. Remember, she already had to put up with my two longest deployments."

"Yes, but this would be safer than being a cop in the city, and you're the most capable soldier I've ever met in my life. Extraordinary!"

"Sorry, but I'll have to pass."

"Instead of the Snake Pit, would you dine as guests of me and the colonel? You could both put on your civilian clothes, if you like."

"I think that might be one too many for the other soldiers, frankly," I laughed.

We all laughed. What a wild trip the last five days had been. It seemed like it had strung out over a month's time. We all headed over to the mess for noon chow. Liz and I moved through the line and looked over to the Snake Pit. Taggert and Bowers were sitting with three other NCOs. I intentionally walked over to them. "Good day, Sergeants. Would you mind if we squeezed in here and sat with Taggert and Bowers? We've sort of been mess mates for a few days, and after morning chow tomorrow, we'll be shoving off." Bowers was genuinely surprised we were talking openly to both of them and admitting to being buddies with them in front of other people.

"Sure," said the other two sergeants, and scooted over on the benches a little for us. "Got enough room?"

"Tons. Thanks."

"So," asked Taggert, "does this mean you've gotten everything sorted out and you're on your way? Transit is complete?"

"Yup."

"Give me your address, Sgt. Ten years from now, when we're both out and whatever it is you're doing right now is declassified, I'd like to get the low down."

Everybody laughed. I just winked at him. He knew better. We had a good, lighthearted meal with lots of laughing and chatting. Finally the other five NCOs got up and made their apologies. It was time to return to their duties. I noticed for the first time, a wedding ring on Taggert's hand.

"Tell your wife 'hey' for me, buddy!"

"You know, I'll do that! I surely will! Maybe we'll see you tonight. If not, have a good tour."

"Hooah!"

"Hooah!"

Liz and I went to dump our trays back toward the kitchen, both of us smiling like the Cheshire cat.

We went back to the room in our area and immediately logged into email.

"Call me in the clear on a phone there. 1-646-610-5000 and ask for me. Let them know who you are, they'll put you right through."

LEAVING AFGHANISTAN BEHIND

"Amelia, what is CONUS?"
"The continental United States."
"Oh."
I gave the laptop to Liz and ran out to the CQ desk.
"Corporal, I need a phone with dialing capabilities to the New York Police Department."
"Right this way." I was led back to a room behind the CQ I'd never noticed before. There were two desks, each with a phone, and each with a notepad and a pen. "This is our COMMS center, Ma'am. You'll be able to direct dial here, you've been cleared."
"Thank you." I dialed the number with butterflies in my stomach.
"New York Police Department. How may I direct your call?"
"Capt. Jernick, please. This is Officer Amelia Gittens, 67th precinct, Flatbush."
"One moment, please."
After a couple of minutes, Jernick's voice, cheery for once, came over the line.
"Officer Gittens! How in the heck are you? I told you we'd get this thing whipped in nothing flat, didn't I? Good old-fashioned police work, but I have to say, you were *brilliant*! You thought on your feet more quickly than anybody I've ever met. I'm damn glad to have you with us here in the department. So what time do you think you'll get back tonight?"
"Actually, Liz and I would just start to hit commuters tonight. We're going to get up at 0430 and take about a ten mile run, eat, and then start back after a shower. That okay with you?"
"You want to stay another day? I think you're nuts, but yeah, that's fine."
"I don't want to seem ungrateful, but I've been on the clock this whole time, haven't I? Just saying."
"Don't worry about it. I'll authorize anything I need to. There are a few little things we'll have to discuss before you can return to duty, though."
"Such as…"
"Such as you two firing on an entire company of regulars! What the fuck were you thinking? You crazy, messed up chick! Please, Jesus, don't ever be my enemy. If that ever happens, I'll just eat my gun and get it over with," he laughed out loud.
"Will do, sir. I'll call you before we leave tomorrow."

"Have a good run in the morning. See you."

I went back into our room.

"You want to go across base to the PX and get some army sweats and a cap to go with your other stuff?"

Liz thought for a minute. "Damn, Skippy!"

"You're eating this shit up, aren't you?"

"Amelia, we kicked some *ass!* Why would I want to turn that down?"

"Okay, so you good with the running?"

"Perfectly."

"Tomorrow, we're going to form up with the last unit and we'll run past every platoon and company all the way to the front, then fall in with the colonel. What do you think? It's not that any one of them couldn't do the same thing, but they have to stay in formation. Us? We don't have the same restrictions. You up for a little showing off? 'Smoke 'em on the trail' is what it's called."

"Wow! You think I can keep up?"

"You haven't let me down with anything else our entire time here, physically or mentally. Believe me, the mental part of it is often the hardest."

"Okay. Let's do this," she said, as we high-fived each other.

We both took a nap we knew we'd wish we had. When I woke up, I had my locker open and was rummaging the pack I brought with me. "Where is it? Where is it?" I kept screaming.

Liz was immediately up and by my side.

"Sweetie, where is what?" she asked, rubbing my cheeks and the backs of my hands with her palms to get me fully awake.

"My Glock! It's not here!"

"The MPs have it. You gave it to Sgt. Hardesty when we came on base. You'll get it back when we leave. Remember?"

I had been down on my knees, but now I fell completely down to the floor, my hands flat under me, like a push-up position, my legs splayed wildly. I was panting like a dog.

"What about that one?" she said, pointing to my web belt.

"But we weren't here. We were in your office. They came through the door, but I had somehow lost my Glock. I already gave my Colt to Officer Taylor and only had my Glock, but I lost it. And they were coming through the door. I couldn't protect you."

LEAVING AFGHANISTAN BEHIND

"Who was coming through the door, Amelia? Who were you trying to protect me from?"

"Them. They were after us. They were after you to get to me... just like Theresa. Everybody was in danger because of me. Don't you see?"

It took about fifteen minutes, but I finally calmed down. Fortunately, the CQ was already accustomed to our "training" noises when shouts and oddities came flying off the walls and echoing throughout the room.

"Let's get you up. It's time to go eat anyway."

"I don't want to be around anybody. Let's go to the chow hall up around Civilian Town."

"You always said the food wasn't as good. I think it would do you wonders to eat here. Just relax, breathe, and let's go eat with our friends."

"Maybe you're right." We went to the battalion mess. While officially an NCO, he was a senior NCO, and that made a big difference. The first sergeant and the sergeant major always ate at the officers' table since they were adjutants to the CO and XO. While we were seated in the Snake Pit, SGM Vetter and the Top Shirt came over to talk to us, holding their trays, which they would return to the dishwashing area.

"Care to take a walk?" Vetter casually asked. We both started to pick up our trays, but he stopped us. "Don't stop eating, just give me your ear a moment." We got up and followed him. "Ever wonder where a design for a non-existent military unit appears out of thin air? What the process is for that?" Both Liz and I shook our heads.

"Somebody takes a database of image files and scrolls through them at breakneck speed. It must be somebody that's able to commit to memory everything he, or she, has seen since starting the slideshow. Then that person has to be creative. They must not only come up with a design that's different, but one that *fits in* with the new unit, such as, say, an Intel unit."

"How did you get the file to her in one day?"

"We moved as soon as we found out you were here. It was Jernick's idea. Amelia, don't sell him short. He's done a lot more than you could ever know."

"Actually, Pete, I do know. And I'll take a lifetime reminding him of that."

"Good deal. You two going to a show tonight? I hear there's a James Bond movie on. Should be right up your alley."

"We might at that. I'll see you tomorrow morning after PT."

"Don't forget, you'll have to give some of that stuff back, including the two nine mils, the helmets, and the armor. You can keep the rest, or donate them to the Salvation Army. Oh, and we'll need your name tapes and your unit badges. They'll have to be destroyed, of course."

"Of course. Good night, Sergeant."

"Good night, Sergeants."

Liz and I did go across the base and watch a Bond movie after picking up some jogging sweats. It was not the latest movie, but more recent than most. About halfway through, Liz leaned over and in my ear whispered, "I used to think this shit was just way too fabricated, too good to be true. Now, maybe not. It's a whole lot more real."

"More than you know," I laughed quietly with her.

When we were leaving the theater, we walked past a group of about seven young, enlisted men. It was obvious that all had been drinking. I was just moving Liz out of their way, by way of putting my hand on the small of her back and gently nudging her to one side. The rudest, drunkest, rowdiest of them all turned around and started talking trash.

"Well, it's pretty obvious that the 'don't ask don't tell' days are over, ain't it boys?"

"C'mon, Jimmy. Shut up. You're going to get us all jacked up. Let it go."

"Hey, you girls want to put on a show for us?" asked Jimmy.

I got right in his face and shoved my grade insignia in front of his face.

"Can you read this? Are you sober enough to do that, Private?"

"It don't matter to me that you're a sergeant. You're still a lezbo and you ain't got no business being in the Arm-"

I had him immediately on the ground in a sleeper hold and he was fading fast. I yelled at one of the other people there to call the MPs as fast as possible. They stood there for a second, then Liz took off for the building to do it. Just as the private started to pass out on me, I felt a boot come up against the side of my face from one of his friends. It stunned me for a second, but I reached out and hooked his foot with my boot, dropping him to the pavement. He fell on his back and I extended my knees, completely knocking the wind out of him. Without waiting, I grabbed the one nearest me by the sleeve of his ACUs and twisted it

LEAVING AFGHANISTAN BEHIND

back around behind his head, pushing him flat over the one I had my knees in. I punched him in the back of the head about six or seven times, without even thinking about it.

I jumped up to my feet. There were still four of them standing. They were all drunk and slightly in shock. I reached out to the two nearest me, bringing my Wellcos up to the side of each of their heads, sort of between their ears and their eye sockets. The first dropped to his hands and knees, the second laid out completely backward. The two remaining enlistees put their hands up in front, as if to offer no resistance, and slowly backed up. Before they could go anywhere, an MP was on site. Apparently they happened to be driving by and Liz didn't even have to call, she just flagged them down. The four of them came up with pistols drawn. No clubs like the old movies. Totally modern, totally professional. They quickly handcuffed all of them, called for two ambulances, and made sure we got transportation back to our area. I suggested that instead of giving us a ride back, he take us to the MP headquarters and call either the SGM or the 1SGT. He agreed. Thankfully, it was Pete that showed up.

"Good Goddamn! Can't you two ladies even make it through one more night without making trouble? I should have made you leave today."

"Actually, SGM, there were seven of them against Amelia, and one of them started it. He actually hit her."

"Well, let me go talk to the captain of their unit and sort this out. Just sit tight, okay?"

"Aye, Sgt.," I said.

Fifteen minutes later, Pete and the captain of the MPs, along with the SFC who was Duty Section that night, came into the room where we were waiting

"Well, Sgt. Plummer, it appears as though you were a victim first, of sexual harassment, and then what was at the very least, felonious assault, and possibly sexual assault. You single-handedly brought four of the seven to a point of incapacitation, is that correct?"

I just shrugged my shoulders.

"That's exactly what happened," Liz chimed in.

"So, what happens next?" I asked, expecting retribution.

"They'll spend the night in the brig. Sometime tomorrow, they'll be given a bill of particulars, which will be filed by one of the JAG officers, investigated by CID, and then given to their COs. Due to the seriousness of the charges, there won't be any Article 15s, it will have to go to court martial. They will, in all likelihood, be jailed for three to six months, fined heavily, reduced in rank to E-1, and thereafter, dishonorably discharged. We've separated them into separate holding cells and have been talking to them. The two you didn't kick the living dog shit out of admitted their group started it all."

"And to me?"

"To you? Why would we punish a victim of a crime, Sergeant?"

"Times have changed. For my last two tours, I had to cover up the fact that I had a girlfriend waiting for me back in the states."

"Ah. They didn't exactly say, they just mentioned that they were taunting you. Are you and Sgt. Sutton girlfriends?"

"No, sir. I merely had my hand on her back, moving her to one side, to avoid the drunken stupidity in the street."

"Well, you handled it well, to tell you the truth. I'm sorry about previous rules. I just enforce them; I don't make them."

"So, I take it you still don't approve, Captain?"

"It's not for me to say, Sgt."

I pulled my ACU coat up from my trousers, loosened my trouser belt, and dropped them down below my tee shirt line. I then lifted my tee shirt, and showed him my battle scars.

"Where are your scars, Captain? I fought for my right to have a girlfriend. I fought for your son's right to be gay. I fought for your neighbor to carry a gun. I fought for your grandchildren not to be raised in a police state. You answer that for me, can you? Where are your battle wounds?"

"Sergeant, I'm certainly not here to start a fight with you about something I have no power over. I've already taken over the investigation from our office rather than wait until tomorrow, and I will make sure that they are prosecuted to the fullest extent of the law. Okay?"

"Fine," I said, dressing back up.

"Sergeant?"

"Sir?"

"For what it's worth, though I don't know the circumstances of your wounds, I am both truly sorry for your injuries, and truly grateful for your service to your country."

LEAVING AFGHANISTAN BEHIND

At that, he gave me a sharp salute, which I returned quickly. I have to admit, it felt good. One of the first times that I thought somebody truly understood.

LEAVING AFGHANISTAN BEHIND

CHAPTER THIRTEEN

Liz and I were driven by the MPs back to the battalion area. It would be our last night in the 2-22. It wasn't just a job, it was an adventure. Wait! That was the navy, right? Didn't matter, it was still true. We walked around a bit outside the building, just talking, enjoying the crisp mountain air, watching our breath form in the air as we talked. We made fun of the fact that back in the city it would be smog, not human breath that made up most of the vapor in the air.

"So, are you looking forward to getting people back on your couch? Scribbling on your notepad? Making sure people are able to deal with the stress?"

"I think so. I'll tell you this... I think I'm much better prepared to go inside people's minds now than I was. School can't ever give the experience of life. My life's experience so far, had only been second hand. Now? I'm more ready than ever to help. I think that now I'm probably more capable than I've ever been. I'll know better what questions to ask. How to formulate thoughts... the same, yet so different."

"At least something good has come out of this whole shitty thing. You know, with your job being related to the city governments, and especially with what's happened, you could probably get a gun permit."

"Please. I think I'll definitely go to a range every once in a while. I can almost guarantee that, but I still don't believe in having guns around the house. For every person that is saved during a home invasion, twenty or thirty are killed by accidents. I especially don't want any in the house around my girls."

"Glad to hear it. I was just asking. 9-1-1 is easy, and usually fast, especially if you know how to ask for it. There are key words to get the highest priority. I'll give them to you in the car ride back tomorrow. Getting cold yet? We should probably go in and get some sleep. We still have one more run in the morning and it's going to be a killer!"

"Hooah!" shouted Liz, grinning. From various, unseen locations outside, there were at least a couple of dozen "Hooahs!" in reply. I couldn't have asked for more.

I gave Liz the laptop first. She read a couple of emails that Keven had sent her, then sent a reply. She knew she wouldn't see an answer until the morning. I got the laptop and there was one message from Theresa. It was concise.

"Yay! You're coming home! I'm going home! It's over. I love you, babe. You'd better get your uniform cleaned. I'm giving you exactly one week to make me an honest woman! X O" I showed it to Liz.

"Yesterday, Keven asked me to marry her."

"So has the not being married thing been your idea, hers, or mutual?"

"Neither of us have been overly-compelled, but I think mostly it's been Keven that's said she doesn't want to be married. She felt that what we have is above and beyond any paper anybody could file at city hall, that we are the important things."

"She's right. I could go either way, but truthfully? I've been thinking about it for almost three months now. It's the biggest thing I can do to show Theresa how important she is to me. Forever. I mean, we've always professed to each other that it's forever, but we also both have exes. I know that theoretically we could end up getting divorced, but it won't ever be my idea. I'm in it for life. This is the first person I've ever felt that way about."

"And she liked it?"

"She went ape-shit nuts! She jumped up and down and screamed and carried on forever. Then all this happened," I said, holding my hands up to my shoulders, aimed out.

We turned out the lights and lay down in our bunks. Sleep was immediate.

LEAVING AFGHANISTAN BEHIND

Washington and I were stuck up in what was an abandoned prayer tower in the middle of nowhere. We overlooked a crossroad though, and the probability of troop movement was high. We had a lot of food and water with us. We each had a Barrett with us on this mission. It was ungodly hot. Out in the sun, it was probably a hundred and twenty degrees. Although the tower afforded us some modicum of shade, it also blocked what little breeze there was, and that made it just stifling.

"Hey, Jervis, tell me again why we do this shit?"

"Hazardous duty pay... Overseas deployment pay... Extra duty pay..."

"Are you serious, dude?"

"Truth? It's so I can prove to everybody in my old neighborhood that I have the biggest dick around."

"I would say you're the crudest person I know, but truthfully you don't even come close."

"Yeah, I don't care what anybody thinks about the size of my dick, except Carol. If she's happy, then I'm happy. And as long as I get back home to her and Jeremy, that's all that matters. So, what's her name?"

"Whose name?"

"Your partner. What's her name?"

"Why do you pigs all assume because I'm a woman doing a 'man's job' that I have to be a dyke?"

"I didn't say dyke. You did. I just meant, you being gay. What's her name?"

"Have you not heard one thing I've said?"

"Gittens, it's not what you say, and it's not what you don't say. It's the way you don't say it back at the FOB. Personally, I think the policy sucks. Other countries don't care, and they seem to work out just fine, with great military efficiency. I'm just asking, what's her name?"

"...Theresa Biancardi."

"Italian, huh?"

"Pretty much."

"I've never shown you a photo of Carol and Jeremy, have I?"

"Not so far."

"Well, I should have. We've been paired up for almost two years. Here, this is them." He got his ID holder out of his pack, and behind his card was their picture.

"Wow. She's gorgeous. What is she? Chinese? Korean?"

"She's a strange mix. She's half Chinese from Hong Kong and half Vietnamese. You usually don't see those two ethnicities mixed. Her dad is a salesman from Saigon. He was always in Hong Kong. Her mom was a flower vendor on the street. He fell in love with her at first sight. He bought six dozen flowers and gave them to her right there. He had already been courting her for a few months when Saigon fell. They got married and he stayed in Hong Kong. She has six sisters and they look like septuplets. It took me years to be able to tell them apart. Still have problems once in a while. They all think I'm an idiot. Maybe I am, but that's my story. What's your story?"

"There's an Italian restaurant/store in Flatbush. The old lady that runs it, we all call her Mama. I was on leave for a week, staying at my mom and sister's apartment. My first day back, I went in. I hadn't seen Mama in about three years. She was so proud of me in my uniform. I'd worn my service dress so my mom could see me. I just wished my dad had been able to see me. He died a few years back. Anyway, I was in Mama's getting dinner for my family and Theresa was in the store. Mama knew that Theresa was gay, too. In Mama's eyes, every gay guy should know every other gay guy, and every gay girl should know every other gay girl, like this big worldwide club or something. Mama virtually came around the counter, sat us both down at a table together, and brought us each a glass of Chianti and some garlic bread. She took Theresa's hand and put it out on the table. She put my hand on top of hers. She looked at each of us without saying a word, her eyes were sparkling. The electricity shot through me like a bolt of lightning. It was very embarrassing and the talk was difficult. Finally, I couldn't stand it anymore. I told her that I needed to get home with the food. She looked a little dejected. She hadn't said anything about a partner or a girlfriend or anything, so I took a chance. I asked her to come back to my place and have dinner with my family that very night. She said she couldn't possibly. I leaned close to her, smiled, and said, 'This may be the only chance we have at this thing. Please don't let it pass us by because you're afraid. I'm afraid enough for both of us. Come with me.' I held out my hand and helped her up from the table. She walked behind the counter and picked up the phone. She called her family and said she wasn't going to be home for dinner. It was fucking magic, man."

"That's got to be one of the best stories I've ever heard. Rock it."

LEAVING AFGHANISTAN BEHIND

"That seems like a million miles away now. You ever hear of the term, 'U-haul lesbians'?"

"Can't say that I have."

"Tend to date for a few days or a few weeks at most, and then take everything they own and move into the other's place. Tend to travel a little light. Before I left for Fort Drum, I made Theresa promise me she wouldn't see anybody else. She agreed. She was still in school so that I couldn't move her, but when she graduated, she got a job for a printing shop, way underutilizing her talents and earning capability, to move to Watertown to be with me. I moved off base and she quickly found out that I'm one of the longest deploying idiots in the world. This is my fourth. She put up with my last one that was 12 months, and it looks like this one will be 15. I'm not going to do a gauntlet. I can't do that to her. I'm retiring."

"So am I. This is only my second, but it's way too dangerous out here, in case you hadn't noticed."

"Oh, you mean like having a gunship raking down both sides of our ravine? Shit like that?"

"Exactly!" he laughed.

It was hard to have conversations like this. We were in the middle of nowhere, seventy-five feet off the ground, and able to see each of four roads for over mile and a half in any direction, but we still had to whisper everything... just in case.

"Liz, hey, wake up," I tugged on her shirt.

"What's going on? Having trouble?"

"No. That's just it. I had a really long, vivid flashback. I relived the entire eight days sitting in an observation point waiting for something to happen. Nothing ever did. My partner and I just talked a little here and there. And nothing happened. You think it's a good sign?"

"Too early to tell. Not the answer you want I know, but that's the answer. What time is it?"

"Sorry. It's about twelve thirty. Go back to sleep."

"Pretty early in the night for you to get a flashback, isn't it?"

"Yeah, I guess it is at that. Anyway, sorry to bother you. Get some rest for the smoking we're going to lay down."

"Hooah," she whispered at me and smiled.

I crawled back in my bunk. I thought I would have trouble falling asleep, as usual, but it only took minutes.

Liz and I heard reveille sound, which meant we had ten minutes to quickly hit the latrine and be out and ready in formation. Today, we fell into formation with the trailing unit. We waited until the entire column was moving, then moved to double time for the run. We started sprinting a little ahead. As we passed the first platoon in front of ours, I sang out at the top of my lungs, "Let 'em blow from east to west!" and the platoon answered with, "The US Army is the best!"

We passed the next platoon in order. I yelled, "Dress it right and cover down," which was quickly answered by, "Forty inches all around!" We were passing a platoon about every forty-five or fifty seconds.

"Motivation check!"
"Hooah!"
"They took away my favorite jeans!"
"Now I'm wearing army greens!"
"Gotta letter in the mail!"
"Go to war or go to jail!"
"Used to drive a Cadillac!"
"Now I wear it on my back!"
"Motivation check!"
"Hooah!"

Every platoon we moved up on, I called out one line of a standard cadence and the entire platoon answered back in chorus. Often the platoon leaders would follow up the echo with "Hooah!" It was my last hurrah, one which I never dreamed I'd get a chance to relive for five days. Never in a million years would I have thought it would happen, and I was eating it up. By the time we'd run about eight miles, Liz and I'd run another half a mile just moving up the column of the entire brigade. It was too bad that we weren't running one of the biannual entire base runs. That would have been too much. I think my heart wouldn't have been able to take it. Not the stress of it, mind you, the sheer joy.

Finally, we were at the front of the entire column and we were running in the first rank. I was on the left side of the staff, showing courtesy afforded by deferring position. Higher ranking officers and NCOs always maintain the position on the right. Liz was on the left side of the second rank, right behind me, running like a regular trooper. If it was hurting her, she sure as heck didn't show it.

"Fine army morning for a run, isn't it, sir?" I shouted to the colonel.

LEAVING AFGHANISTAN BEHIND

"Outstanding!" Everybody was smiling as we ran. Everybody. Finally, we got back to battalion. After we were dismissed, Liz and I got a quick shower and a change of ACUs. We moved into the dining facility. In the food line itself we were right behind Taggert and Bowers, along with a few other NCOs.

"Hey, guys. Well, this is the last meal we'll share with you. We're moving out in thirty minutes for Philadelphia, St. Louis, Kansas City, and points west…" Everybody laughed. A way to say "We're going away and we're damned sure not going to tell you where."

Bowers turned to me. "You know, you've been under arms practically since you've been here. I'm not sure if it's because you never want to take your hats off, even in the house, if you're afraid of something, or if maybe you two are the biggest bad asses I've ever come across. In any case, I don't think I'd want to break into your quarters at night." Liz got a mortified look on her face, but I tried to laugh it off.

"Yeah, one of those. You'll have to choose which one."

"No thank you, no-sirree!" Everybody laughed.

We ate, then said our goodbyes to Taggert and Bowers and the six NCOs immediately next to them. After we had put our trays up, I approached the officers' area and requested permission to approach. After that was granted, I addressed Pete, telling him that we needed transportation to the armory, then our outgoing inspection.

"Very well. I'll meet you at your quarters in twenty minutes. After we finish all of our business, we'll go to the major's office… if that's okay with you, Major?"

"It is. It is indeed. Let me just say, Sergeants, it's been a pleasure having you both with us this week.

And this morning's run? That was an outstanding performance. Already heard about it from about every platoon leader. Outstanding!"

"Thank you very much, sir. We'll return to our quarters and make ready." We both saluted, turned on our heels, and went back to our room at the CQ. We put our helmets and body armor on the top bunks. We packed all our gear and got out a change of civilian clothes. We wanted to be ready so after we returned from the armory and the major's office, we would be able to change clothes and leave immediately. As soon as we got a driver, we went back to the armory to turn in our Berettas, clips, and rounds. The same sergeant that checked them out to us, checked them back in. He not only inspected them visually, very carefully, but he also took both weapons back to the test box and fired a round from each to make sure they were serviceable. What a dick, but at least he didn't say anything.

When we got back to the room, we had the CQ Runner call the SGM to give us our out-processing inspection. Pete verified we had our helmets, body armor, winter coats, name tags, and unit insignias ready to be picked up, lined up on our bunks to turn in. "Amelia, it's sure going to seem dull keeping these troops trained up without you around stirring things up. As for the spanking you gave our little FTX boys? Um... Yeah, there's going to be a little, tiny change in training instruction on that bad boy! But I'm glad you were here and I'm glad we could help."

"Pete," I said, shaking his hand, "I'm glad I wasn't locked up. My plan was actually to get locked up with the MPs for two days, buying me some time. I never dreamed you'd be here and it would actually work out. Thanks for everything you guys have given us."

"And you, Liz, you must feel pretty good about Amelia doing as good a job as she has, taking care of everything. And then, when you do show up, you perform brilliantly. I mean brilliantly. You're both young enough; you should think about enlisting. Amelia, you'd keep your grade and Liz, you'd start out as a captain."

"No offense, Pete, but if I couldn't do what we've been doing, I don't think I'd want to be in the army. If I only wanted to be a psychiatrist, I'd just go home and go to work," she laughed.

After talking for about fifteen minutes, Pete left us to change clothes. I'd taken my boots off already, then my ACU top, and I was standing there in my trousers and tee shirt. Liz came up to me and ran her fingertips along my neckline, then up and down my arms. "May I help you?" I asked her.

"It's just amazing to me. You're so muscular, so strong, but you have such soft, beautiful skin. It's wonderful. Unlike me, the fricking albino, I bet with your dark skin you never, ever burn, do you?"

"One of the few advantages of being black."

"I better get dressed so we can go see the major and get out of this here town. I bet he'll be glad to see us go."

"Actually, we had already crossed our last line. I think if we hadn't been cleared today, you would have gone to WITSEC and I'd have gone home to work the case. I do think we were on his last nerve, but

LEAVING AFGHANISTAN BEHIND

hey, we had fun, right? In spite of all the things going on, we had fun, don't you think?"

"Hopefully, the type of fun we'll have in the future is the weekend in the summer at the boardwalk with me and my three girls, and you and Theresa and your children, with hotdogs, cotton candy, sodas, popcorn, candy, and stuff like that."

I smiled and nodded my head. That did indeed seem like a wonderful thought. We both got changed and went out to the CQ. He did a double take when he saw us, especially Liz. She was wearing her professional clothes, albeit with tennis shoes, and I had changed into my black jeans and shirt, throwing on a little of Liz's lip gloss. "What's the matter, soldier? You've never seen a woman before?" I said straight-faced.

"No, ma'am. I mean, yes, ma'am. I mean, I mean no disrespect, ma'am…"

Liz and I both started laughing at him then and he got very embarrassed.

"That was mean of us, I know. Sorry. I couldn't help it. It's been a pleasure. Hooah?"

"Hooah!" he said in return, along with Liz.

Our driver took us over to the major's office where we spent about twenty minutes just shooting the breeze. Again, I was complimented for my brainwork behind our hiding out in plain sight among thirteen thousand rifles, cannons, and mortar tubes. Finally, our driver took us to the armory where we turned in our guns and night vision goggles. Then we swung by the MP station at the far side of the base. We had to inspect the car before we could sign for it, to make sure it hadn't been damaged in any way during its temporary storage. We got the keys and a round of handshakes wishing us well.

"Uh, sergeant? Aren't we forgetting one itty, bitty thing?"

"Not that I'm aware of, Officer Gittens."

"You're holding onto my Glock 27. I bought that with my money, not the department's, and it's got a nickel-boron slide. Either try and find my gun, or write me a check for eight hundred dollars, if you would?"

"Oh, that information would be kept in a different location. Normally we don't have people bringing weapons on base that are *approved* in a roundabout sort of way like yours. So it's not on a standard contraband list. Wait one…" He returned a couple of minutes later with the gun in an evidence bag, sealed, with four clips of rounds in with it. "Like the car, inspect the weapon before you take possession, please."

I pulled the slide back making sure the chamber was empty, then pulled it back fully and let it slam home. I pointed it straight up and pulled the trigger, hearing a very solid snap. Ah... my own gun! He handed a sheet of paper across the counter for me to sign, then went to make a copy of both the paper for the car and the gun, bringing them back to me.

"Good luck, ladies. Have a safe journey home to the city."

"You too, Lieutenant."

We got into the car, headed for the west gate and back to Watertown, then south to the city. I stopped about two hours south to fill up the tank and get some snacks.

"You're sure a lot more at ease than the last time we stopped."

I just smiled. We drove, pretty much in silence, for the next few hours, stopping once more for gas right before we hit the city. It was early enough in the day that the traffic was light. Light for the city of New York, that is. We drove straight to the dealership and returned the car.

"Goodness, gracious, I'm so glad you two are done with this whole nasty affair. It's been all over the news, you know."

"Thanks, Magpie. We mean that. Thanks! You were an integral part of us being able to carry out our mission."

Maggie reached into her drawer, pulled out the contract, put it through a paper shredder, and gave me a sealed envelope. We got on a bus to go back the precinct, and while we were riding I opened it. It was the entire amount of money I'd given her as a deposit. Despite my being completely jaded, it just goes to show there are a few people out there that are genuinely good people.

Entering the precinct, Liz and I had to get visitor's badges, since mine was back in my locker. I put her in an interrogation room, got my gear from the locker, and returned to the front desk. I had the desk sergeant let the duty captain know we were back. The three of us chatted for about an hour, with Jernick joining in on speakerphone for the second half.

"We'll have you come into the precinct tomorrow, Officer Gittens, about 1300, if you don't mind, to talk more in depth about this. I'm not sure if we'll do the final debrief with everybody coming in here, or if

LEAVING AFGHANISTAN BEHIND

we'll go over to 1PP. I'm assuming that right now both of you would like to go stretch out on your own couches, am I right?"

"That'd be nice, actually," I replied.

"Okay. Talk to you ladies tomorrow then. Bye."

"I'll get a squad to take you both home instead of trying to wrangle transportation. Give me about fifteen minutes."

"Thanks."

Right then, a uniformed officer came into the interrogation room to get us and all our gear: Liz with one pack, and me with my two.

"Hi. Rick Collier. You're Gittens?"

"Yup, and this is Dr. Elizabeth Feynman, the department shrink."

"Pleased to meet you both. Where are we going first?"

"Drop her first," I said, pointing to Liz.

We drove through the streets, through the traffic, through the noise... despite how much I loved being in the woods up north, I'm really a city girl at heart. To tell you the truth, I could go out for six months at a time into the wilderness, but if I knew I wouldn't ever get to come back, I think I'd just kill myself on the spot and avoid the Christmas rush. We approached Liz's house. There was already a squad on site.

"Is somebody already here as a detail?" I asked Collier.

He was about to answer, but he was getting up and out of the squad.

The officer in front of Liz and Keven's house got out of his squad and smiled at us. Liz and I were right behind Collier, and started walking up the walk toward the house, toward the smile of the waiting officer. Then in a flash, the officer in front of the house drew his weapon and shot Collier in the head, instantly dropping him. He turned to Liz and pulled the trigger, sending a round directly into her heart. I quickly realized what was happening, but still had the disadvantage of my Glock being tucked into its pocket in the front of my hoodie. By now, though, I had him in my sights, and threw ten or so rounds at him. We're always trained to use deadly force as a last resort, but at that point, head shots are the most lethal. He was definitely down.

I ran over to Liz, who was lying on the ground, clutching her chest, screaming in pain. I had to pry hard to get her arms back out of the way so I could unzip her winter coat. I rolled her over onto her back. There, in the outer layer of my Second Chance that she'd been wearing, was the flattened bullet that had been meant to take her life. I grabbed her by the arm holes of the vest and began lifting her off the ground.

"Breathe!" I yelled at her. "Liz, breathe. Breathe in! I know it hurts, but breathe in! You've got to breathe! You've probably got a couple of shattered ribs, but you gotta breathe, baby!"

It took about half a minute, but she was finally able to catch her breath. She was still writhing in pain. I laid her back down and ran to the car to call for backup with the radio. I called an ambulance as a precautionary measure. I got down on one knee beside Collier. "Hey, are you all right? Shit, you're bleeding like a pig." I pulled my pack out of the squad and folded up a tee shirt to make a compress. "Here, hold this tight to your head. Man, that's going to need stitches. A *lot* of stitches. Really, I mean hold it tight as you can. Can you get up and walk okay? Let's get you out of the street." Collier gritted his teeth, and with my help got up, gripping his head with my shirt. "I'm taking your cell phone for a minute. Sit down here in the grass and lie back flat. Don't keep your knees up high or it will make the bleeding worse. Okay?" He nodded his head at me. I walked over and gave Liz the cell phone. The dead man was up closer to the house.

"Collier?" asked Liz.

"He'll be okay. He's hollering like he got his thumb hit by a hammer. That's not the sound of a serious wound."

"The other officer?"

"Dead. He may have been a real cop, but he was definitely on somebody's payroll. It's a good thing we're here before anybody else got home, you know. You probably ought to give Keven a call and tell her to take the kids somewhere else until we get this sorted out. It's not something they should have to see."

It took only minutes for sirens to start coming in from every direction. We got six squads and two ambulances. There were also two unmarked cars that came up within about twenty minutes. Jernick got out of the back of one of them. I didn't recognize the other officer. It turned out he was the director of the Gang Task Force, Captain Carmichael. They walked over to the dead man.

"That piece of shit?" said Capt. Carmichael.

"I take it you know him?" asked Jernick.

"We all but brought him up on criminal charges. Name's Diaz. He was given the *opportunity* to leave or go to prison, basically.

"So, this might actually be over? This was a stringer?"

"A stringer?" asked a patrolman standing beside Jernick.

LEAVING AFGHANISTAN BEHIND

"That's a round that's defective, causing the trajectory to be affected in some way rather than following the twists induced by the rifling, and the drop in height from physical properties," said Jernick.

"You know, you're starting to really impress me, Captain. Please forgive me, everything I've said to you, any time that I've acted at all inappropriately, everything."

"Don't worry, Officer Gittens. I understand that you did it because you were close to the problem. You just wanted to protect your family. I guess this is our first live debriefing, in a way. What a genius plan for hiding out. You must really have some pull with those people."

"Actually, I fully expected to be put in jail, but I figured it would have given us at least two nights in jail there until DHS and WITSEC could be contacted directly. Thank you also, for being so supportive of our little... camp out?" I said.

Everybody chuckled at that, despite the situation. The paramedics were still checking Liz. I waved to the brass and walked over to the back of the ambulance.

"Gentlemen, those are my baby sister's tits you have hanging out in the wind, and it's a little cold out here. Now that you know she's not going to die on you, how about you get these doors closed, huh?" One of the paramedics immediately did so. It took another thirty minutes for the CSI crew to show up. We would have only got the ME's office, except this was obviously a scene that needed a little more looking at. It was just starting to get dark. After the body had been removed and the tape was taken down, I got in the back of the ambulance to see how Liz was doing. Tired, that's how she was doing. Hurting, that's how she was doing. Still scared, that's how she was doing.

"I've got to finish up a few things. When they finish with you, get your things out of our squad and let's go inside. It's official. This guy was an ex-cop who was trying to make his bones with a gang. Guess he didn't pass Go and doesn't get to collect two hundred dollars. I just checked with Collier, sitting in the other ambulance. He's got thirty-eight Steristrips on his head. They're probably going to take him to the ER, remove the strips one by one, shave his head in a little row, and then put in stitches. That'll keep him busy for a little while. That's what he gets for bleeding all over one of my favorite shirts," I laughed.

Liz barely managed a laugh, but reached up and took my hand.

"Amelia, is it really over?"

"Yeah. It's over. It's not even eight o'clock yet and your girls will be here soon. Ready for them? Remember, we'll still have to go to the ER later to get X-rays to make sure there's no splinters in your ribs. I'm pretty sure they're either separated or broken from the impact of the slug. Bulletproof doesn't mean pain-proof!"

She didn't say anything. She just nodded her head and tears started streaming down her face. We went up to her house and she dialed in the number to the electric lock, letting us in. Wow! Their place was beautiful and palatial compared to our apartment. They also had two floors, whereas we had one. I kicked my shoes off at the front door and followed closely behind Liz. She dropped her purse and coat on the floor at the end of the couch. This was unlike the rest of the house, which was immaculate, with not one single thing out of place. She plopped down on the couch, laid her head back, closed her eyes, and sighed.

I moved up in front of her and sat on the coffee table. I pulled her feet up one at a time, removing her shoes. After I had them off, I started rubbing her feet.

"I'll give you exactly one hour to stop that!"

"I could stop sooner if you'd like?"

"God, no, it's wonderful. I may go to sleep…" those were her last words before she went to sleep. I continued to massage her feet. We remained that way until I heard a noise as the door opened. Then there was squealing, little footsteps running across the floor, and pouncing on the couch, which woke Liz up.

"Mommy, Mommy, Mommy!" both Alyssa and Clarisse shouted together. Her arms wrapped around both of them, holding them in tightly, hugging them, as tears started rolling down her cheeks.

I turned to Keven, offering my hand to her.

"I don't think so," she said. I knew she might be angry with me for getting Liz involved in all this. "If she's your little sister now, that would make me your sister-in-law, and a handshake won't cut it," she said, giving me a bear hug and kissing me on the cheek. "Thank you so much for taking care of my Little Lizard."

"Lizard Breath?"

"Ha. She showed you that, did she?"

"Yup, KayKay," I giggled.

"You know, for a doctor, she doesn't exercise that part about confidential information very well, does she?" she laughed.

LEAVING AFGHANISTAN BEHIND

"Well, everybody needs a few nights alone at home to get back to a schedule, especially your girls, but what say about Sunday, you four come over to our place and have lunch? We'll grill some chicken, make some potato salad, and maybe some deviled eggs... Theresa should surely be home either tonight or by tomorrow at the latest. Or not, just a thought."

"A great thought, Amelia. I know Theresa well. She is one of the best students that I've ever had. It would be a delight."

I walked over to Liz and tousled her hair. "I won't take up your family time, but we'll see the four of you at our place on Sunday for lunch. Okay? I've already talked to Keven. I'll talk to you tomorrow; I'll call your cell during lunch. Have a good night." I leaned down and kissed Liz. The kids didn't seem to notice the strange lady kissing Mommy at all. They were just so happy to have her home. They'd cleaned up the dead body and the crime scene, then sent one ambulance back on its service rounds. The one with Collier in it went to the hospital so they could work on him. There was the one squad from Diaz that they'd taken away on a transporter for further investigation. They needed to see how he'd gotten the car. And lastly, there was the squad that Collier was driving us in. They'd ferried another officer over to drive me.

"I can drive myself to the station, then take a bus home from there."

"Nope," Jernick said to me, gesturing his hand toward the unmarked car he was in.

I put my packs in the trunk and we drove off. I was watching out the window at the buildings moving by and hadn't been paying much attention. "This isn't the way back to the precinct, and it sure as hell ain't the way to my apartment. Where are we going, Cap?"

"34th Street."

"What's over there?"

"You'll see."

We drove for about half an hour. Once we got there, we took the elevator all the way to the roof. It was a huge waiting room with padded benches and outside the doors was a marked helipad.

"VIPs coming in tonight?" I asked him and the detective with us.

"Very much so. Should be here within the hour. Sorry about the wait."

"It's all good. After all the help you've given me, it's the least I could do," I said. I sat back in a chair and closed my eyes. I drifted off within minutes.

I was standing in formation on the parade grounds at Fort Drum during an early autumn day. The air was slightly breezy, crisp, and clean to breathe and a few wispy clouds dotted an otherwise bright blue sky.

"Staff Sergeant Gittens, Mrs. Gittens, Cheryll Anne Gittens, present yourselves to the commander."

I came running up from the assembled troops to the head of all the companies for the entire brigade. The general in charge of the entire 10th Mountain was standing beside the brigade commander, who was a bird colonel. My mother and sister joined them, facing the formation and me.

"Sgt. Gittens, with the authority of the Department of the Army, upon advice from the US Military Command, and with the approval of the congress of the United States, because of valor shown in battle, on 04 April 2007, having been confirmed by the Commander, US Army Central Command, while exposing yourself to grave danger and sustaining wounds in battle, you did exhibit such valor, that you are being awarded your second Bronze Star for Valor."

He stepped back and saluted me; I returned the salute. This is one of the few times a superior will salute the lower grade first. Then they had my mother pin my new medal on my uniform on the pocket underneath my name. This was temporary, until I could get the oak leaf cluster with V added to my existing medal.

"Staff Sergeant Gittens, called before the attention of the US Army Staff Headquarters in Washington, D.C., for actions performed in conditions of battle, decision capabilities, leadership qualities, and extraordinary standards of military character, you are hereby being relieved of your grade of staff sergeant in the US Army," he said.

It's too bad I wasn't in ACUs. They would have been tearing off the velcroed SSGT stripes and I would be getting to hear that awesome sound of the rip. With the Service Dress Blue ASU uniform the stripes are sewn on usually, but I was wearing the alternate coat today with shoulder boards for immediate change. Not as nice as hearing the rip of the Velcro, but replacing the shoulder boards, instead of the sleeve insignias, was still a pretty nice feeling. And for my mom to do it? Absolutely the best! I pointed to the sky and said a quick prayer for my

LEAVING AFGHANISTAN BEHIND

father. The general handed me my first set of stripes for my combat uniform. There wasn't a prouder parent in America that day than my mother, the immigrant from Barbados.

I was awakened with the distant thud-thud-thud of a helicopter coming in for a landing.

"Officer Gittens, I know it's been a long day for you, but I need your attention for just a few minutes."

"Sure, Cap, but am I really dressed for this?"

"Hey, your sweats do say NYPD, right? And your stocking cap? I'd say you're in a perfectly good uniform, representing your department pretty well. Don't worry about it."

As it approached, I could see it was a Sikorsky S-76. It flared, then wobbled just a bit as its wheels touched down. The oleo shocks compressed momentarily before coming to a standstill, then the loud whine of the twin engines started winding down. The three of us went out onto the tarmac on the rooftop to await the passengers getting out. First was a black man holding a suitcase and a garment bag, followed by a Hispanic gentleman also holding a suitcase and a garment bag. They left the door open and just as the two men were about to greet us, out popped the third passenger. A dark-haired beauty carrying a sports bag, an aluminum case for her laptop, and a gift bag. It was my Theresa!

She came running to me, dropping all her gear including her laptop, and jumped up in the air with her legs around my waist and her arms around my neck.

"Baby, baby, baby, baby, baby. Don't you *ever* pull a stunt like this again, do you hear me? Ever! Oh, I missed you so much. I could barely stand it. Where were you, anyway? We never did get word on that," she asked.

"Fort Drum, with the 10th Mountain. Back on base."

"With Liz? How'd you pull that off?"

"We were in uniform. Special Detail."

"Those designs were for you two?"

"They were indeed. They were made that day. We wore them and now they've been destroyed already."

"Aw, I would have wanted to keep them. Of course, I did it on their machine so there's no way I could copy anything."

"So where were you?"

"Toronto."

"In Canada? That was a good move."

"I couldn't tell you anything about Toronto. The only thing I saw was the airport gift shop. Danny over there loaned me the money to buy you this, since I couldn't have any money or credit cards," she said, handing me the gift bag.

I pulled out a tee shirt that said, "My wife went to Toronto and all I got was this lousy tee shirt!" I hugged her. It was so perfect for us.

"Well, we already have a meeting scheduled for tomorrow. What about everybody going home now? This time for real, no ruse," Jernick said, winking at me.

"Thanks, Cap. Thanks a lot."

"No worries."

Finally, Theresa and I were in our own bed. We were in our PJs and the lights were out.

"What else haven't you told me?"

"Are you seriously going to do this tonight?"

"And every damn day for weeks!"

I laughed at her, pulling her into me so hard we molded into a single form. That night I had no flashback, no dream. And after that they were infrequent at best, and rarely as bad as they had been, just snapshots of 'a day in the life', so to speak. Maybe I'd finally gotten it through my subconscious that the bad things that happened over there weren't my fault. They were just bad things that happened.

Theresa went back to work on Monday. I showed up at her office at lunch, wearing my dress uniform with all my awards. As soon as she saw me walk in the front door, she squealed and jumped up and down.

"We're going to do it! We're going to do it today!"

"What are you talking about?" asked Sarah, who sat directly across from her.

"We're getting married. Friday we got our license, but I wasn't sure when we would do it. We had to wait twenty-four hours. And that's all Amelia's waiting. Oh, it's wonderful!"

I walked up to her desk and stood in place, not saying a word, just smiling. I took off my hat with one hand and my other I held out to her. She took it and stood up, grabbing her purse.

"Hey, everybody, I'm leaving for the day. I'll be back tomorrow." She scribbled something on paper and handed it to Sarah. "Here's my new name. Would you get me new cards and a new name plate? Thanks."

LEAVING AFGHANISTAN BEHIND

CHAPTER FOURTEEN

We probably see Liz and her family every other weekend. Liz and Keven waited until spring break from school to get married, just for convenience and ease of taking time off. The little girls were wearing pink Easter dresses. Liz wore a black and white dress and Keven wore a black brocade patterned dress. They looked wonderful together. We were their witnesses. We have all become inseparable. There's that old saying that "With your family you get what you get, but you get to pick your friends."

It was a strange set of circumstances that gave us our new friends, but from the beginning Theresa and I didn't consider them friends... not even life-long friends. They were truly our family. Of course, when we went to a big holiday shebang with anybody's family, everyone was just absorbed into that family unit. This included Liz, Keven, Alyssa, and Clarisse, Theresa, and I. All equal shares.

I did go to the VA to see the doc with the absolute newest in treatments, but I still have the ability to call Liz at lunch and talk to her about bad nights when they do occur.

~ THE END ~

About the HollyAnne Weaver

Ms. Weaver has worked for many years in a scientifically-based career writing technical documents. An avid reader from a very young age, she gradually began writing poetry and fiction, one of her current passions. Growing up, Ms. Weaver was always fascinated with books and the ability of an author to write fiction. A sequence of emails with a close friend led to her writing longer pieces, eventually culminating in her first novel being completed in 2010. Ms. Weaver's main writing focus is on lesbian fiction, although she has projects for mysteries and historical fiction already planned.

❧ THE PLAID SKIRT ❧

If you have enjoyed **LEAVING AFGHANISTAN BEHIND** please look for HollyAnne Weaver's novel **THE PLAID SKIRT**
from
Shadoe Publishing:
We have a chapter here for your enjoyment.

"Put down the skirt and move away!"
"What?"
"I said, put down the skirt and move away."
"Are you talking to me?"
I couldn't keep a straight face anymore; I broke out laughing. She had the cutest look on her face. Perplexed, confused, angry…
"I'm sorry," I said as I held my hand out to her. "I'm Alison Lockewood. I saw the skirt coming in the doorway and thought it was perfect. I'm going to a club to hear a band. I'm looking for something new to wear. I didn't mean to upset you."
"You scared the crap out of me," she said as she shook back. "I'm Alexandra Aronov. Call me Sasha. I don't have an occasion. I just thought it was pretty." She still looked a little rattled.
"Seriously, I'm sorry. I've never done that to a stranger ever in my life. I don't know what came over me. Please forgive me. I'm so sorry."
"That's okay. I'll get over it. Sometime," she managed with a little laugh.
"I'm a size twelve. You?"
"Ten. Perfect. We'll both get what we want."
"Great. I'm so sorry to have freaked you out. Really, I don't normally do that."
"Don't worry about it. I've already forgotten it."
I got a top to wear with the skirt and some tights to wear under it. I also found a scarf that looked like it was made for the skirt. I walked up to the counter to check out. Sasha was already in line just ahead of me.
"Hi again."
"Oh, hi."
"Listen, do you have somewhere you have to be?"

"Not particularly, why?"

"Do you have time to let me buy you a cuppa to make up for my silliness? I feel pretty guilty. I'd feel better if you'd let me."

"That's really okay. You don't have to."

"I know I don't have to, I'd just like to. But I understand if you don't. I guess I'd pass as well. Well anyway, I hope you have a nice day."

Sasha paid for her clothes and walked away from the counter. I put my purchases on the counter top and handed the cashier my card. When I got to the door, Sasha was standing just outside.

"I changed my mind. I do have time for a coffee. If the offer is still there that is."

"Yes. It is. Do you want to go to the bookstore? The coffee bar there is pretty good and not too expensive."

"Okay."

We made a little small talk while we walked to the bookstore.

"So, Sasha… Do you mind me asking what you do?"

"Not at all. I'm a social worker. Mostly I work with children. Sounds pretty dull, huh?"

"No, it sounds… Noble, frankly. I work with computers and networking. Most people would find that boring. But I like it."

"You must be pretty smart then. If you're good at it anyway," she said with a little grin.

"Are you sure I'm not keeping you from anything? Husband? Kids? Boyfriend? I know it's Saturday but I imagine you had some sort of plans for the day."

"No husband, no kids, no boyfriend. No plans."

"I'm sorry. I have a habit of putting my foot in my mouth. Saying something without thinking. It's not one of my more desirable traits, my mother always told me growing up."

"Don't worry about it. What about you? Husband? Kids? Boyfriend?"

"Nope. I have friends that I go out with every once in a while to clubs or to dinner, or shopping sometimes. "

"I guess we're just not one of the 'popular' girls."

"I guess not. I never have been for the most part. I've always been a bit of an outcast. All through school and college."

⚜ THE PLAID SKIRT ⚜

"I find that hard to believe. You're too pretty for that to have ever been. You weren't an ugly duckling that's now a beautiful swan, are you?"

I blushed. I mean really blushed.

"So we share the same trait. I can put my foot in my mouth, too. I don't mean to put you on the spot. It's just that my life was a lot like that."

"That's okay. What about your family? Do you have brothers and sisters?"

"Two brothers older than me and two sisters younger than me. We don't get along very well though. Actually, they get along pretty well but they don't get along with me. They don't really approve of me. What about you?"

"I'm an only child. I'm an ultra-liberal born to ultra-conservative parents. We don't get along very well either. Holidays are just a chance to belittle me. I've actually started having 'emergencies' at work to get out of some of them. Except for Christmas and Easter. I'd rather spend the time with my friends. Much happier that way, and it really pisses off the folks. That's just a bonus," I laughed.

"I haven't spoken to my parents in almost six years. Not once. They can't accept the fact that one of their daughters is a lesbian."

I froze in my tracks. I guess I was just wide-eyed.

"Did I shock you? Does it bother you?"

I couldn't answer for the longest time. It was totally awkward.

"Maybe I better go now. Thanks for the coffee. It's been a pleasure."

Sasha stood up to leave and picked up her purse and her bag.

"No, please don't go."

I grabbed her purse to keep her from turning around.

"Sit down, please. I want you to stay. I just didn't expect it, that's all. I don't have a problem with you at all. In fact, it's something more than that."

She sat back down, hesitantly.

"Sasha, I'd like to tell you something. It's something that I've never told anybody before. Never in my life."

"Why me?"

"Because…"

"What is it?"

"I've never had a boyfriend. Ever. Not in Junior High. Not in High School. Not in college. I don't find boys attractive. In a romantic sense."

"You've never told anybody? Not even a best friend? Your parents don't know?"

"No. I don't think I'm as brave as you."

Sasha picked up her coffee cup and held it in her hands, staring at it for the longest time, without saying a word. Then she put the cup down and folded her arms onto the table.

"Are you sure you want to have this conversation with a total stranger? Don't you think this is something that you need to discuss with your parents or even your friends or something? Maybe even a therapist. Doesn't anyone even suspect?"

"I've been trying to say this to somebody forever. I've started to a million times. There have been times I've just wanted to stand out on the street corner and shout it out to the world. I've just always been too afraid."

"Afraid of what?"

"I suppose disappointing people. Or driving them away."

"Alison, if that's what will happen, don't you think those people don't deserve to be in your life?"

I just stared at her face for the longest time. I couldn't talk. I couldn't move. Then it happened. Tears started streaming down my cheeks. Not just a few. A constant stream. I just couldn't stop crying.

"Alison, trust me, the first time you say it is the hardest. And it's good that you chose today to be weird. We wouldn't have met. And you wouldn't have told me. And you might have gone on living your life in misery and alone. And feeling like you're cheating yourself out of life and love. In my case, I was lucky enough to have gotten caught in Junior High fooling around with another girl. It caused a lot of problems at the time, but it's made my life a whole lot easier in the long run."

Sasha stood up once again to leave. Then she opened her purse and pulled out a business card and a pen. She turned the card over and wrote another number on it. Then she handed the card to me.

"Here's my phone. My cell phone is on the back. If you need it. Ever. Day or night. Call me. I mean it. Do you understand me Alison?

THE PLAID SKIRT

She reached down and squeezed my hand lightly. I had finally managed to control the water works. I was barely able to nod my head a little.

"My friends call me Aly."

"Okay, Aly. Day or night. When you need the support, call me. About anything."

I nodded again, holding the card. While Sasha walked away from me, I kept the card in my hands, looking at the front, then the back. Then the front again. Back and forth. Finally, I put the card in my purse and got up myself and headed back to my apartment. The afternoon had gotten away from me and I needed to get ready to go out.

I turned the key in the lock and opened my door. My apartment was almost oppressive tonight. I didn't see Lilly, my cat, anywhere. She was hiding behind or underneath something. I dropped my bags and purse on my bed. Then I went into the kitchen and got a pouch of cat food and opened it. That got Lilly running into the kitchen. She jumped onto the counter purring. I put her down on the floor and emptied the food into her dish and refilled her water. If it weren't for my kitty I don't know how I'd ever have survived. I'd had her for eight years. I had her in the dormitories against regulations during college and managed not to ever get caught. All three of my roommates that I'd had were cool about her.

After feeding her I glanced over at the clock. By the time I'd gotten on the subway and then bus and back home, it was almost five o'clock. I got undressed and brushed my hair out. I got dressed in my new clothes, added a pair of knee high brown boots, a silver metal belt, and put on my makeup. I don't think I'm great looking by any stretch of the imagination. I know that I'm heavier than I should be for my short height. I'm only five feet-three. But I think I look okay. I wonder if anybody will ever look at me and like what they see. Somebody that I would be able to love and that would love me. Another woman.

Somehow I felt different now than I had in my life. Meeting Sasha was wonderful. I'm not stupid. I know there are gay men and women everywhere. That live openly as such. I just wish I could. I wondered if I ever would be able to. I took most of the cash out of my billfold and put it the top drawer of my dresser. Then put it and my lip gloss in a clutch that more or less matched my boots. Along with Sasha's card. Then it was scratch Lilly on the head and locked the door behind me.

Normally our group all met up on a Friday evening. I'm not sure why we were doing it on a Saturday this time. It would prove fateful for me. I caught the bus to Lexa's apartment and together we caught the subway to Manhattan and walked about twenty blocks to the club. We went inside and looked around, quickly finding the table with our friends sitting around it already. We joined them and ordered drinks. I loved the local band that was playing tonight. We'd heard them several other times. The music was just right. Loud enough to take over your senses but soft enough that everybody could hear what the other was saying.

After we'd been there about an hour and a half, Brianna stood up and wiggled her finger at me, beckoning me to follow her as she walked back to the Ladies' room.

"Okay. Spill it. What's going on? You've been moping around all night like somebody kicked your dog. What's bothering you?"

"Nothing. Really, it's nothing. I guess I'm just sort of tired."

"Bullshit. What's going on with you? I've known you for four years. I know there's something wrong. I'm your best friend in the world. I can tell there's something up."

It was show time. Time to face my fears. Something I would never have been able to do if I hadn't met Sasha. Something that never would have happened if I wouldn't have been if a crazy mood in the clothing store. There were butterflies and knots and God knows what else in my stomach. I felt sick. I wanted to throw up. I wanted to turn tail and run away.

"Brianna, there's something I need to tell you. Something I've kept to myself for the longest time. It's just that... It's just that... Well... I don't want what I tell you to ruin our friendship. You know that I love you to death."

"Okay. You know you can tell me anything. And no matter what you tell me, we'll always be close. I don't have to tell you that."

"Here's the thing. I'm... I'm... I'm a lesbian."

"No shit. Like we don't all know that. Well, pretty much all of us anyway. We've known for a long time. Why haven't you talked to me before now? Obviously it's been bothering you."

THE PLAID SKIRT

Then the tears came back. Brianna put her arms around my neck and pulled me in close. The dam was starting to burst for me. This was an admission to somebody I knew. Somebody I cared about. Somebody I was close to. And she didn't care. And I wondered, how did she know?

"Danny and I have talked about this at home before. We both figured if you didn't want to tell us, then it was your choice not to. We're cool with it. I love you. Danny agrees with me. He loves you too, you know?"

I just cried and cried while Brianna and I held each other. Women came and went from the bathroom, I'm sure, but I never took notice. Finally I was able to screw my head on straight, fix my eyeliner, put on a new pass at my lip gloss, and make myself presentable. Brianna put her hand on my cheek and stroked it with her thumb.

"Honey, do you want this to stay just between you and me? If that's what you want, that's what I'll do. I won't even tell Danny. And my husband knows pretty much everything."

"Truthfully, I don't want to hide it anymore. Ever again. I don't want to brag about it or get up on a soap box or anything. But it's been bottled up inside me for ten years. I just can't take it anymore. The only people I really don't want to know yet are Mom and Dad. I'll have to find the right way to break the news to them. They really, really won't like it. They're perfect little conservatives."

"Okay, let's get back to the table. Everybody will start to wonder."

~End Sample Chapter of THE PLAID SKIRT~
For more go to www.Shadoepublishing.com to purchase
the complete book or for many other delightful offerings.

~ *Because a publisher should stand behind their authors*~

Lawyered
K'Anne Meinel

Discovering that you don't have everything you thought you wanted is a surprise. Getting a promotion, finding new friends, learning you are attracted to women....

Nia Toyomoto has worked hard all her life to prove she was the best; she graduated early from high school, college, and got the dream job in Manhattan. Becoming a partner at the tender age of thirty she thought she had it all until the law firm made demands about her personal appearance and a few other things that made her change her life for the promotion. Then she realizes having everything isn't all that it is cracked up to be without someone to share it with...

A successful lawyer in the big city, choices have to made, sacrifices and surprises await this beautiful and talented woman....does she make the right ones though?

www.shadoepublishing.com

~ Because a publisher should stand behind their authors~

What do you do when you meet someone who changes everything you know about love and passion?

Paige Harlow is a good girl. She's always known where she was going in life: top grades, an ivy league school, a medical degree, regular church attendance, and a happy marriage to a man. So falling in love with her gorgeous roommate and best friend Alyssa Torres is no small crisis. Alyssa is chasing demons of her own, a medical condition that makes her an outcast and a family dysfunctional to the point of disintegration make her a questionable choice for any stable relationship. But Paige's heart is no longer her own. She must now battle the prejudices of her family, friends, and church and come to peace with her new sexuality before she can hope to win the affections of the woman of her dreams. But will love be enough?

www.shadoepublishing.com

~ Because a publisher should stand behind their authors~

Coming out is hard. Coming out in the public eye is even harder. People think they own a piece of you, your work, and your life, they feel they have the right to judge you. You lose not only friends but fans and ultimately, possibly, your career...or your life.

Cassie Summers is a Southern Rock Star; she came out so that she could feel true to herself. Her family including her band and those important to her support her but there are others that feel she betrayed them, they have revenge on their minds...

Karin Myers is a Rock Star in her own right; she is one of those new super promoters: Manager, go-to gal, agent, public relations expert, and handholder all in one. Her name is synonymous with getting someone recognized, promoted, and making money. She only handles particular clients though; she's choosy...for some very specific reasons.

Meeting Cassie at a party there is a definite attraction. She does not however wish to represent her despite her excellent reputation. She fights it tooth and nail until she is contractually required to do so. In nearly costs them more than either of them anticipated....their lives.

www.shadoepublishing.com

~ Because a publisher should stand behind their authors~

As I watch the wormhole start to close, I make one last desperate plea ... "Please? Please don't make me do this?" I whisper.
"You're almost out of time, Lily. Please, just let go?"
I look down at the control panel. I know what I have to do.

Lilith Madison is captain of the Phoenix, a spaceship filled with an elite crew and travelling through the Delta Gamma Quadrant. Their mission is mankind's last hope for survival.

But there is a killer on board. One who kills without leaving a trace and seems intent on making sure their mission fails. With the ship falling apart and her crew being ruthlessly picked off one by one, Lilith must choose who to trust while tracking down the killer before it's too late.

"A suspenseful...exciting...thrilling whodunit adventure in space...discover the shocking truth about what's really happening on the Phoenix" (Clarion)

www.shadoepublishing.com

~ Because a publisher should stand behind their authors~

When Delaney Delacroix is called to locate a missing girl, she never plans on getting caught up with a human trafficking investigation or with the local witch. Meeting with Raelin Montrose changes her life in so many ways that Delaney isn't sure that this isn't destiny.

Raelin Montrose is a practicing Wiccan, and when the ley lines that run under her home tell her that someone is coming, she can't imagine that she was going to solve a mystery and find the love of her life at the same time.

www.shadoepublishing.com

~ *Because a publisher should stand behind their authors~*

HEART OF VENGEANCE

DAWN CARTER

WARNING ~ book contains graphic violence towards women

 A serial killer plagues the gay community and leaves a trail of dead bodies across state lines. Agent Danni Pacelli and Agent Parker Stevens rush against time to catch their killer and stop the body count from increasing.
 Agent Parker Stevens life was perfect when transferred to a new city and new location which offered her solitude from the grief of losing her partner and children to a predator. But, while hunting down her suspect, she meets Samantha Petrino who takes the once closed off Stevens and opens a world to new love. The charming advertising agent breaks down her defenses, and no matter how hard she fights to protect her heart, she finds herself falling for the beautiful and intelligent woman.
 New to the FBI, Agent Danni Pacelli's struggles to balance her personal life along with the job, to save her relationship, she convinces her new partner to bring in Annabel and utilize the young detective's skills to track down their killer or risk losing Annabel all together.
 The heroic efforts of two agents who hunt down a serial killer, but find more than they bargained for.

www.shadoepublishing.com

~ Because a publisher should stand behind their authors~

FRANKIE

PRUDENCE MACLEOD
IN COLLABORATION WITH
CRYSTIANNA CRAWFORD

Carrie flees from the demons of her present, trying to protect the ones she loves.

Frankie hides from the demons of her past, and the memory of loved ones she failed to protect.

A modern day princess thrown to the wolves, Carrie's only hope is the rancher who had spent the better part of a decade in self imposed, near total, isolation. Frankie's history of losing those she tries to save haunts her, but this madman threatens her home, her livestock, her sanctuary. She knows she can't do it alone, has she still got enough support from her oldest friends?

www.shadoepublishing.com

~ *Because a publisher should stand behind their authors~*

  In a world on the verge of being told that everything they once thought was merely myth is real, can one teenage girl cope with life changes she never saw coming?

  Seventeen year old Kyndle Callahan began her year as a typical high school senior. Well, as typical as a girl can be while living life as a werewolf. She wasn't bitten or scratched as most people believe all werewolves are made, no, she was born into the pack that's always been her extended family. She's never seen the people she grew up with as the monsters of myth and legend but everything in her life is thrown into a tailspin when her father springs some shocking news on her. Suddenly, reality as a werewolf is much scarier than the stories humans tell. Stunned by the prospect of spending her life bonded to someone she can't even stand sharing the same space with and devastated at the thought of losing the only love she's ever known, can Kyndle settle into who and what she is in time to set things right? Can the girl that grew up knowing only pack law stand up, embrace her true calling, and become the woman she was meant to be despite going against everything her family believes?

  With the help of her best friend Abbey, Kyndle must navigate a confusing world of wolf culture, teenage drama, and coming out in a group that believes her lifestyle is unnatural. Follow her journey through pain, heartache, several states, and the fight to be with the girl she loves and take her place in the world.

www.shadoepublishing.com

~ Because a publisher should stand behind their authors~

THE DEATH ROOM
RACHEL MALDONADO

Roberta Pena finally has her dream job of being a Biology Teacher at the high school that she once attended, but something sinister lurks in her classroom. She begins to have unusual paranormal experiences. Is she simply losing her mind or is there a ghost trying to make contact? How will she deal with the mystery of the room that often smells of death and where she has begun to have so many unsettling and ghastly sightings? Will she solve the mystery or be forced to leave her career that she worked so hard to achieve? Might she find love in the process?

www.shadoepublishing.com

~ Because a publisher should stand behind their authors~

RIDING THE RAINBOW

GENTA SEBASTIAN

A Children's Novel for ages 8-11

Horse crazy Lily, eleven years old with two out-loud-and-proud mothers, is plump and clumsy. Her mothers say she's too young to ride horses, she can't seem to get anything right in class, and bullies torment her on the playground. Alone and lonely, how will she ever survive the mean girls of Hardyvale Elementary's fifth-grade?

Across the room Clara sits still as a statue, never volunteering or raising her hand. To avoid the bullying that is Lily's daily life she answers only in a whisper with her head down, desperate to keep her family's secret that she has two fathers.

Then one day Clara makes a brave move that changes the girls' lives forever. She passes a note to Lily asking to meet secretly at lunch time. As they share cupcakes she explains about her in-the-closet dads. Both girls are relieved to finally have a friend, especially one who understands about living in a rainbow family.

Life gets better. As their friendship deepens and their families grow close, their circle of friends expand. The girls even volunteer together at the local animal shelter. Everything is great, until old lies and blackmail catch up with them. Can Lily and her mothers rescue Clara's family from disaster? Or will Lily lose her first and best friend?

www.shadoepublishing.com

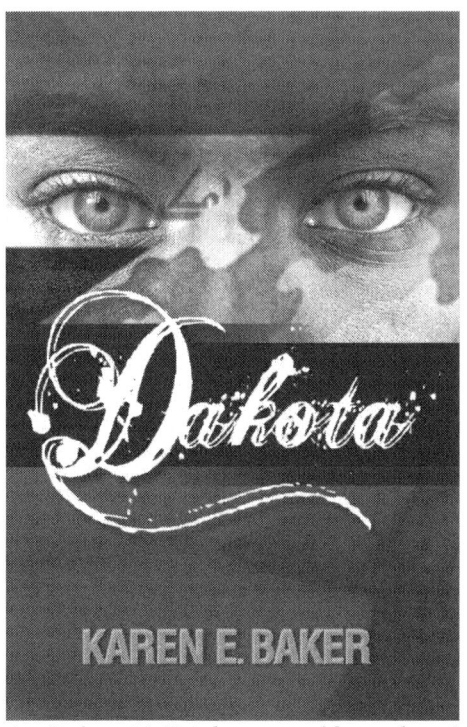

~ *Because a publisher should stand behind their authors~*

Dakota

KAREN E. BAKER

When U.S. Marine Dakota McKnight returned home from her third tour in Operation Iraqi Freedom, she carried more baggage than the gear and dress blues she had deployed with. A vicious rocket-propelled grenade attack on her base left her best friend dead and Dakota physically and emotionally wounded. The marine who once carried herself with purpose and confidence, has returned broken and haunted by the horrors of war. When she returns to the civilian world, life is not easy, but with the help of her therapist, Janie, she is barely managing to hold her life together...then she meets Beth.

Beth Kendrick is an American history college professor. She is as straight-laced as they come, until Dakota enters her life, that is. Will her children understand what she is going through? Will she take a chance on the broken marine or decide to wait for the perfect someone to come along?

Time is on your side, they say, unless there is a dark, sinister evil at work. Is their love strong enough to hold these two people together? Will the love of a good woman help Dakota find the path to recovery? Or is she doomed to a life of inner turmoil and destruction that knows no end?

www.shadoepublishing.com

If you have enjoyed this book and the others listed here Shadoe Publishing is always looking for first, second, or third time authors. Please check out our website @
www.shadoepublishing.com
For information or to contact us @
shadoepublishing@gmail.com.

We may be able to help you make your dreams of becoming a published author come true.